THE
DARK
SIDE

THE
DARK
SIDE

CHRISSIE F MICHAELS

DEDICATION

I dedicate this book to my husband, Lee, who has supported me for over twenty-five years while I have pursued my very demanding, but enjoyable career.

I dedicate it also to my mum and dad, Chris and Mike and my sister Annette. I so wish that my mum was alive to read it and it is in large part due to their unending love, support and commitment that I was able to pursue my dreams.

I also wish to thank all those who have worked with me throughout my career, and my friends for putting up with me, you may recognise yourselves in some of the characters.

Our beloved dog Harley features throughout this book. He was the most loyal friend for over twelve and a half years, and we miss him dearly.

THE MAJOR CHARACTERS

THE PRACTICE
Caroline + Alex
William + Michael
Seb + Ian + Sandra

THE GANG
Robert
Kyle
Dale

THE DOG WALKERS
Paula and Joe – Couple with two black labs named Barney and Bailey
Anthony – Male in his sixties, owner of a beagle called Millie
Christine – Teacher with golden retriever Clive
Julie-Ann – Bubbly, in her forties, owned by French bulldog Lola
Marie – Senior lady with cockerpoo Oswald

THE PRISON
Louise and Dave

CHAPTER ONE

THE FIRM

Caroline sighed as she swivelled round in her chair and looked out of her office window. The police station across the road was barely visible through the rain lashing down on yet another wet, dreary, grey day in November. On checking her phone, she was shocked to discover that it was nearly one o'clock. She'd been sat at her desk since seven that morning pouring over a seemingly endless number of client files. It was all the normal stuff, clients accused of thefts, criminal damage, assault and an array of what had now become to Caroline mundane, boring nonsense. Having been a criminal defence solicitor for twenty-five years, the entire system thoroughly jaded her.

She stood up and stretched, noticing a lot of clicking and cracking. *A sign of old age,* she thought wearily.

Caroline was forty-eight years old and not unattractive, with thick, long, wavy, dark hair that fell halfway down her back, an athletic figure and a pretty but drawn face. She had dark circles under her eyes and had long since given up trying to find a concealer to hide them. She yawned while she pondered what her life had become. There were the clients. Some were lovely, in desperate need of help after making a big mistake in their lives. That was where she made a real difference to the direction of their future. Others, and these were the most troublesome cases, faced accusations of things they'd not done. That level of responsibility was overwhelming and exhausting, but was what she lived for. With those clients, you built up a genuine bond, especially when they faced serious accusations.

Bending to touch her toes and stretch out her back, she recalled the murder cases she'd handled over the length of her career. She'd handled over forty such cases, quite a lot for a rural solicitor, and most had resulted in convictions. There were a couple, though, where she'd done some actual legwork, far beyond what most solicitors would have done, and she and the clients received the right results to go with it.

The first was a man accused of murder in a rough town in the county. All the prosecution witnesses had previous convictions, but it was clear there were others involved, and others who had relevant knowledge who the police had not spoken to. Caroline had realised at the time that if she instructed an enquiry agent to locate these people, they wouldn't speak to them and would go to ground. This required her going personally, visiting some dangerous people in less salubrious parts of the town to persuade them they weren't grasses, that someone was facing over twenty years in prison for something she was sure he hadn't done.

It was fascinating what she'd uncovered; a web of lies by the prosecution witnesses to incriminate her client when they, too, had been involved. It was still the only case in her career where she'd ever served her own witness statements on the prosecution. The defence was only required to serve the names and dates of birth, not the details, but in this case, she was so certain of her position she needed the prosecution to investigate it, not wait for the trial and the jury. The prosecution reviewed the position and offered a Manslaughter, the right offence for the client in the circumstances and he got four years instead.

The other case was a female with children. As was the case in all but very exceptional cases of murder, she was on remand awaiting her trial. The separation from her children was very difficult for all concerned, but especially the children. Every time Caroline saw her client, which was weekly, she'd lost weight and looked more drawn and haggard. Again, on painstakingly going through the case and visiting witnesses on many dark nights in winter, it became evident she was just in the wrong place at the wrong time, not involved in the gang killing that had gone down. She knew the parties involved but had played no part in what had taken place and indeed had fled the scene, fearing for her own life. Caroline persuaded the prosecution to treat her as a prosecution witness instead of a defendant and she went home a year after first being remanded.

Those were the cases that had kept her up at night worrying, but were also the reason she went into the job. To fight for the underdog against the system, to test it robustly, to ensure to the best of her ability that justice was done.

'How can you represent guilty people?' she'd been asked so many times it got boring and predictable.

'It's worse representing the innocent,' she always replied. 'I don't make up stories for guilty clients. I make sure the evidence is there. The worrying thing is when they are innocent, and you're trying to stop the full force of the law hammering down on them. People lose their jobs, families, homes and often their liberty when false allegations are made. There's no recompense if the state gets it wrong in most cases.'

Caroline stretched, sliding her arms down her left side and then her right side and rolled her head and neck, trying to release the tension and stiffness that came from sitting for so long in one position.

I must set a timer on my phone to remind me to move and take a break, she thought to herself.

Her movement had disturbed her beloved pet dog, Harley. He came out from one of his happy places under Caroline's desk for a stroke, but not before he'd done his downward and upward dog stretches himself.

'You a bit stiff too, lad?' Caroline said to him softly and affectionately, stroking the top of his head and along his back. He shook himself and licked her hand. 'Don't worry, I'm not going anywhere. Chance would be a fine thing. I'm just stretching.'

As if he understood exactly what she'd said to him, he flopped back down on one of the many beds strategically placed in his favourite spots. He liked to be under the desk of his chosen human, but with his head poking out so he could keep an eye on the door and whoever else might be coming in and out. Caroline knew it was to make sure he had all treat avenues covered.

She continued with her musing and thought about one of her clients fondly who'd been in this terrible situation of being accused of something he hadn't been guilty of. The allegation was he had sexually assaulted his two stepdaughters. Caroline had known him as a regular client over the years, but not for that sort of offence. He could drink too much and get into a fight in a pub, but this wasn't something she could ever imagine him committing. When she went to the police station for his interview, he'd been so upset. She'd never seen him cry before; he was a tough, bald-headed, thirty-something-year-old man. However, here he was, understandably, besides himself.

'I didn't do this, Caroline,' he'd said as soon as she walked in. 'You gotta believe me.'

'I do,' she replied simply, but the relief on his face had been overwhelming. 'If they'd said you'd killed someone, I could have believed it; whacked someone a bit too hard, maybe, but not this. It's not you, I know that.'

Together they'd built his defence, and he'd been successful, acquitted on all counts. She was horrified to discover a few months later he'd taken his own life. He'd been on remand while awaiting trial and during that time he'd lost his job and his home. She'd later found out from one of his friends what had finished him was that his name had been in the local papers. Everyone knew of the accusations, and despite his acquittal, in the local community they were saying "no smoke without fire" and he simply hadn't been able to cope with that.

Caroline shook, feeling shivery as she recalled how she'd felt physically sick when she got the news. All that effort to stand up to the system and it was a pyric victory. He'd lost everything and paid the ultimate price because of tittle-tattle and rumour. Absorbing people's problems all the time was very tiring, but it was this case more than others that had weighed heavily. It had made her question whether any of what she did was worth it and whether, in fact, it made any actual difference at all.

That question was something she asked herself almost daily now as most clients were very different to this man. He'd been so grateful for everything she'd done; he just hadn't been able to live with the aftermath. Most were self-centred, whinging, whining, pathetic specimens who were rude, abusive, obnoxious and entitled. Even though the vast majority of them were legally aided, it didn't stop them from shouting down the telephone at the poor reception staff that they were "paying their fucking wages".

Still staring out the window but not seeing what was out there, lost in deep thought, she recalled the initial excitement she felt when she was embarking on the career she'd wanted to do for as long as she could remember. She'd called her mum the first time she'd gone to represent a client at the police station by herself. She was beside herself with excitement.

The buzz when she received her first phone call for a murder case at the police station had been as if an electric current was coursing through her body. Likewise, when she attended her first identification parade at the police station. It was a bit like she'd seen on the TV.

They were good fun, she mused, *not digital like they are now.*

Her friend had been one of the stooges on one of her parades and she grinned to herself as she recollected the surprise on his face when he'd seen her attend as the solicitor. She'd had great fun making sure the stooges were as close to her client as possible, changing clothing, wigs, a make-up artist drawing on false beards and scars.

The good old days, she thought, then laughed to herself. *Christ Caroline, get a grip, you're turning into a right old fart.*

She remembered the first time she represented someone she knew. It had happened a lot over the years, a by-product of working where she grew up. It was a friend from school, Amanda, and she'd mitigated her heart out. She'd only been qualified for a few months. The problem was, she'd persuaded herself that Amanda shouldn't go to prison. When she did and they were in the cells, it was Caroline who was upset, not Amanda.

'That was not the right fucking decision,' Caroline clearly remembered herself saying, choking back tears.

'I was always going to prison,' Amanda replied matter-of-factly.

'They should have given you another chance,' Caroline said, trying not to cry.

'I've had more than my fair share,' Amanda answered, putting her arm around Caroline, the wrong person doing the consoling and needing to be consoled. 'You were brilliant; you made them think. But you can't change the facts; I'm still on the drugs and it is what it is.'

That was the start of Caroline toughening up and growing the backbone and the rhino hide she would need to do her job successfully.

Her desk phone interrupted her ruminations. She answered it and Sandra, her loyal and very hard-working secretary, said, 'Hi Caroline, I have Roland on the phone. Do you want him?'

Caroline's brow knitted in confusion. 'Roland who?'

'I don't even mean Roland, do I?' said Sandra, laughing. 'I mean Robert,' and they both laughed.

This was typical of Sandra. She never got anyone's name right. Caroline had once gone to court, calling out for David Beckham in the foyer. The client was, in fact, Paul Beckham and the entire foyer had erupted with laughter. Fortunately, the client had seen the funny side too.

It amazed Caroline that Sandra even got her name right. *She'd make a terrible police witness although a good one for the defence,* she thought, smiling to herself.

'Absolutely yes I do, you know I do,' Caroline replied, and the next moment Robert was in her ear.

'I have good news for you, there is lots of interest–'

'Stop Robert!' Caroline shouted. 'You know we cannot discuss anything on the phone. The line from prison isn't secure, even to solicitors. Why are you even ringing me on this phone? I'll arrange a video link to speak to you as soon as I can.'

Caroline could hear the disappointment in Robert's voice at the way she had spoken to him. 'Well, see you do,' he said gruffly. 'We need to talk.'

'I said I'll sort it and I will,' Caroline retorted.

'Quickly, Caroline,' were his parting words as he abruptly hung up.

Caroline sat back in her chair. A tingling feeling ran down her spine. This was potentially so dangerous, but also so profitable. She'd slaved for a quarter of a century, barely making a living and working relentless hours and this was her opportunity to build herself a big nest egg quickly and get out. She'd given so much of her life, and this was a real chance to get some of it back.

However, Robert was a big part of that, and his manner with her had made her feel uncomfortable. Caroline didn't like the way he'd spoken to her. She'd talk to him about that. She was the boss of this outfit now and he had better remember that.

Also, why hadn't he rung her from his mobile? she mused to herself.

Prisoners weren't allowed mobile phones, but there were many ways they could get hold of them. Robert had one and changed it often. He always rang her from his. She wondered what had happened to it.

Nothing bad, she hoped.

Even switching phones and SIM cards often weren't foolproof. There would be evidence of calls to her on the phone. It was an offence to speak to a prisoner on a mobile, let alone what she was speaking to him about, but she needed the regular contact with him, despite the risks. The people they were involved with were not people to mess about with. If it went wrong, it would go horribly wrong.

She glanced down to where Harley slept soundly at her feet. Thankfully, her shouting hadn't woken him. She could feel him twitching against her as he dreamt and made cute whimpering sounds.

'Chasing those rabbits again, Harley,' she whispered, bending under the desk and stroking his head and ears, 'although knowing you, it's probably a ball.'

Harley opened one eye, acknowledging her before returning to his slumber.

Her mobile ringing snapped her out of her deep thought. It was her business partner of five years, Alex.

'Hi,' she said, answering his call. 'How is court going today?'

Alex was six feet tall, blond, forty-five years old, with a boyish smile. He was a brilliant solicitor, attending the Crown Court daily with his higher rights, but was such a chaotic operator. Common sense and logical thinking weren't his best qualities and when he was in the office there was a trail of destruction wherever he went, paperwork and clothing that he just seemed to abandon en route. In fact, it was almost as if it had abandoned him. If he was a burglar, his apprehension would be inevitable, the only one known to leave more at a scene than he stole.

'Well, the day has got better.' He sounded jovial and started chuckling. 'I got halfway to court this morning and realised that I'd left my court files at home, so I had to go back for them. Not that I needed them for court itself. I know the cases inside out, but of course the packages were inside. Then, as I got out of the car in the car park, I noticed I had one brown shoe on and one black. Good job they're the same style. No one said anything, but I got a few funny looks. The final straw was when I got into court and realised I'd forgotten my robe. I had to borrow one from a chap who's about five foot three. I looked bloody ridiculous.'

Caroline laughed out loud. 'How did I get into business with such an intelligent scatterbrain?' she howled. 'When God gave out organisational skills, you must have been in the toilet. Seriously though, you cannot be leaving those files around, even at home. No one can look inside them. Forget about client confidentiality. We have far more serious things to worry about.' Her tone became quiet and very serious.

'I know,' Alex said, 'my heart rate and blood pressure shot up when I realised Rhi is working from home today, but they were in my case, and she doesn't go in there.'

'We just cannot take any chances,' Caroline whispered. 'Things are going so well. We play our cards right, we make a fortune, we get it wrong, and we're going where our clients are for free board and lodging for a long time and that's not what either of us wants, especially you with Rhi expecting. I spoke to Robert briefly on the phone earlier. He has the potential to be a loose cannon now he's back in there. I know we can't do this without him, but his mouth is too big for my liking. Discretion is not in his repertoire.'

Alex immediately retorted, 'He's not stupid. He'll keep his mouth shut when he needs to, and he's got the angles we need.'

'I know,' Caroline said softly, 'but he worries me. He thinks he's brighter than he is. Don't forget where he is. He wasn't so clever in the end, was he?'

'He was unlucky, but he's not in there for anything connected to this. Nothing bad will happen to us. We know the pitfalls; we've planned and been doing this for a while. We'll be fine.'

'Absolutely, we will,' Caroline responded positively. 'Failure is not an option. But he did phone me from the prison phone to the office line today rather than his mobile. I don't know why, couldn't ask him. I'm getting a video link with him to find out what the hell is going on.' Changing the subject, she asked, 'Did you shift it all at court today?'

'Yes, I did, and I could have sold more. A couple of them were asking if I had more. We might need to think about increasing what I take to court.'

'No way,' Caroline said quickly and firmly. 'You have your card to get past security at court, but that doesn't mean you're totally safe. Someone could see you with the client or look in your case and we don't want too much direct connection with clients. We cannot trust any of them. They'd sell their own grandmothers if they could.'

Horror quickly filled Caroline's mind. The only way this would continue to work was to keep as much distance from clients as possible and limit the numbers they had direct contact with. Caroline did not want Alex going against the plan by finding potential clients or changing the agreed-upon amounts. Robert identified the ones they could trust, and that was risky enough. They would sing like a canary the minute the police spoke to them if it suited them. If Alex started too, she'd never know who was involved. There were risks and there were risks and this one had catastrophe written all over it. No, this was not the way to go.

And Alex, with his butterfly mind would leave his case in the robing room open for all to see what was inside or leave his files in court or an interview room and goodness only knows who might look in them and see either drugs to be distributed or cash received. No, Robert was a potential liability, but Alex was equally one, if not more so.

'We've got to keep this tight-knit and just deal with people at court that Robert directs us to. He steers the clients in our direction. He knows when they're in court. We are not approaching anyone directly or changing the agreement. It's just too risky.'

'OK. I agree,' Alex said reluctantly.

Caroline could sense Alex's disappointment with the way she received his money-making idea. She guessed he was thinking it was all very well for her sitting in the office, plotting and giving orders, but he was out on the front line, exposing himself to risk. She was concerned he was getting complacent and might think that he could make the scheme more worth his while.

*I'll have to keep a close eye on him as well as Robe*rt, Caroline thought, massaging her temples.

'I actually don't know which one of the two of them is worse,' she said peering under the desk at Harley.

He opened his eyes with a look that said, 'double trouble as bad as each other.'

'Sadly, Harley, I think you are spot on,' Caroline sighed.

CHAPTER TWO

CAROLINE

Caroline drove home after a dull afternoon in the office, sorting out the other major element of her job, running the criminal contract. It involved such exciting things as training plans for all the staff, which is what had occupied her along with Sandra's appraisal. If she was completely honest with herself, she could see the importance of this sort of stuff. It was easy to get bogged down in the work created by the clients and forget about the development of the staff. However, that was something she had always been very passionate about. It was why one of her greatest achievements was building a criminal practice with loyal staff who worked hard in what was a very difficult industry. Over the years, she had done her best to reward them with bonuses when she could, something which Alex was in favour of too. They had the same mentality regarding the staff. That was one of the many reasons they worked so well together, she had to admit to herself.

Sandra's appraisal was absolutely pointless though, going through the motions and ticking the relevant boxes. She had been with Caroline for more years than either of them cared to remember and wouldn't be going anywhere until she retired. That was something she threatened on almost a daily basis over the last few years as the clients got more and more abusive.

She often said, 'I don't need this shit, I think I'll retire,' and of course, was there promptly the next morning.

It was almost part of her coping mechanism, and they had all had to find ways over the years to manage the stress as best they could. They'd had a good laugh together this afternoon, though. Sandra had written on her form that the only reason she came to work was to babysit Harley and the day he retired so would she, unless she became a multimillionaire first in which case she'd immediately retire and take him with her.

Caroline said to her hopefully that status wouldn't be too far away now, and then they could share Harley between their mansions. 'Good job the auditors will think I'm joking, isn't it?' Sandra said, grinning. 'It can't come quickly enough, can it?'

'No, but we have to be a bit careful. I think Alex wants to expand things even further and I'm worried the wheels might come off,' she had confided.

'No chance,' Sandra had responded confidently. 'With you in charge, it's a no brainer. That's why we all agreed. You're a born leader and you have always looked out for everyone here. That won't change. Trust your gut as you always do, and we'll all be fine.'

Caroline had replied with one of her usual dry, witty retorts for which she was famous – 'let's hope I don't get a touch of gastroenteritis then' – and they'd curled up laughing.

Caroline was known for being cutting and witty but kind, absorbing not only her own problems and those of her clients but also her staff. That's what had got her down over the years. It was the constant level of stress that she was operating at. Even now, with the real prospect of making money and getting out of the rat race, she was under tremendous pressure to deliver for all of them, and she wanted to.

At least there was an end in sight, a light at the end of the tunnel. *Just hope it isn't a train heading towards me,* she thought.

Caroline missed the cut and thrust of court, but someone had to be in the office and that someone had ended up being her, how she couldn't now recall. Lawyers hated being office-bound, especially criminal lawyers. Their days were unpredictable, never knowing how many clients would require help at the police station or how many would ask for the firm at court. The total opposite of that unpredictable working lifestyle was the working life Caroline had now. She was desk-bound and coped with it about as well as a caged tiger.

'All of this is exactly why I have to get out,' she said to herself out loud as she was pulling up on her drive. 'And I have to keep Alex, as well as Robert, under control. It feels like supervising children in a nursery,' she moaned, feeling more tired by the moment.

Come on girl, it'll be worth it. You've got this, she said to herself firmly.

It was her concern about what Robert would be like when he went inside, and Alex and his scatty nature and the overwhelming responsibility that she felt for all her team that had led her to set up her sideline that Alex knew nothing about. She liked him and trusted him to run the practice, but couldn't be sure he wouldn't get them caught. Likewise, with Robert and his unpredictability now that he was in custody, and she had less control. She intended to have enough stashed away so that if either of them dropped her in it, she could leave everything and go. There were just too many moving parts for her to control if one of them went off piste, however much faith Sandra and the rest of the staff had in her.

The only bonus of being desk-bound was that she took her faithful best friend to work with her every day. Harley was a black, nine-year-old springador. When she first got him, everyone said he would be a nightmare, being a combination of a bouncy springer and a busy, chewy Labrador. In fact, he had proved to be the total opposite. He didn't mind whether he was at the office or home as long as he was with his mum and also had his ball. Caroline had said ever since he was a puppy that if a burglar broke in, he'd let them take everything as long as they brought him some new balls and didn't try to take his old ones.

The bond between Caroline and Harley was very special. They went everywhere together. If the invitation did not include Harley,

Caroline simply didn't go, and all her friends knew that. Most of them were doggy people and felt the same. Caroline preferred dogs to people. In fact, she often wondered how she ended up in a job where she was forever dealing with miserable people and their even more miserable problems. She dreamed perhaps she would have been better off working with animals. The only problem with that would have been when animals were sick, or worse still, needed euthanising. Caroline knew she would be absolutely hopeless with that; therefore she was stuck with the people.

Having Harley had also introduced her to her idea of the sideline. On the weekends, she went on long walks to different places with Harley. He was a water baby. Whether it was the sea, the lake, the river, he really didn't mind as long as he could swim with his ball. In the water he looked like a seal and grunted like one and Caroline was certain if he could live in water, he would.

Her favourite times were when she took Harley away to the beach or when she took him to the local 'doggy daycare', which had a pool, and they got to swim together. Harley got so excited when his mummy was in the water with him. He still chased his ball, of course, but wanted her to swim alongside him. He grinned at her, and every fibre of his body shook with excitement.

'This is the reason we are doing this,' she said to him as he sat in the passenger seat looking at her, 'so we can be together all the time and do nice things.'

Harley barked, confirmation that he completely understood what was going on and why. Caroline often thought he understood her better than anyone in the world. Mind you, he ought to with the complaining she'd done to him over the years. To and from work, he sat in the passenger seat listening to her moaning and groaning while she vented and tried to get everything off her chest.

'You keep a confidence, boy; you're reliable, not like people,' she said stroking his ears. 'You're my therapy dog, best friend and partner H, you know that, don't you?'

Harley looked at her as if to say, 'oh yes, and it's a big job, so keep the treats coming.'

However, in the week with heavy work commitments, longer walks were not possible, especially in the darker months or poorer weather like now. As a result, Caroline had found a pleasant route around the estate where she lived. It took in a little park known as the "pocket park" as it was a lovely little pocket of grass with trees in the middle in one part of the estate. The walk took around twenty minutes, allowing for Harley to sniff every blade of grass to see who'd been there since he last went round there the day before. When she was in a hurry, Caroline got frustrated by his attention to detail but at other times found it highly amusing.

Because of the nature of her job, Caroline had always paid attention to people and over the years realised that the same people took their dogs on the same route at pretty much the same time each day.

Pathetic creatures of habit we all are, she thought more than once.

For the first few encounters, there would be no interaction. Then it would lead to nodding and smiling. Then comments on the dogs and now, with many of them, full-blown conversations. In fact, several she regarded as friends. She knew all about their families and their lives. People were quick to divulge a lot about themselves, she discovered.

Caroline was the polar opposite and kept her cards close to her chest. She didn't know whether dealing with clients and the criminal world every day had made her more guarded or whether she'd always been like that. She assumed she had got worse due to her career because her mum often used to comment on it.

Caroline had become quite close to one couple, though. They had two black Labradors, Barney and Bailey. Harley loved them, apart from when they tried to steal his ball. Then he gave a low growl, and his hackles went up. He may have been the eldest of the three, but they knew not to mess with him when he did that. Paula and Joe turned out to be the parents of a client. At first, she hadn't made the connection. She knew them, and their son Tom, from the estate, but not knowing surnames she had never realised they were from the same family.

It was during the case they mentioned to her she representing their son, Tom Reynolds. Because of client confidentiality, she couldn't say anything at all, as he hadn't given his permission to speak to them. Caroline simply told them she couldn't confirm or deny it because of confidentiality, and they understood that. She could see that they were terribly worried about him and understandably so as he hadn't given them any information about what was going on and didn't want them coming to court. It had worked out well in the end, though. Originally arrested for possession with intent to supply, she'd persuaded the prosecution to take simple possession. He was on a community order under the supervision of probation. Paula and Joe were so grateful to her and bought her flowers, despite her saying it was just her job.

During another restless night about eight months ago, mulling everything over that was happening in her life, she formulated an idea in her mind. As a result, she made more of an effort with the dog walkers. Caroline had many restless nights; she was a very light sleeper. It came from going to bed but being on semi-alert all the time. The police often rang in the middle of the night for her to speak to a client on the phone or attend the police station.

Criminals and the police work twenty-four hours, and she often felt that she did the same. On many occasions, having been in court or the office all day, she spent all night in the police station and then went to court the following day without ever going to bed. Rest periods didn't apply to solicitors, they didn't have a tachograph.

Caroline knew that being a lawyer was like being an actor. She performed in court for the benefit of the client to persuade the audience, whether that be judge, jury or magistrates. She had always been very good at that, building up a large client base, and realised she was equally good at playing any part she chose. Therefore, she started talking to the other dog walkers regularly, being more friendly and networking.

Anthony was a single male in his sixties. He clearly doted on his beloved beagle, Millie. She had a selection of collars in pink, red and purple and in the winter, a little jumper or coat to match. She was a complete diva, treated like one and behaved like one. Anthony referred to her as "Millie the Duchess" because she was so demanding but had to concede it was his fault. Harley liked playing with Millie up to a point, but occasionally she behaved in a way that clearly made Harley think she wasn't his type of dog. Caroline could tell.

'She's too high maintenance for you, lad, isn't she?' Caroline had said to Harley when they'd first met.

Harley had looked at her with his beautiful brown eyes and said, 'too right.'

When Millie wore her matching coats and collars, Caroline was sure she could see Harley laughing and rolling his eyes as if to say, 'really what do you think you look like?'

Christine was in her thirties and was a teacher at a local secondary school. Her class had thirteen- and fourteen-year-old students in it and Christine seemed to suffer the same stress and abuse that Caroline did. That was one reason they had bonded so well. Her golden retriever, Clive, loved the water as much as Harley. His light, long coat made keeping him clean much harder work than Caroline had with Harley's coat. Christine didn't mind though; like Caroline, she was single, and Clive was her focus. Her dad, a widower, came in to see Clive during the day when she was at work. He treated Clive like his grandson. Christine often joked about coming home from work and Clive not being there because he was round the corner at her dad's lying on the sofa.

'We share him,' she told Caroline on one of their meetings walking the circular route. 'I don't have a choice, otherwise he'll just dog nap him, and I don't think Clive would mind.'

'Of course he wouldn't,' Caroline laughed. 'I've seen your dad with him. You spoil him, but he takes it to a different stratosphere. He actually asks him where he wants to go on his walks. I've heard him.'

Caroline described the similarities with the relationship Sandra had with Harley. Whenever anyone asked Sandra whose dog Harley was, Sandra smiled broadly and informed them he was all of theirs, but Caroline paid his bills. Everyone always laughed at that, but it was so true.

Lola was the Frenchie, owned by Julie-Ann.

'Well, that's not right because you never own a Frenchie. They are like cats. They own you,' Julie-Ann told Caroline when they first met.

Like Millie, she could be a diva, but she was also a tomboy and loved rolling in mud and fox poo, much to Julie-Ann's disgust. Harley didn't mind sniffing Lola's rear end, but he didn't really have much time for her. The grunting got on his nerves; Caroline could tell. When they saw Lola, he often looked at Caroline with an expression that was asking if she came with a volume control.

Julie-Ann was in her mid-forties, Caroline would guess, a couple of years younger than her and divorced. She was an extremely bubbly character, always very jolly, but Caroline soon realised that it was a mask. Underneath, Julie-Ann suffered with low self-esteem and anxiety. She kept it to herself and did her best to deal with it, but Caroline recognised the signs. *Probably because of her job,* she thought. Caroline really liked Julie-Ann. She hadn't got a bad word to say about anyone and always tried to cheer up everyone she met, even when she was clearly struggling herself.

The final dog walker Caroline had become close to was Marie. She was a senior lady with a cockapoo called Oswald. Caroline didn't know her age and didn't like to ask, but she'd guess she was in her late seventies. Her walking wasn't so good, so she went out with Oswald on her mobility scooter. Sometimes he trotted along happily at the side of her. They could go at a fair old pace Caroline discovered when they first met, and she was trying to keep up with them.

However, whenever Oswald, who was only seven, felt in the mood, he hopped onto the scooter and sat by her feet. Or, on a good day, when she could, Marie would pick him up and pop him in the basket. Harley looked at him as if to say, 'you are so pretentious.' However, on a couple of occasions he jumped on and hitched a ride through the park, looking thoroughly pleased with himself. Oswald was extremely spoilt and in charge of Marie and they both knew it. In fact, neither of them tried to hide it.

It was seven months ago that Caroline had approached Robert with her plan. At first, he was very sceptical, saying that she was mad coming up with such a hairbrained scheme, and it would never work. Caroline thought at the time it was something her mum would have said, and it made her smile. However, she could be very persuasive when she wanted to be. She'd helped Robert out of more holes than either of them cared to remember, especially the current one in more ways than one, so it didn't take long to twist his arm.

CHAPTER THREE

ROBERT

Robert had spent the afternoon lying on his bunk in his cell, annoyed at how abrupt Caroline had been with him on the phone.

She needs to remember who she is fucking dealing with, he thought to himself angrily. *I know she's helped me out of some scrapes over the years, but she wouldn't be doing what she's doing now without me,* he ruminated as he looked up at the dirty ceiling. At some point, it might have been white, but that was years before Robert had occupied the cell. Now it was heavily stained with brown and yellow, and he didn't want to imagine what bodily fluids might have caused such a terrible pattern.

Robert had known Caroline since he was eleven years old. She had been at the start of her career when she had attended the police station for his first arrest for theft. He had stolen some beers with his friends from the local corner shop and been easily caught. They were quite difficult to hide discreetly under his small coat. The firm Caroline worked for at the time had represented his father for years. He had later learned for many offences ranging from theft to armed robbery and eventually murder. He'd gone to prison for sixteen years when Robert was six years old. Robert remembered that day as if it was yesterday. It was the day his heart broke, and his world changed forever.

He couldn't always remember his dad from when he was a child much anymore. His life since seemed to have obliterated most memories, and however hard he tried, he couldn't always bring them to mind. Now, though, he reminisced about his dad putting him on his shoulders and running around with him laughing. He remembered them rolling on the floor in fits of giggles, the best of friends. He remembered that. His mum would say they were 'as thick as thieves'. At the time, he hadn't understood what she was getting at, but it made his dad laugh, so he knew it was a good thing.

Then one night, the police came and said something about a fight in the pub the night before. His dad, always so happy and larger than life, looked ashen. Robert had noticed that day that his dad had a very red and swollen hand. It had lots of cuts on it, and he looked in pain. Robert had asked him about it and his dad had ruffled his hair and told him not to worry about it, he was a big boy, so it didn't hurt that much. Robert remembered how sick and frightened he felt seeing his dad like that when the police handcuffed him and took him away, totally defeated. Crushed was the word. That was the last time he ever saw him in the house.

His mum didn't tell him much about what was going on with his dad, even though he screamed and cried to know. She said it was best that he forgot about his dad. He wouldn't ever be coming home. How could he forget about his dad? He'd never understood why she said that, how she thought he could do that. He was his best friend, the person he loved most in the world gone, supposed to be just forgotten. Robert couldn't do that.

Robert's mum had always been a bit of a drinker and it just got worse after his dad was no longer there. He recalled she would be in her dressing gown all day; her lank hair straggling down her back rarely washed. She would always seem to have a cigarette hanging out of her mouth and the house got grubbier and grubbier. Overflowing ashtrays, unwashed crockery everywhere, piles of dirty clothes. Robert's stomach growled as he stared at the walls of his cell and remembered it growling as a child. He would look in the cupboards for food and there would be little to eat. He would open tins of beans or soup and eat them cold, not knowing what to do with them. Or he would dig his hand into the cereal packet and eat handfuls of stale Rice Krispies or cornflakes. There was never any milk to go with them.

Several times on the way home from school – when he went, which got rarer as time went on – he would look in people's bins and take out any leftover food that he could find. He did this at school, eating what other children threw away and was often laughed at and taunted for it. At school, he was bullied by other children who would say that he smelled as he rarely bathed, and his clothes were hardly ever washed.

Robert had realised that to survive, he was going to have to get tougher. He started fighting back at school and got a reputation for being a hard nut. He liked that. Some older boys asked if he wanted to hang around with them. Robert was thrilled to be asked to be part of their gang, as they were about fourteen or fifteen. He felt like he belonged somewhere for the first time since his dad went.

That's how the first arrest came about. There was a group of four of them who decided to steal the beer. Robert was nominated to go into the shop and take four bottles, one for each of them. Unsuccessfully concealing them led to the store owner stopping him and calling the police.

I was a stupid little twat, Robert thought to himself, *but then if that hadn't happened, I wouldn't have the going on I've got now.*

When he got to the police station, Robert recollected overhearing a conversation when his mum was talking to a friend about his dad's case. He remembered the name of the solicitor, Simon Cross. It had been an easy name to remember as he used to play "Simon says" with his dad and so he just thought of that and his dad being cross. He smiled now, thinking how clever he thought he was remembering the name at the time.

When the police officer had asked him if he had a solicitor, his face had the look of amazement when he responded 'Simon Cross' aged eleven as if he was a seasoned visitor to the police station. Robert grinned, recalling the moment. Little did he know then that over the next twenty-five years he would be a reasonably frequent visitor, but not as regular as some.

Of course, Simon, an important and experienced solicitor, didn't attend the police station for an eleven-year-old arrested for theft. Caroline did. She was young, enthusiastic, in her early twenties then. She was pretty; she was kind to him, but most of all, she was tough with the police. Robert thought at the time that his dad would like Caroline very much. He had asked her if she had met his dad, and she hadn't. She knew of him and his case, but she hadn't dealt with it.

Over the years, Robert's path had crossed with Caroline's as his offending continued. During his childhood it was petty stuff, more shoplifting, some criminal damage and a bit of fighting. Caroline had always attended for him; they had a bond. She knew how difficult his home life was, but she didn't see him as a victim. She just tried to help him. Caroline had encouraged him to attend school and try to get himself more in life. She had also kept him up to date on his dad's appeal case as much as she could. He would always be grateful for that. His dad would send messages to him through the firm, just that he loved him and not to worry. It meant the world to Robert to know that his dad was still thinking of him. He sent messages back.

He'd had no other way of contacting his dad. Mobile phones were in their infancy and certainly not available to the likes of him as they were now. His mum didn't even have a landline after his dad left. She stopped paying the bills. If his dad wrote, he never knew about it and he didn't know how to write back. Caroline had said she would help him, but his writing was poor.

'He won't mind,' Caroline had encouraged when he told her why he didn't want to write. 'He'll just be pleased to hear from you.' But Robert wouldn't.

Sometimes now he wished he had, but no point dwelling on the past.

'Stop going over old ground,' Robert said sharply to himself. 'It doesn't do any good. Get a fucking grip. It is what it is. You are in here for the next couple of years, so you need to make the best of it. Caroline is the way to do that. We've got a good thing going on and that's not going to change. You'll be all set up when you get out.'

He got up from his bunk and dropped to the floor and banged out a hundred press-ups. It was important to keep mentally alert and physically fit in prison. It wasn't the first time he had been here, but he was hopeful it would be his last, that he'd secured himself a better future with enough money when he got out to move away and start a new life.

However, he knew from previous experience that there was danger at every turn in prison, and he always needed to be on his guard and at the top of his game. To most inmates, Robert's reputation preceded him, and he had no bother, everyone kowtowing to him. But he was smart enough to know there would always be someone lurking in the shadows to try to replace him, both on the inside and the outside. It was not an option that anyone would succeed. He needed to remain top dog while he was serving to build up what he needed. Then the next man could step up to the plate, see if he could do any better. Until then, it was his and that was that.

Dripping with sweat after his press-ups, Robert wiped his face and neck on a towel that had definitely seen better days. It was as hard as sandpaper and was a dirty, unwashed grey. It reminded him of the towels at home when he was a child.

He looked out of the window, smeary with rain marks and grime between the bars, and sighed. It was dark and raining. He could hear it hitting the window and see the big drops running down, slowly to begin with and then as the rain got heavier making runs down the window until he could hardly see out of it.

He could hear the wind and thought to himself, *The weather is as fucking miserable as I am. I need to shake myself out of this. I'm still in control on the outside and I'm creating on the inside, fucking way to go.*

As if he could read his thoughts, Dave, a screw, opened the door. 'Whatcha up to, Robert?' he enquired.

'Just done a workout but I can drop and do another hundred if you want to join me?' Robert replied laughing at Dave, who started guffawing.

Dave was a reasonable guy, even if he was a screw. He'd been on the job more years than he cared to think about, and Robert had seen him on several of his visits. However, a less likely candidate for the gym you were not likely to meet. Dave was in his late fifties, quite overweight, with a reasonable belly hanging over the top of his belted trousers.

'Jesus Christ,' he'd said to Robert when he first saw him for this stretch, 'I'd bloody hoped not to clap eyes on your ugly mug again.'

'Right back at ya, Dave,' he'd said. 'You looked in the mirror lately?'

They'd always got on well, and Dave was obviously genuinely disappointed that Robert hadn't stayed out of the system. He told Robert as much to which Robert had retorted, 'someone's gotta keep you in line.'

Dave was a trustworthy nice guy. Got to be watched, of course, because he was a screw after all, but Robert had thought since he first met him that if they'd met down the pub, they'd have been mates. He got the feeling that Dave felt the same. Dave watched out for him, came to chat to him about football or what was on TV, just the regular stuff that people talk about. For a short period, it made Robert forget where he was and feel normal. That was very important when he was younger and less sure of himself. Now it was good because it distracted Robert from his wallowing, helped pass the time and it also meant that Robert got his post double quick, which was important.

Post was a serious issue in prison. Even if letters were sent by recorded delivery, they seemed to vanish into a black hole only to reappear days later when the prisoner had kicked off and the family or legal team, whoever had sent the letter, had complained to the

Governor. Not so with Robert. Since he'd been back, he'd made it clear to Dave that he needed his post getting to him asap and Dave had facilitated it brilliantly. He was a reliable soldier.

'I told my missus I've spoken to you,' he said to Robert, a little nervously.

'Have you?' Robert replied, raising one eyebrow. 'What did she say?'

'I didn't say you were involved in anything, or that you could help us or that we could help you. I just said that I'd offered if you needed anything.' Dave was tapping his foot anxiously, clearly dancing around the subject wanting to get a feel for the situation from Robert.

'And what did she say to that?'

'She said I need to be careful; inmates aren't to be trusted, but that she trusts me and if I trust you, she will too, so she'll help if you want her to.' Beads of sweat were forming on Dave's forehead.

'I didn't say I was involved in anything Dave, be careful what you say and who you say it to. However, if I or anyone I know needs help, you'll be the first to know, I promise.' Robert was firm. He didn't want Dave blabbing to anyone about anything, but he might come in useful. That was one of the things he wanted to talk to Caroline about. He silently prayed that she had sorted the video link and it happened quickly.

'Sure,' said Dave. 'I haven't said anything to anyone, only Louise, and I wouldn't. It's just I do need the money so …'

'I know you do mate; I promise I'll see what I can do,' Robert reassured him. They chatted a bit about how diabolical the weather was, and Dave left.

Robert felt sorry for Dave. He'd confided that his dad was in a nursing home with dementia. He'd burned through most of his money from the sale of his house; well at £1,800 per week, that's going to happen pretty fast. Dave was very concerned as to what was going to happen when the money ran out. There was talk of moving him to a cheaper facility when the state took over payment,

Dave had explained to Robert, almost in tears.

On a good day, his dad still recognised him, and it was obvious that Dave adored him. He was very worried that a change in facility, and to one that wasn't as good, would be very detrimental to his dad's health. Other than the dementia, he was as strong as an ox, the doctor said, but a stressful move like that could set off many problems. They had crunched the figures, but there was no way he and Louise could fund the home on their incomes, not for any length of time.

Most people thought Robert was heartless and ruthless, but that was only one side of him. He had a softer side that he kept very well hidden most of the time, but Dave had touched a nerve with him. He was a good man, and his father seemed to be too. It was such a sad situation to be in having dementia in the first place, let alone all of this. Robert had been a little envious of the bond between Dave and his dad, but he also loved his own dad and thought about what he would do if it was his dad in that situation.

No brainer, he thought, *got to try to cut him in somehow.* Now he just needed to talk to Caroline about this, and the other small matter, his own dad.

CHAPTER FOUR

THE PLAN

It was about twelve months ago that the plans first started, and the operation began a month after that, slowly at first. Robert was sitting in Caroline's office discussing the case for which he received the prison sentence about six weeks ago. He had seriously beaten up a man, breaking his nose, several ribs, his right leg and his left wrist. He'd given him a good kicking. Robert was confident that the man wouldn't grass him up. 'He wouldn't fucking dare,' he had said in a threatening tone.

However, he hadn't noticed the CCTV camera outside the shop across the street. Unfortunately for Robert, the police had done a proper job for once and canvassed the area and secured the CCTV. Caroline knew that in a lot of cases, they failed to do this. No such luck for Robert this time. Even more unfortunate was the fact the shop had a genuine camera that recorded the incident. It was handed to the police without being recorded over and it was good enough quality to appear in a Netflix show. Robert was bang to rights, and he knew it.

'How could you have been so bloody careless, Robert?' Caroline had said to him, exasperated.

She knew there was no way of fixing this and that Robert would be doing some time.

Robert knew the same. He didn't need the look on her face to tell him that he was an intelligent man, and the overwhelming evidence hadn't escaped his attention.

Caroline's exclamation woke Harley, who was asleep under her desk. He'd greeted Robert when he came in with a wag of his tail, ensuring he received the obligatory biscuit and stroke, but then returned straight to his bed. He now looked at Robert as if to say, 'what have you done now?'

'Did it not occur to you to have a look about and just see if there were any cameras? It wasn't exactly hidden, was it?'

Robert is not an idiot, she thought. *How could he have been so bloody foolish?*

Caroline immediately thought of one of her clients who she had represented as a young boy. He had been in the police station every other day, or so it seemed. His penchant was for burglaries, although he wasn't good at them. In fact, she was at the police station so often with him and his mum that she referred to his mum as "mum". They'd had a few laughs over that. She had told this client that he was so rubbish that he either ought to stop offending altogether or at least buy some gloves. He was leaving his fingerprints at every scene, making it inevitable that he would get caught.

The next time she saw him, in the police station no less, she said to him, 'You clearly didn't take my advice then?'

'I did,' he said indignantly. He was being the stroppy fifteen-year-old he could be on occasion.

'In what way, then?' Caroline asked him. 'You clearly didn't stop offending as here we are again, and you clearly didn't buy any gloves because guess what? Your fingerprints are at the scene again.'

'Yes, I did,' he'd fired back at her. 'I bought gloves.'

'But your fingerprints are everywhere in the burgled building, the point of entry, on drawers that have been rifled through. Did you take your gloves off?' Caroline questioned him.

'No,' came the very meek reply. 'I bought fingerless ones.'

Caroline had laughed uncontrollably when the client revealed this and was smiling at the memory when she was jolted back to the room by Robert saying defiantly, 'That rat had to be taught a bloody lesson and fast. Challenging my authority, he was, can't fucking have that, not then, not now, had to send him a fucking message he'd fucking understand, and keep the other bastards in line while I was at it.'

Robert had sat arms folded, jaw jutting out, challenging anyone or anything that thought he could have done things differently. 'Anyway, the main thing is the old bill doesn't have a fucking clue what it was all about. Lewis won't dare speak to anyone about it, so it's no biggy.'

Caroline just looked at him, opened her mouth and shut it again and then opened it to speak.

'No biggy. You do realise you are going down for this? The cops might not have any idea what it's all about and what you are involved in, but if you are being challenged now, what's going to happen when you are off the scene? You're finished, aren't you?'

She looked at him, thinking, *clients never seem to learn from their mistakes.* She had given a lift home to a client for whom she had secured a community order, saving him from a prison sentence. He was incredibly fortunate, as his rap sheet resembled a child's Christmas list. His penchant was for stealing cars, which he usually crashed, leaving behind his fingerprints or DNA to be linked back to him swiftly afterwards. As he was being taken home, he sat in the passenger side of her car and had the nerve to try to take apart her crook lock. It was the latest model, and he hadn't seen one, so he hadn't had the opportunity to work out how to get round it.

Robert leant back in his chair and folded his arms behind his head. He was a big built man, six-feet-four tall, thirty-five years old, stocky but not fat, with rippling muscles. He worked out a lot and Caroline had no doubt he also took steroids. Robert had always had attitude, but when he was on stuff, he was more aggressive and unpredictable. His head was bald, deliberately so, and his thick neck, dark goatee beard and tattoos made him look instantly like someone not to mess with. Caroline hated the tattoo on his face, a spider's web with a spider hanging from a thread down the left side of his neck. He smiled. 'I'll be fine and dandy Caroline, don't you worry about that. I just need your help in another way. I have a cracking idea that would be good for both of us, but you'll need to think outside the box.'

Caroline looked at him, bemused. 'Thinking outside the box is my specialty. How do you think you've escaped convictions as much as you have?'

'I'm not knocking yer, keep your hair on,' he laughed. 'This is thinking well outside the box.'

'Come on then,' Caroline challenged, 'what exactly have you got in mind?'

Robert explained he ran a drugs ring. He'd been doing it for about five years. Caroline was astonished. She'd had absolutely no idea. He wasn't flash with watches, a fancy car, a nice house, or anything of that nature. Robert worked in the gym where he clearly spent a lot of time working out, and his lifestyle had always seemed to match his income. He was well connected. He often referred clients to her, but that wasn't unusual. It was a small town, they'd both grown up there and gyms brought lots of connections with all sorts of people.

'How exactly does it work?' Caroline asked, intrigued. 'And how have you never been caught?'

'Simple,' replied Robert. 'I know what I'm doing. I'm not greedy and I'm well connected.'

Caroline was aware that the county lines ran through Northampton, the town where Robert lived, she lived, and her practice was. Many years ago, it had been a lovely market town, but now it was run-down, overpopulated and lacked amenities. Drugs ran through from London to Birmingham, Manchester and Liverpool, and then further north. Northampton was a town with city crime Caroline knew, where knife crime was rife and gun crime was on the increase.

Robert divulged drugs came into the country at the ports. The higher part of the hierarchy was involved in this part, including customs officials and border control. That's how the drugs got in. They were concealed in vehicles and allowed to pass through. They then made their way up to London, where a lot of dealing and drug gangs were involved.

'Far too fucking dangerous to be involved in any of that,' Robert said. 'There's always fucking turf wars. You're more likely to get fucking stabbed to death or shot than lifted by the old bill. I know about it, but I have nothing to do with that part. I don't know names and I don't want to. The operation seems fucking reliable, and that's as much as I want to know.'

He paused and took a swig of his tea, *which must by now be stone cold,* Caroline thought. She didn't say anything, not wanting to interrupt him. She was intrigued, more than she knew she ought to be.

Robert knew he had her hooked. He could see it in her eyes. He knew she was bored, disheartened and discontented with her life and had been for some time, often commenting to him she wished she was in court more and not stuck in the office but even the court didn't interest her in the way it used to. He had counted on that. He knew from the moment he had given Lewis the kicking that he shouldn't have, and he would likely go down for it.

He hadn't planned it in advance. He'd learned just moments before that Lewis had hinted to one of the others he could run things better than Robert and he might try to take over. Thank god Kyle had told him. Kyle wasn't the brightest button in the box, but he was fiercely loyal, and Robert would take that any day over brains. Robert was the brains. He needed loyal foot soldiers to just do as they were told, and Kyle did that brilliantly. The trouble with Lewis was that he was greedy and too ambitious. That was dangerous, as they operated low key to stay off the radar.

Robert had been struggling to keep him in check for some time and so when he learned the news from Kyle, he had to deal with it fast. He knew where Lewis would be and ambushed him. He never said a word to him, just kicked the shit out of him.

He knew it had to be done, but wished he'd thought about it and planned it better. Robert wasn't a dweller, though. He'd learned in life that shit happened and it was how you deal with it that counted. Lying in bed on the night he'd been released on bail, he knew he was going to prison and knew he needed to safeguard what he'd built up. He wouldn't be away forever. For the most part, he could trust his men. He just needed someone in overall control.

That's when he'd thought of Caroline. She'd always had a soft spot for him, and they'd got to know each other quite well over the years. He knew she was married to her job, initially because she loved it and now because too much time had passed, and she couldn't get out of it. She wasn't happy and wasn't in a relationship as far as he knew. In fact, she didn't seem to have much of a life other than her beloved mutt Harley. Robert had smiled when he thought about Caroline with Harley. He wasn't her dog; he was her baby. He'd once said that to her, and she'd said that he was better than a baby. He wouldn't grow up; he'd always love his mummy and she wouldn't have to worry about exam results and girlfriends. It was sad, really, he thought. She'd have been a good mum. Perhaps that was why they'd bonded. She kind of mothered him and, if he was honest, he liked it.

'The drugs come to me in bulk at the gym,' he carried on. 'The guy has the London connections; I don't ask about them. I pay £22,000 for a kilo of heroin. I take it home and bulk it out with cutting agents and take it back to the gym. I sell it on in ounces at £1,000 to the retail dealers. I can clear it quickly cos this is to bigger suppliers who sell it on to users who, as you know, buy it in individual wraps or quarter kilos.'

'Ah yes,' interrupted Caroline, 'the nine-bar.'

'Spot on,' said Robert, grinning. 'I buy cocaine for the same per kilo, and I sell it at £1,200 per ounce. I am shifting about a kilo of each a fortnight.' Robert stopped speaking and continued looking at Caroline, who just looked back at him, trying to absorb everything she had just heard.

'You are making over £40k a week, over two million a year!' she exclaimed, hardly believing what she was saying.

The maths was easy. She was used to doing the calculations for clients' cases, remembering that there were thirty-six ounces in a kilo. Why large amounts were measured in metric and divided up on the imperial scale she could never fathom, other than to make her brain ache when she first started.

'Yet you drive a five-year-old Ford Focus and live in a rented house. Are you winding me up?' she said, thinking, *he's pretending to be something he clearly doesn't seem to be.*

'No way I'd wind you up,' he replied. 'Straight up, this is what I do. I haven't been earning it for three years, of course, it's taken time to build it up to what it is now. And I told you I'm not stupid. Old Bill sees Robert driving round in a fucking Porsche and living in a fuck off house they'll be all over me. No, they think I'm too fucking thick to be anything other than a petty criminal and a hothead, and that's how I like it. I've got a fantastic accountant; he's got the money offshore for me. I did think about crypto, but the guys I deal with ain't bright enough for that, so cash works.'

'How do you move that amount of money in today's climate with everything going more digital and cashless?' Caroline asked, concerned about how interested she was in all this.

'Dealers and druggies ain't digital,' Robert said, laughing. 'The druggies get their benefits, take the money out the bank and buy their wraps from the dealers. The dealers use that to pay me. I use that to pay my supplier and I give the rest to the accountant. He knows a guy in a casino who washes it for a percentage and the rest comes back to the accountant. He puts it in accounts in Belize, the British Virgin Islands and the Cayman Islands. They are top for confidentiality, and we spread the risk. The accountant and casino cost a bit and my men cost me a bit, but I'm still making over a million a year and I've got nearly half a mil in each account, so I'm cushty.'

Robert looked very pleased with himself, and Caroline could

not believe her ears. She knew Robert wasn't stupid, but never imagined that he was bright enough to get involved with something like this and pull it off. Mind you, look at him now. One hot-headed mistake, and it looked like it might all unravel.

'So why are you telling me all of this, Robert?' she asked.

'You know why,' he responded, looking her directly in the eyes. 'I'm on to a good thing here and I don't want to lose it. If I don't take care of it, it'll be gone by the time I get out. I trust you; you could run things for me while I'm away.'

'What?' Caroline exclaimed. 'That is absolutely bloody ridiculous. I'm a solicitor, I could get struck off, go to prison. And anyway, I don't know the first thing about drug dealing. I'm not connected to the gym. I don't know who you associate with. This is like something out of a movie,' she went on. However, inside she felt quite excited. She hadn't felt anything like that for more time than she cared to think about.

Caroline's reaction had disturbed Harley again. Now he was off his bed, standing next to Caroline, with his head in her lap, looking at her.

'It's alright lad,' she whispered to him patting his head and stroking his back, 'mummy is OK, just a bit surprised that's all.' She bent down and kissed the top of his head, and he looked up and kissed her face with wet licks.

'You and that dog,' Robert said, smiling.

'I love Harley more than anyone or anything in the whole world,' retorted Caroline, 'and no one had ever better forget it.'

'Woof,' said Harley in agreement and laid down on the floor next to her, as if confirming the position.

Harley's intervention had taken the temperature in the room down a few notches. Robert took the opportunity to continue setting out his plan.

'It doesn't matter what you don't know, it matters what you do. You are an intelligent lady; you know damn well how county lines and drug dealers work. No one would ever suspect you. I'm on bail.

This is going to the Crown Court. We both know that. I'll take it to trial and plead on the day. You don't need to tell me about credit for a guilty plea. I know all about it, but time to get this set up is more important than time I'll end up serving extra later. That'll give us months to get things properly sorted.

'The way I see it happening is that we'll get the London guy to deliver to you rather than me. Just think about where you want that to take place and he'll sort it. Kyle and Dale are the two of my team I trust the most. They'll take it from you and cut it and deliver it back. We'll agree on a rate we pay them for that. Then rather than dealing with the dealers at the gym, you can deal at court.'

'How on earth are we going to do that?' Caroline was incredulous. This was getting more and more silly by the minute.

'Easy,' he replied, as if she was foolish for even asking the question. 'You have cards, so you don't get searched going into court. You take in the drugs. I'll organise who is going to collect the drugs that day. I'll tell you and you take them into an interview room. They'll have the money hidden on them, probably in their trainers or sewn into the lining of their coats. You'll do the swap and that'll be that.'

'You've seriously been thinking about this, haven't you?' Caroline was a little worried about the intricate detail Robert was going into. He clearly expected her to do this.

'Absolutely I have,' Robert said enthusiastically. 'No way this can fail with the two of us in charge. I'll sort the deal with the accountant and casino as it is now. The accountant can set up accounts for you, same as for me, and move the money as he does now. None of that needs to change. It's just location change, nothing else. It'll involve a few more people as we can't have the same faces turning up at the court in the way we can at the gym but leave that with me. I'll figure that bit out. I've enough connections.'

'And what if I say no?' Caroline said.

'You won't,' Robert said, clearly very sure of himself. 'I'm making over two million a year before expenses, of course, but even paying those I'm clearing around a million, we'll split it 50:50. I'm not negotiating on the amounts. I've thought hard about this. I need to make some, but it needs to be attractive to you and you need to realise I am serious about this.'

Caroline took what she thought was the deepest breath she had ever taken. This was so dangerous. She trusted Robert as much as you could trust any client, but he could be a hothead, current case in point.

What would he do to her if she said no? Did she want to say no?

A hundred thoughts were flying through her brain all at once. It sounded quite easy, and there was a lot of money to be made. It wasn't just the money that was drawing her, though; it was the excitement. While he had been talking, she could feel it in her stomach rising through her chest and now fluttering butterfly-like at the back of her throat. She noticed that her heart was beating hard and fast in her chest, and she was breathing more rapidly.

Get control of yourself, she thought to herself firmly, *decide in haste repent at leisure.*

'This is a hell of a lot to take in, Robert,' she said forcefully. 'You are asking me to take my life in a direction I have never ever thought about, not in my wildest dreams and imaginations. I need time to think.'

'Not a fucking problem,' Robert replied, smiling inwardly.

She was in. He knew it was just a question of letting her play it all out in her mind, feel in control. If it was going to be a no, she'd have said it straight away. But he'd known deep down she would agree. It was just a matter of setting it all out and letting her see how easy it would be and how much money she could make and how fast. She'd have a couple of million in no time, and if she wanted to that would be more than enough to quit and do whatever she dreamed of doing other than work.

'How long will you need?' He didn't want to push her too hard, but he couldn't afford to hang around either, this was going to take time and effort to get right, and it had to be right before he went away.

'I'll ring you as soon as I've decided,' she replied. 'I know you need an answer, but I need to consider it all. It'll be days rather than weeks.'

'Good enough,' he replied, standing up. He bent down at the side of the desk to stroke Harley, who lifted his head. Robert smiled at him and winked at Caroline and left.

CHAPTER FIVE

THE DECISION

By the time Robert left the office, it was well after normal closing time. When Caroline opened her office door, she was surprised to see Sandra still at her desk, typing away.

'Everything OK?' she asked Caroline. 'You look a bit flustered.'

'I'm alright,' Caroline replied, 'just a bit tired. I thought everyone would be gone by now.'

'I just had a couple of bits I wanted to finish up now the phones have finally stopped ringing. What a day it's been. No one ever rings to say thank you anymore, do they? It's all complaining and moaning when they are the ones who've got themselves into the mess. If we don't have the answers they want, they shout and swear. I asked one young lad this afternoon if he'd rather I just bullshit him, tell him what he wants to hear and then wait for it to all go wrong in court.'

'What did he say to that?' Caroline asked, smiling.

'He told me to fuck off and hung up, cheeky little sod,' Sandra said. Although she was smiling now, Caroline knew how much this sort of thing upset Sandra. 'We all do our best but more and more now the clients seem to think it is OK to behave in this totally inappropriate manner.'

'Go home Sandra,' Caroline said. 'It's late enough. The rest can wait until tomorrow. You've earned a large glass of wine; go and put your feet up and enjoy.'

'I will,' Sandra replied. 'And if I don't speak to another human being until tomorrow, I won't be sorry,' she laughed. 'See you tomorrow.'

'See you tomorrow, and thanks Sandra. You don't deserve the hassle they give you on the phone and I really appreciate all that you do. I couldn't do it without you,' Caroline said genuinely and honestly.

'I know you do,' Sandra replied. 'That's why I still put up with it. Well, more importantly, so that I can see Harley,' she added, stroking his ears, and kissing his nose affectionately. 'See you tomorrow.'

Sandra left and Caroline did a check of the building before she left the office with Harley and walked to her car. She thought about how tired Sandra looked. Sandra was a petite lady in her early sixties. She had beautiful skin and did not look her age. She looked more exhausted today than she normally did, and Caroline thought to herself that one day soon Sandra would have had enough and quit.

On the drive home, she was thinking about the conversation with Robert and discussing it with Harley. All her decisions were made with him. He sat in the passenger seat on the way to and from work, listening to her moans and groans, dreams and desires. He was her closest confidant and keeper of all her secrets.

'Well Harley,' Caroline glanced over at him and there he was looking at her, so pleased as he always was to have her attention. 'If anyone had told me what was going to happen today, I would have told them they had taken something they shouldn't,' she said, laughing. 'Now I'm thinking it might just be the best idea anyone has ever come up with. I cannot put up with any more moaning and groaning from these clients. I just cannot do this until I retire and without this plan, I don't know if I could ever afford to retire. When you are young, you think you can change the world. I certainly did. Looking back, though, I've changed nothing at all. I've just got older, more tired and grumpier. Time to look out of the box and get out of it.'

'Woof, woof,' Harley barked.

'Well, that's settled then if you agree,' Caroline laughed and stroked his head and ears. 'I'll get Robert in tomorrow once I have thought through the finer details.'

As usual, Caroline had difficulty falling asleep when she went to bed, but this time it was not because of a client's case that was worrying her, or an audit, or a problem with a member of staff. It was how her life could be changing its trajectory. She felt almost schizophrenic. Part of her wanted this because of the excitement and financial opportunity to get out and do something else with her life. On the other hand, it was one hell of a risk, colloquially getting into bed with a client, crossing the line, becoming a criminal. She smiled as she thought that no one would ever believe that strait-laced Caroline would contemplate such a thing, let alone be seriously planning how she might carry it out successfully.

Even when she fell asleep, she wasn't asleep for long. She was soon awake, mulling everything over in her head.

Could she really make this work? Could she live with herself? Could she avoid getting caught? Caroline worried about what would happen if she was caught. *Prison for sure and for a long time, they'd make an example of someone bringing the justice system into such disrepute. Who would look after Harley? How would he cope without his mummy?*

He wouldn't, she was sure of that, and she certainly couldn't cope without him. She'd just have to make damn sure she didn't get caught. As if to confirm this, Harley snuggled right into her, and she put her arm over him. He was lying on the left-hand side of the bed on his left-hand side like a person. She smiled to herself in the dark. While she loved Harley more than words could say, she rarely got a good night's sleep because of him, although she would never stop him from coming on the bed. He had an uncanny knack of lying on his back and stretching out his legs in a starfish shape, using his sharp elbows to nudge Caroline over so that she ended up on a very small strip at the edge of the bed.

'The price you pay for love,' she laughed to herself as she listened to Harley snoring.

At nine the following morning, Caroline rang Robert from the office phone. She was not taking any chances. He was a client and, although they rang clients all the time from mobiles and out of hours, she wanted this to be a very clear client/solicitor relationship should anyone start digging around in the future. He was obviously surprised but pleased to be hearing from her so soon. She asked him to come into the office for an appointment at four that afternoon so that they could discuss matters further.

She then told Sandra of the appointment who said, 'You only saw him yesterday,' in a surprised tone. 'Is his case that complex?'

'Oh yes,' Caroline replied, 'more than I realised.'

At ten to four, Robert was in the reception waiting for his appointment. Caroline was sitting in her office and was free to see him then but kept him waiting for the full ten minutes. She wanted to be in control of their relationship and was determined to start how she meant to go on. Caroline had never had any business connections with a client before and her whole working life she had been in control. She did not intend to let that change. Caroline knew she could not afford to show any weakness. Robert could be unpredictable, as his current matter showed. Doing business with him was a risk, and she needed to minimise that risk from the outset.

'Sorry to keep you waiting, Robert,' she said as he came in. 'It's been one of those days.'

Robert came in with Harley, who'd been out in reception with Sandra. He was licking his lips and Caroline realised that Robert had clearly been feeding him biscuits. Harley looked very pleased with himself and took his regular spot under her desk.

'Well, make the right decision,' he responded, 'and those sorts of days will be as limited as you want them to be.'

He looked directly at her, trying to figure out what was coming next. He was certain that she would go for the idea, but she seemed more confident and more in control than yesterday. That was only to be expected though, that was what had made her so good at her job all these years.

'I was absolutely shocked yesterday when you approached me with this, Robert, I'm not going to lie,' she said looking him directly in the eyes, 'but having mulled it over I think we can come to a very convenient working arrangement for both of us. In broad terms, I think what you have worked out and the financial split is fair, and I won't haggle with you about that. However, for me to make it work this end I'm going to have to bring in a few of my team. As you know, I run the practice. I don't want to, but I do and there is no one else to do it. Your scheme, while potentially making us very rich in the medium term, isn't going to make me a millionaire overnight, so the business must keep going. That means I need to stay put in the office.'

Caroline paused to see how that went down. Robert said nothing, clearly waiting to see how she planned to make this work.

'We will have to cut Alex in on the deal,' Caroline explained. 'He is the one who goes to court, so he is the one who will have to be the carrier of the drugs and the recipient of the money.'

'No way,' Robert said. 'He's a brilliant lawyer, but he couldn't find his way out of a fucking paper bag. The last time he dealt with me at court he'd forgotten his cufflinks. He had bloody bulldog clips keeping them together. It was funny at the time, but how can a fucking buffoon like that deal with this? The people involved ain't nice, you know. Fuck up and you get your throat slit. He'll drop us in the crap the first bloody week.'

Caroline had expected this reaction. In fact, it had been her own reaction when she was first thinking it through, but she didn't see any other way of doing it. Some risks would have to be taken whether they liked it or not, and this was one of them.

'Robert,' she said firmly, 'I know what he's like more than most. I'm taking an enormous risk and I won't make it any more dangerous than it has to be. But like it or not, he's got to be involved, otherwise the court angle is a no-go. It will also have to involve others of our staff too. You well know how unpredictable courts can be with volume of cases and length of cases. I can't guarantee Alex can be in the right place at the right time all the time. This needs to be seamless.'

'How many staff are you thinking?' Robert asked. 'The more staff, the more risk of being found out and also the more people that need paying from all of this. I'm making good money, but the risks are high. There's no point doing it if the risks are increasing, and the reward is disappearing.'

'I'm thinking of a bigger operation,' Caroline said confidently. 'And I want to cut in my most loyal members of my team. Criminal defence work is hard work, Robert. Long hours, poor pay and ever increasingly unreasonable demands from the government. Ridiculous decisions made by people who have never done the job and could never do it. I wouldn't have my firm without my team, not all of them, but my core people. I want to give them a payday. Alex and a couple of the other solicitors can take care of the court side. I'm also thinking of connecting with those in prison who get remanded. We could get drugs into them under Rule 39. We could then continue that with you when you are inside.'

'Holy bloody moly,' Robert exclaimed, rubbing his hands together. 'You are thinking of a right little empire here, aren't you? I like the Rule 39 angle though. Bloody clever that, I'm kicking myself I didn't think of it. Stamp Rule 39 on the outside of the package and the screws can't fucking open it. Drugs are in with the papers. Nice angle. I'll have a think about who we can use until I'm sent there. We'll want a few practice runs.'

'Also,' continued Caroline, keen to keep the flow going as Robert seemed receptive to her ideas, 'I want to keep the gym part going too. There's a fair few mouths to feed here, as you've already rightly commented on. Let's go large or go home. My trainee would be perfect for the gym drops. He'd rather be at the gym than doing his work, so I might as well make use of him. He doesn't seem to realise this is a 24/7 job sometimes with courts and police station call-outs. He'd rather be working out so he can work for me while he's doing that.'

Caroline was pleased to feel she would be getting something out of Seb at last. He was a typical millennial in her eyes. Talked the talk but couldn't be bothered to walk the walk. He liked the idea of the title of a solicitor without the hours of extremely hard graft that were needed to bring it about. He wanted the pay of a CEO but to work about two hours a week.

'Wow, this is a very big plan,' Robert whistled through his teeth. 'So, we have got the gym part going I've got now, we've got deals at court and drugs going into prison. Course we'll make double bubble on the stuff going inside so that'll be a great markup. How much are you thinking we are going to be making?'

Robert was intrigued with the whole idea while thinking, *could he increase the amount he was getting in? Would the supplier be able to do that? Would they find enough buyers?* His head started spinning. He certainly had not been expecting all of this.

'Well, we hope the gym will make us about 40k per week as it is now. If we pay Kyle and Dale out of that bit, we should clear about £25k per week easy, probably more. The only other one to pay is Seb. Once we are up and running at court, it depends on who you think we can use to move the stuff and how much you think we can shift. I would hope it would be about the same amount, but we'd have Alex plus William and Michael to pay out of that. You know them both. They are my most reliable solicitors, and we'd need them both. I reckon £10k to Alex, and £5k to the other two so we'd clear £9k there. Sending stuff into prison is just my secretary, Sandra. I'd want her to make some money out of this. She works so hard and with obnoxious clients; her job gets tougher by the day. I also want my police station rep Ian to be in on this. He works incredibly hard and can fill in any gaps. Then it's whoever you think in prison and how much of a cut they want for it. You can do it once you're in there. At least that will make your stay worthwhile. If we move half of the amount in there, we'll still get the same for it. Overall, I think we can make £90k per week, £45k each, which isn't bad.'

Caroline sat back in her chair and drew a breath. There it was out there for Robert to digest, the ruminations of a very sleepless night while she had tried to pull it altogether with the figures to make it work.

'Far bigger than I could even think of, let alone run,' Robert said, full of admiration. 'But that's why you are where you are, and I never made anything of school or exams. You think you can keep control of all of this cos my brain is fucking boggled just thinking about it all?' he said, scratching the top of his bald head. 'If you can, I'll be making over two mil a year, the same as I am now. I won't lose anything even though I'm sharing half with you. I can't fucking believe it.'

'Alex calls me the thin controller or commander,' she said, laughing. 'It has wound me up not only because I hate being the controller, but also because I don't enjoy what I am in control of anymore. I need job satisfaction. All my life I've been driven, now I'm just being driven mad. This will give me exactly what I need, a real challenge. I want more than fifty per cent, though. You'll be in custody, and I'll be the one trying to keep it all together.'

'Absolutely bloody not, no fucking way,' Robert replied angrily. 'Yes, your ideas, if they work, expand the business, but you wouldn't have anything to expand if it wasn't for me. I'll still be sorting things in prison, especially if you want deals at court and moving drugs into prison. In fact, as you pointed out, it'll work better when I am in there. No fucking way, it's half or nothing,' Robert glared.

'Alright, alright, keep your wig on, oh you haven't got one,' Caroline chuckled, patting Harley, who had stood up at the shouting and was standing at the side of her. 'You can't blame a girl for trying. Half each it is, but we won't let on to Alex what we are earning. We'll need to keep the figures away from him. Ten thousand pounds is a lot and if we give him more, it reduces what we get. It's our baby and we'll keep it between us. You need to keep your two boys in check, Kyle and Dale, and make sure they are on board. You will need to get Seb set up for the gym and work with me on how we are logistically going to sort the courts and prison. I describe my practice as an octopus, lots of legs to keep under control, so I've had plenty of experience.

'I'll sort Alex, William, Michael, Ian and Sandra. We'll need regular contact, though; you can't have too many appointments as not all the staff are going to be in on this. I don't want to ring you from my mobile or the landline. The less record, the better.'

'Ahhh, for once I'm ahead of you,' Robert said proudly.

She had placated him with backing down over the money. He had expected pushback from her, more so in fact, perhaps she was a little scared of him. Rightly so, he wouldn't turn on her unless he had to but each man for himself and all that.

He reached into the rucksack he was carrying and handed over a burner phone.

'This is yours. I've got one. Your number's in mine, mine's in yours. Any concerns ever, dump the phone and we'll get another. Kyle and Dale have burners, their numbers are on your phone. When we get the rest of the team organised, I'll sort burners out for them. We only communicate through them. I only want to deal with you from the office side of things. You deal with me for my side until I go inside, then it'll be Kyle. He ain't the brightest, but he'll do exactly as he's told, which is what you want. You don't want the likes of him thinking outside the box, ever,' he said, laughing and winking.

There was a glint in his eyes. This was better than he could have ever hoped for. All his Christmases had come at once with her agreeing to run things while he was inside, so he didn't lose what he'd built up, but this was even better. He'd be coming out to a real empire.

Caroline could see that Robert was pleased with what she'd put together. She would need his help with the client side of things, as they had to be incredibly careful who was involved. That is where there was a real risk. If the police picked any of them up and they thought it was worth their while to spill the intel they wouldn't think twice. She could also see that she'd made it attractive to him, building it up, so he'd have something even bigger to come out to. Well, that's if she was still around by then. She hoped to make it big before that and then just vanish off the grid, but no harm in keeping everyone sweet and right where she wanted them.

'How easy do you think it's going to be to get everyone on board?' Robert asked.

'I'll persuade them, and it won't take long,' Caroline replied immediately. 'We don't have long to get this up and running to make sure it all works,' she added. 'I plan to speak to Alex as soon as he is back from court today.'

'Good luck with that,' Robert replied. 'I'm not sure he's as good as you at thinking outside the box.'

'Maybe not,' Caroline responded, 'but I can be very persuasive when I want to be. I'll be in touch when things are in place this end.'

'Woof,' agreed Harley.

CHAPTER SIX

ALEX

Alex came straight into Caroline's office as soon as he got back from court, as he always did. He slumped down into the chair opposite her and sighed.

'I'm getting too old for this shit,' he said, half-jokingly.

He took off his jacket and slung it over the back of the chair. Caroline knew that is where it would stay until either he needed it again or she at least hung it up on a hanger, so it didn't look like he'd slept in it the next time he wore it. His waistcoat was missing a button or two, not because he was too portly for it, but because he had caught them on something and lost them. Then she noticed he had bulldog clips for cufflinks again and she smiled, thinking back to what Robert had said about him.

'What are you grinning at?' Alex asked.

'Your accessories,' Caroline retorted.

'Forgot my fucking cufflinks again,' Alex laughed. 'I must put a set in my bag, so I've got spares.'

'They won't be there for long,' Caroline said, grinning. 'You'll need them the minute you put them in there, then leave them lying around or lose them and you'll be in the same pickle again. I don't know why you find dressing so difficult. Just put on everything you need when you get up.'

Caroline knew that would be impossible. The mess he left in the office must be a tiny window into the world of his house. She didn't know how Rhi put up with it. She'd find it very difficult when the baby came, as she already had a big one she was constantly looking after. Caroline didn't envy her.

'I really need to talk to you,' Caroline said, looking directly at Alex. 'I need you to listen to me without interrupting at all.'

'Sounds serious,' Alex said, sitting up straighter in the chair. 'What's this all about? You are worrying me.'

'Nothing to worry about, but it's a lot to explain and a lot to take in. You won't see the complete picture if you don't let me set it out.'

'OK,' said Alex anxiously.

As if to reinforce the importance, Harley put his head in Alex's lap. Alex stroked his head while focusing on Caroline. It took Caroline the best part of thirty minutes to set out the conversations that had taken place with Robert and her plan. She could see Alex was having real trouble keeping quiet and a couple of times he had opened his mouth to say something, and she had just held up a finger to silence him. She continued with her monologue, not giving him the chance to interrupt her. His eyes, saucer-like, got wider and wider with incredulity as she was speaking. His pace stroking Harley had got faster, although he was clearly not aware of that.

Now she had finished, she sat back in her chair, waiting for his response. He opened his mouth, but nothing came out. For the first time, he was speechless. If it hadn't been so serious, she would have laughed out loud. Alex always had something to say. Whether it was a story he was regaling from court, or a witty one-liner, he was not known for silence.

Harley, obviously feeling he'd been stoked hard enough, crept under Caroline's desk to the sanctuary of his bed.

'Say something,' Caroline said, the quiet beginning to unnerve her. 'Usually, I cannot cope with the endless stream that comes out of your mouth, but the silence is worse.'

'You are joking, aren't you?' Alex finally responded. 'This is a wind-up, isn't it? You are not seriously thinking about this, are you?'

'I'm deadly serious,' Caroline replied, her voice low but stern. 'It might be alright for you. You still get out in the cut and thrust. You have fun at court and get the thrill of winning legal arguments and cases. I am trapped in this office supervising cases I don't care about anymore. In fact, I'm struggling to remember if I ever did. Constantly chasing the prosecution for CCTV, papers, etc. because no one seems able to do the job they are paid to do anymore.

'No one ever has to chase me, but no one ever seems to think about that. Do you know Michael was criticised at court last week when he did a trial and asked for an adjournment because the prosecution hadn't supplied the footage they should have done? The District Judge had the audacity to say that we should have chased it more. Three telephone calls and four emails clearly aren't seen as chasing these days, yet two unwanted contacts can get you arrested for harassment. The world has gone mad. Good job I wasn't the one in court because I'd have said no one has to fucking chase me to do the job I'm paid to, so why don't you criticise the lazy bastards for not even having the courtesy to reply?'

'That's why you don't go to court often,' Alex said, laughing loudly. 'Otherwise, I'd be getting a call from the cells to say you'd been arrested for contempt.'

He looked at Caroline and she knew he could see what had been obvious for a long while now. She hated her job. She was a brilliant advocate but sadly a brilliant manager too and no one else was capable of that job. To keep a government legal aid contract, it wasn't just about helping clients and doing the work on cases. In fact, that seemed to be less and less important. It was more about business plans, manuals, policies, appraisals and endless form filling. Caroline knew he would hate to do it and also be useless at it. She appreciated he understood why she hated it so much. She knew he avoided discussing it with her because there was no straightforward solution to it. They couldn't run the business without her doing what she did. Caroline knew it, and so did he. Knowing this fact didn't make it any easier to handle.

'I know how unhappy you are,' he said softly. 'But we've spoken about this before and there isn't any other way of doing things.'

'Maybe not until now,' she replied quickly. 'This is my way out and you are not stopping me.' She glared at him. 'I am sick of doing what I am doing. I have sacrificed everything, the best years of my life for this job, and I have little to show for it.'

She hated saying it out loud. Caroline was not someone to feel sorry for herself and didn't like others pitying her either. She also didn't like voicing that she thought she'd made a terrible career decision and wasted her life.

'You have a lot to show for it, Caroline,' Alex coaxed. 'We have a very successful practice, and the clients still love you. It is largely down to you we have the firm we have. The clients wanted you at court because you were tenacious and proactive, and you are the same running the office. We get amazing results for people that need us. We win trials. People's lives go in a more positive direction because we get the right decisions. Not always, I know, and it is terribly sad when someone is convicted, and we don't think they did it. We also have our fair share of arseholes to deal with too, I know that. I also know you get the brunt of that when they ring the office moaning. But we fight for the underdog. That's why you came into this and that hasn't changed.'

'But things have changed, Alex,' Caroline said sadly. 'And I've changed. The clients are more and more difficult. Millennials don't seem to want to do a stroke of work and think the world owes them everything. A lot of them don't even ring up anymore, it's too much hassle and they are usually in bed all day, so their stupid mothers or girlfriends ring up on their behalf. The ones that do bother tell us they are paying our wages out of the fucking taxes that we pay them for their benefits. It's all I can do not to put my "Mr Tickle" arms around their throats and strangle them. It's all "mental health" being used as some excuse for just being fucking rude and obnoxious. Clients have had mental health problems for my entire career. Now it just seems to be a convenient label for unacceptable behaviour. Sure, we get the odd client that is different from that. They need us and are grateful for what we do, but they are getting fewer and farther apart. Ask Sandra, she had a right gutful of it yesterday.' Caroline paused, gathered herself and continued.

'I've changed too. You start off all enthusiastic in your twenties thinking that no one before you has got it right, you have the newest and best ideas, and you can change the world. Twenty-five years later you turn round, you're single, you've had no kids because you've been married to the job and the world has just got worse. You've changed absolutely nothing. All that has happened is you've got older and more bitter because you believed the bullshit that working hard and fighting a good cause would make you a better person when, in fact, it just makes you mentally and physically exhausted. That's me, that's my lot. And I don't even have anywhere near enough to think about retiring. Money's not important, they say. Well, those who are saying it are saying it because they have plenty of it. I should have listened to my lecturers at uni, they desperately tried to change my mind, make me go into a more profitable area of law but I wouldn't have it. I was the great Caroline, and I was going to do great things.'

Caroline stopped. She didn't do this; she was normally a positive person trying to find the best in every situation. Caroline hated herself for being like this but realised that in fact all she did was put a veneer on each day, put on her make-up, her court face, but it didn't change what was underneath. She had just chosen not to think about it and certainly not voice it until now. It was always there at the back of her mind, but she was a believer in not dwelling on what you couldn't change. That's why it was all coming out now. Robert had given her a way out. He'd given her the plan to change, and she knew that there was no way things could stay the same now.

Caroline saw Alex had the lightbulb moment at the same time. He now appreciated she had put up with it because she didn't see a solution. This was the way her life was supposed to be, she had assumed. Now a completely different route was available to her, and she knew he could see she wasn't going to be diverted from it however much he tried.

'Caroline, you have done great things,' he implored, 'you just can't see it. You took over and expanded this practice and have a large client base. You run the contract, which is complicated, and we do well at our audits because of you and your organisation. You find witnesses on cases that make a real difference and there are people out there living their lives because they were not convicted of what they were accused of. That's down to you. Have you forgotten about Lee? On remand for murder and a terribly sloppy job done by the police. A few criminals named him, so he's in the frame. It was you trailing round finding the others who were there, getting statements from them that meant he got four years for manslaughter instead of about twenty years for murder. What we do matters, we matter, you matter.'

'Like I said, the odd case where we make a difference, but it's not enough compensation for the rest of the tedious grind. This way we can do both until we make enough money. Then I'm out. You can do what you want after that,' Caroline said emphatically.

'You know that if we do this, there is no way out of it until we've made enough to change our lives totally. There's no going back to running the practice the way it is now,' Alex said seriously.

There it was, the change in tone, the change in words. It wasn't a *no now*; it was an *if we do, we can't go back*. This was what Robert had seen in her and was when he knew he had her. She was sure of it. Now she was beginning to draw Alex in. Time for the final kill.

'Alex, you are ill all the time,' she said kindly. 'You know I worry about you. You've had that constant cough for over a year now. I know the doctors say it's nothing to worry about but it's a sign your immune system is constantly fighting something and that's not good for you long term. Every time a cold goes round court or the office you get it, heavens only know what you'll be like when the baby comes. They get every bug going. We both work ridiculous hours. The court days are long enough, but we both work on cases at home every evening and weekend. Then there's police station call-outs on top. This pace is not sustainable. We don't eat well. How many times have you gone home, and you haven't eaten a thing all day? I'm the same. We spend so much time looking after other people we aren't looking after ourselves and I don't care what you say, those people don't appreciate it like they used to.'

'You are right, I know,' Alex said, and he suddenly looked exhausted. 'I'm constantly tired but wired on coffee. I love Rhi but she often says I care more about work and the clients than I do about her. It's not true, of course, but I can see her point. I hardly spend any time with her. I'm always reading cases and when we are together, I'm usually falling asleep. We go to watch a film and ten minutes in, I'm snoring my head off. I know I am not good company; she makes a joke that she's amazed we found time together to make a baby, but I know it gets to her. I'm thrilled we are having our little boy, but worried too. I'm an older dad and I've barely got the energy to get up in the morning. The thought of sleepless nights caused by anything other than work worries me and I wonder where the hell I'm going to get the time and energy from to be a proper dad.'

Alex looked sad. Caroline understood he'd just voiced the worries he'd kept suppressed. She knew until now, every time it had nagged away in the back of his head, he'd thought *it'll be fine.* He'd just distracted himself by thinking about something else. She knew this because that's exactly what she had done too. Now voicing his fears had made it sound even worse than it had in his head, just as it had for her.

'That's why we have to get out,' Caroline jumped in. 'We are not getting any younger. We live on our nerves, constantly in fight-or-flight mode. We never get time to relax and do things for ourselves or better still just do nothing at all and recharge our knackered batteries. I've missed out on so much and you are falling and will continue to fall into that trap if we don't change trajectory. You'll never see the baby and when you do, you'll be too tired to enjoy it. You'll have to work longer and harder to pay for your family.

'We are like hamsters on wheels going absolutely nowhere, but now we are getting so tired that turning the wheel is getting harder and harder. What's it all for? Put in as many hours as you can to miss out on so many other aspects of life? Why is work time so much more valuable than leisure time and family time? It isn't, but you get on that treadmill at school, and you believe the crap they feed you, that we have to work hard, we have to get a good job. Why? To pay your taxes and die before you retire and start taking money out of the system. No, not us, not anymore. We are bright Alex; we know the cock-ups that clients make that get them caught. We won't. We've joked about it before that we'd make much better criminals than they do. This is a good plan. This will work. We won't be greedy, and we are as bright as we think we are. We can do this. You don't want to look back when your son is eighteen and you've missed everything, and his childhood has gone by in the blink of an eye.'

'I'm worried about Robert. He's a hothead at times. Look at him now. I hear what you say about why he's in this mess, but we can't afford for him losing his shit and somehow this coming out. I trust you implicitly. That's why we run our business together. Robert's a client when all's said and done and I know he's clearly got away with a lot, but he's been caught a fair few times over the years.'

'I understand your worries, I truly do. But he's the one with the operation that we are expanding. We need to learn from him and then adapt and expand as per my vision. We'll be reasonably safe when he's in custody. He'll be getting money for doing not a lot, so it's in his interests to keep his trap shut. The same before he goes in, if we don't master it, he'll have fuck all to come out to. He needs us; we need him. That's why it'll work.'

'How much are we going to make out of all of this?' Alex asked.

'Well,' Caroline replied. She'd been expecting him to ask of course and wanted to make sure he got enough information, but not too much. She was determined he wasn't getting the same as her. It was Robert's idea, so he deserved his half. She would be the one with the headache of running it and expanding it. There was no way Alex would be capable of doing something like this. She would be lucky if he did his part without totally cocking it up. '£10k for you per week and £5k for everyone else. We are the bosses, so we are taking the bigger risk, but they'll still be getting a good whack.'

'Half a mil a year,' Alex whistled. He clearly thought she would get the same from the way she had phrased it, as he didn't question her further.

'Minimum,' Caroline added. 'If we can get the prison part properly up and running, there's serious money to be made there.'

'Yes of course, it's double, isn't it?'

'Absolutely, and with Robert headed that way, it'll get easier not harder for us.' Caroline continued the hard sell.

'Alright,' Alex said. 'Let's do this. Tell Robert I'm in and we'll get the staff on board. He needs to get the burner phones and we need a meeting to start getting each bit up and running. We don't want to be doing it all at the same time, otherwise it's going to go tits up. We've got time before he goes to prison, so let's use it to learn the ropes and get this set-up foolproof.'

'Woof, woof,' said Harley, and licked his hand.

'I think he's confirming I've made the right decision,' Alex said to Caroline, winking at her.

CHAPTER SEVEN

THE TEAM

Three days later was the soonest Caroline could make sure all the players were together in the office. The unpredictability of the job was one of the fundamental problems with criminal law work. Planning was very difficult. Much of the time, all those working in the criminal law field had to be reactive, which was partly why everyone was so stressed and exhausted. No one knew who was going to be arrested and when and how long the case would take at the police station. Cases were booked into the magistrates' court and Crown Court, but some clients only asked for the firm on the day, assuming that by some process of osmosis Caroline would know they were in court and ensure representation. In the magistrates' court, it was especially challenging because of the unknown factor of how many prisoners would be held for court. The magistrates' court was the accident and emergency department of the court system Caroline often thought, and after slogging there day in day out in the past felt as worn out as a junior doctor. The hours were certainly comparable.

That didn't even factor in clients being arrested and taken to police stations and courts out of the area which always added drama to the rich tapestry of the working day. There was also the unknown element of how long cases would take. Would the bail application or sentence take ten minutes or an hour? Would the trial in the Crown Court take the estimated four days or, in fact, turn out to be eight? Caroline had always said you might as well pick a number out of the air because nothing ever ran to time, especially when lawyers were involved. Too many of them were full of their own self-importance and liked the sound of their own voices. The Crown Court was more like the operating theatre, but Caroline guessed surgeons would have to be far more accurate with timings than the lawyers ever were.

There was no fancy meeting room or conference room. This was a criminal practice. Space was at a premium and every part of the building was maximised. There wasn't a desk for everyone, but the nature of the job meant that rarely, if ever, was the entire team present. Some advocates could go several days without making it into the office. Thank goodness for digital working, Caroline often said. The logistics of moving files weren't as bad as it used to be, although there would have to be more movement now to hide the money and the drugs.

William, Michael, Seb, Ian and Sandra were all gathered in the Crown Court office. It was the biggest room, so it was where meetings occurred when everyone was in person. It was rare for everyone to attend meetings these days. When they happened it was the usual office meeting that took place every three months, as the government required. Half the staff were normally missing as they were in court or the police station and most linked in on Zoom from those places if they could between cases. It was most unusual to be called together like this, where they all had to attend. It was out of hours, not that they minded; they were all used to putting in extra, but they didn't know why they had been summonsed or why it was just them.

'Where's everyone else?' said Seb.

'I don't know,' replied Sandra. 'I don't even know if anyone else is supposed to be here. I just got told by Caroline to be here. There wasn't the general email to everyone that normally goes out about a meeting, was there?'

They all agreed that there hadn't been and in fact they had all been told in person to attend by either Caroline or Alex. It hadn't occurred to them to ask each other whether they were attending. They had just assumed everyone was going to be there. The level of intrigue was growing.

'This is quite odd,' William mused. 'I wonder what it's all about. I hope we are not having another surprise audit and we've been selected to help. I can barely keep on top of the paperwork I have with the court cases, let alone anything else,' he grumbled.

William was your archetypal solicitor. He looked the part and acted the part. Mid-fifties, white, with dark greying hair that made him look distinguished. Not fat, but stocky and tall. He was an imposing figure physically and commanded a room when he spoke. He was kind and witty, but was coming towards the twilight of his career, and could occasionally be ground down with the stress of the job to the point he was off sick.

'Tell me about it,' Ian, the police station rep, chimed in. 'I'm going from case to case in the police station. I just about have time to write what I need to on the forms, the basics mind you, and then I have to set the files up on the computer and do all the letters afterwards. It's very time-consuming.'

Ian was brilliant at the police station. He could crack through several cases while making the clients feel they were the only ones needing his time. He stood no nonsense from the police and was not at all intimidated by them. Ian knew the law better than most and fought hard for every client. He was not one to back down from an argument. The police hated him, and the clients loved him.

'I'm sure it'll be nothing like that,' Michael said softly.

Michael was the oldest of the team at the spritely age of seventy-three. He used to have his own practice but had given that up a number of years ago. He got fed up with the management side of things and just wanted to do the job he loved. Caroline and Alex snapped him up. Technology was a bit of a stumbling block, but he was as sharp a lawyer as ever. When it suited him, he gave the impression of a bumbling old man only to cut the legs out of the opposition, who have been foolish enough to believe it. Married with a grown-up family, he worked because he liked it. He didn't desire holidays, reading, gardening, relaxing or any of the normal retirement hobbies. Caroline had never understood this, dreaming of retirement daily herself, but counted her blessings every day that he continued to be part of the team.

'I'd rather be at the gym,' chirped Seb. 'I'm not on call for the police station tonight. This is my evening to do what I want to do for a change. I wish they'd hurry up.'

'Relax,' said Michael, 'plenty of time for the gym, son. Don't get stressed.'

Caroline had often thought Michael wouldn't know stress if it hit him on the nose. Michael was the most laid-back, easy-going person she had ever met in her life. She wished she could be like him but found life just too frustrating.

Seb was Caroline's trainee. She found him exhausting as she did most young people. He was constantly late, seemed permanently tired, although he put in fewer hours than anyone else in the office and seemed to take ages doing the simplest of tasks. When he shadowed Michael at the police station, he went home halfway through the night tired, leaving Michael to carry on alone. Caroline had torn a strip off him for that. A twenty-four-year-old going home tired leaving a seventy-three-year-old at the police station fighting the fight. Caroline said they'd never win a war now as all the youngsters would get sick notes or get their mums to ring up, making excuses for them. It would be the likes of William and Michael on the front line, the average age being late forties. It was funny as a joke, but it wasn't funny. Seb was the epitome of the youngsters. He wanted to earn a fortune and be the boss by doing as little work as possible.

At that moment, Caroline, Alex and Harley came into the room.

'So sorry to keep you all,' Caroline said sincerely. 'We do appreciate you all staying late, but we think you will be very interested in what we have to say,' she continued, smiling, and making eye contact with all of them. 'What I am about to tell you will only work if we all agree. It must be kept absolutely confidential. Only this group and others that you will become aware of will know about it. No one else here can know about it and no one outside can know. That means you're nearest and dearest, anyone at all.'

They were all looking at her, barely breathing. You could have heard a pin drop. She was certain she had captivated all of them, so she told the story just as she had to Alex. She expanded on what she had initially told Alex, repeating some of the exchange they'd had following her setting out the plan so that they could understand the reasoning behind why they were both up for this even though it was so risky.

As she was talking, Harley sat with her bolt upright. Not his usual position. He stared intently at them all as if he knew the importance of what was taking place.

'So,' Caroline said, coming to the end of her explanation for the meeting. 'This is the plan that we have designed and now you know why each of you has been chosen and how you fit into it. What do you think?' Caroline looked around and it was like looking around Madame Tussauds. No one moved, no one even seemed to be breathing. 'Say something someone,' she urged.

'Woof, woof,' interjected Harley, by way of encouragement.

'Come on guys,' Alex interjected. 'I was as shocked as you are now when Caroline first told me. I thought it sounded like something out of the fiction section, but we've thought this through very carefully and tweaked the original set-up a lot to maximise return and minimise risk.'

'I don't even know where to start,' said William. 'I just cannot get my head round this. I feel like I am in a dream. This isn't a wind-up, is it?'

Alex laughed, 'That's pretty much word for word what I said when Caroline first told me about it. But no, it isn't. We are deadly serious. We all work very hard. Often it feels like we are chasing our tails, achieving very little and earning a pittance compared to all the hours we put in. Here's a chance to make some real money and quickly.'

'How much money are we talking about?' Seb asked.

Caroline had anticipated he'd be the most interested. He'd like the idea of maximum return for minimum effort and having to go to the gym would be right up his alley. The part was made for him, and she could see that was exactly what he was thinking, too.

'I mean, there's some risk to me, ain't there?' he said. 'I'm the only one operating on the gym front, the young black man, the one the cops are most likely to be interested in out of all of us.'

'Now that's stereotypical if ever I heard it,' Caroline responded. 'I picked you for that role because you love the gym. You already go there because it's across the road from the office. You'd live and work from there if you could, anyway. Plus, it's the part of the operation that's been successfully running for years now. No reason that should change. Your part is lower risk.'

'Quite,' said William. 'Also, I can hardly run the operation at the gym. Don't think anyone's going to be fooled that I work out, do you?' he said, laughing.

'Nor me,' chimed in Michael. 'Not unless they are holding a fittest oldie competition.' They all laughed at that.

'Five grand a week each is guaranteed, more if we make more. We are not here to rob anyone, and everyone is needed to make it work. That's why you've been chosen and that's why we've expanded the operation in the way we have so that everyone can make a lot of money.' Caroline looked at everyone individually to see their reaction.

'I never ever thought I'd hear myself saying this, but I'm tempted,' said William.

Caroline was also surprised. She liked William a lot but thought he would be far too straight for this and would need a hell of a lot of persuading.

'I think I've got about another five years in me,' he continued.

'If we can keep it running that long I'll make over a million, maybe even more.' The cogs were whirring in his head doing the sums while he was speaking. 'That'll be far more than my pension I've been paying into all these years. It'll firmly safeguard my future. I'm in.'

'Well,' said Michael. 'Of all the meetings I've ever been to in my career, I can honestly say I've never been to one like this.'

Caroline was also worried about whether Michael would be on board. He didn't need the money at his time of life. He didn't work for that. Michael did it because he enjoyed being part of something and didn't want to be at home too much with his lovely wife. They'd survived fifty years of marriage, he said, because they'd only seen each other for the equivalent of half of that. If he was at home, there were jobs to do, so he'd rather be out at the police station or court. He still enjoyed the cut and thrust of it all. The attitude of the clients didn't seem to bother him in the way it did everyone else. Nothing phased or flustered him ever. He was the kindest man Caroline had ever met, but she wouldn't want to be on the other side of a case to him. 'The smiling assassin' the prosecution called him, and they weren't wrong. You didn't see his move coming until it was too late. That is why she had chosen him. No one would ever suspect him in a million years.

'I'm in the twilight of my life. I still do this because I enjoy it but I've less to lose than the rest of you. I'm nearer to the end in any event,' he said philosophically.

'Christ, that's a bit morbid, Michael,' Ian piped up.

'Not at all,' Michael replied. 'It's just reality. I'm lucky I'm fit enough to do this, but I know that won't last forever. A blast of excitement and helping you all out in the process works for me. I don't need the money though, so put my share in the extras pot and divvy it up each month. I think we can make this work, but it'll have a shelf life. Then we'll need to pull the plug so the more money we can make and the quicker we can make it, the better.'

'That's so kind of you, Michael,' Caroline replied, and it was typical of Michael.

73

The words 'team player' summed Michael up. Nothing was too much trouble, and he was always thinking of his family and colleagues, never himself. His happiness came from the happiness of others. He was just a different type of human being to anyone else she knew, and she so wished she could be more like him. He took each day at a time and seemed to enjoy it. No stress and he didn't take any tablets, most unusual for someone of his age. No high blood pressure, no risk of a heart attack or stroke for him. Caroline just didn't know how he could be like that, he was wired differently to her, she was certain. She just wished she could plug into his system every now and again.

'What do you think, Ian?' Alex asked.

Ian had said nothing up till now, and that was rare for him. He was a very hard-working police station rep who lived with his partner and had two girls in their early teens. He was always saying how hard he worked and that his money seemed to disappear faster than he was earning it. Ian never moaned about his family, but with the cost of living, everyone always seemed to be chasing the next buck. No time to stand still and pause. That's what Caroline didn't like, the constant treadmill of life, no time to relax and just be.

'It's got its risks,' he said thoughtfully, 'but I can't say it's not attractive. I could squirrel that money away for the girls for university or a house deposit, bung a load in my pension and let that work for me and it guarantees my retirement and the future of my family. I want to think about it, but I'm very much leaning towards being in.'

William clapped him on the back. 'We've got each other's backs,' he said genuinely. 'Always have and always will. A criminal firm isn't like any other place of work. We are a family, and we look after each other like we look after ourselves. None of us will take unnecessary risks and we'll all speak out if we are worried about anything. Caroline has always said you'll never get into trouble for a genuine mistake, you'll only get into trouble if you don't own it. As long as we follow that, we can't go wrong.'

Sandra joined in. 'If you'd suggested this to me a few years ago, I'd have thought you'd all gone stark staring bonkers. But now I don't. I stay because I love you guys and I enjoy working with you, well Harley, not you, but I absolutely hate my job most days now. Every day I have clients shouting at me on the phone. It's not just the odd one or two, it's continual. Rarely does anyone ring up to say, "good job people, thanks so much for all your help." No, it's a constant stream of moaning or abuse. I've learned words on reception I'd never heard before and to be quite frank, I could have lived happily without ever hearing. Why it's my fault their court time is too early, and they'll still be in bed, or it's not fair they shouldn't be in court for this, or we are shit because the prosecution is late with the evidence I don't know. And,' she continued, 'why people have to shout and just cannot speak in a normal tone of voice is absolutely beyond me. Just make sure my role is simple. You know what I'm like with names. The wrong person will get the wrong thing and that wouldn't go well,' she laughed.

'To be honest, I've already thought of that and worried about it,' said Caroline, laughing out loud. 'But I'll double check anything that's being sent to prison to make sure it's the right person and the same with papers being collected from the office. They are only to be collected when I am here, so we'll be certain the right person is getting the right stuff. We'll also not let Seb write the envelopes. With his handwriting, who the hell knows where the packages will end up and who will get them?'

They all laughed. Seb was known for having the worst handwriting in the firm and that was saying something, as most lawyers wrote like doctors. He was the youngest and everyone commented he must have been absent on the day they taught handwriting, now that schools relied far more on technology. It looked as if a spider had fallen in ink and dragged its eight legs across the page, and that was on a good day.

Seb quickly responded, 'I'll be too busy working out in the gym now to be worrying about writing anything.'

'Oh no,' responded Alex, 'this is not a free pass to spend all your time there. You've got case work to do as well.' Seb huffed and pouted, pretending to be offended, and they all laughed.

'It's always annoyed me,' Caroline said, 'that we are seen as "the dark side" of the criminal justice system. We are fighting for the underdog and keeping the powers that be tempered and under control. However, the police and prosecution think that we are in league with our clients. I think we'd come up with better stories if we were. At least now we'll deserve that label and be making a shed load of cash. Truth and justice seem to matter less and less in the system now that statistics drive everything, and the clients are less deserving and grateful.'

'It's time to put ourselves first,' Alex said enthusiastically.

'That'll make a delightful change,' Sandra added.

'To the dark side,' William said, and raised his hand as if he had a glass in it and was making a toast.

'To the dark side,' they all chimed in unison and Harley woofed, his tail wagging furiously.

'And don't forget teamwork makes the dream work,' Seb piped up. This was his favourite expression, which got on everyone's nerves whenever he said it, which of course only made him say it more. Everyone groaned in unison and Harley howled.

'Trust you to lower the tone,' Caroline said, grinning.

CHAPTER EIGHT

THE OPERATION

After thinking about his position overnight, Ian confirmed he was in. Everyone was committed to the cause, and Caroline was delighted. 'It wasn't anywhere near as difficult as I thought it would be,' she mused to Alex. 'I thought they would be more concerned about the risk, especially William and Ian.'

'Me too,' agreed Alex, 'but they've followed you into plenty of battles with complex cases and audits, so if anyone could convince them, it's you.'

'Audits and cases are quite different,' Caroline replied. 'This is serious stuff, mixing with some very dangerous people. Not to mention illegal. I thought they'd all, but particularly William, take a lot more convincing.'

'It sounded to me as if they are all as sick of the job as you are. And they know you plan everything to the nth degree, so if they're ever going to take a risk, it's with you.'

Two days later, the same group was gathered in the same room in the office. The only addition being Robert. This time Harley was lying down fast asleep on one of his many orthopaedic beds. The details of the operation were clearly of no interest to him.

'Here are your burner phones,' he said, handing one out to each of them. 'All contact to do with this op goes through these phones. You all have each other's numbers in those phones. You see each other a lot, so keep contact to a minimum. It's all traceable somewhere somehow. I know you legitimately contact each other on your own phones but keep that contact purely about normal work and stuff. Nothing about this. That way, if the old bill ever become suspicious and get a wiretap, they'll be nothing to incriminate us.'

'You need a lot of evidence if you are the police to bug a phone, Robert,' Alex said. 'It's not like the movies.'

'I don't give a shit,' replied Robert. 'We ain't taking any risks. You ain't got my number in there, just each other's. Any issues for me, your point of contact is Caroline. If she thinks I need to know anything, she'll get in touch with me. If you think your phone has been compromised for any reason, tell her and we'll sort a new one. Don't take unnecessary fucking risks. Play your part and no more. Don't go off script, there are no retakes if it goes wrong,' he said seriously.

'Do we keep these phones on all the time?' asked Seb.

'No,' said Caroline. 'You just turn them on when you need them. We don't want them ringing in court because someone forgot to switch them off, and attention being drawn unnecessarily to additional phones. I know where you are, so if I desperately need you, I can ring the courts or police stations. I'm always chasing you guys down over something so that won't look suspicious. I won't do it about this op unless I absolutely must. This is just so that you can get in touch with each other or with me if you need to.'

'Good job it hasn't got to be on all the time,' joked Seb. 'Michael would never have it on, anyway.' They all laughed.

Michael was not a fan of 'newfangled tech' as he referred to it, and although he had a mobile phone, it was an old Nokia brick. It enabled him to make and receive calls. That was it. He had no access to the internet on it, and no desire to have it. He wasn't part of the office WhatsApp group, and he used his mobile infrequently. Michael turned it on when he wanted to make a call, and when the call ended, he turned it off again. He couldn't be persuaded to leave it on, which was incredibly frustrating when trying to get hold of him when he'd just left a police station or court to reroute him.

However, for this purpose, his usage would be perfect.

'See, this is what I've been training for,' he said proudly. 'You'll be leaving them on when you shouldn't, I won't.' Everyone laughed.

'OK,' Robert continued, drawing the group back to the issues at hand. 'I'm going to start with the gym first for a couple of weeks. Get you up and running, Seb. We take delivery of the heroin and cocaine on the second and fourth Tuesday of each month.'

'Why a Tuesday evening?' asked Seb.

'Why fucking not?' said Robert. 'Drug dealers don't keep fucking office hours, you know. We are a small part of a much bigger op. Probably something to do with when the drugs come into the port. How the fuck should I know? All I know is delivery is on a Tuesday evening between seven and nine. So, you gotta be at the gym then. You'll see the guy. It's always the same one. Don't know his name, don't want to, don't need to …'

'What if he's sick?' Seb interrupted.

'For fuck's sake,' Robert was getting exasperated. 'What's with all the fucking questions? He ain't been fucking sick in all the time I've been doing this, so let's assume he ain't gonna be now. He'll drop call your burner when he arrives. You make your way to the lockers and get out your gym bag. He'll have an identical one. You take out yours with the cash in and put it on the floor. He'll put his with the drugs in next to yours. He takes yours; you take his, simple as. Same bags swap back the next week and so on, clear so far?' he questioned Seb.

'Crystal,' Seb replied.

'Then either Kyle or Dale will be at the gym in the evening and will take the drugs off you. They'll cut them and bring them back in the same bag the following evening. They will drop call you as you'll be working out normal like, and you'll go to the changing room. You'll take possession of the bag ready for the deals to be done.

'I have the same buyers every fortnight at the same time. That's why this works so well. They come into the gym, do their work out.

I'm in there doing my workout. We go to the changing rooms and discretely, while we are getting changed, bags get put on the floor and the money and drugs move. I trust them, they trust me. No one fucking dares rip anyone off because they know what the fucking consequences will be. You must make sure they trust you, too. No fucking trying to rip them off. No taking off any of the drugs. It works, so don't do anything to fuck it up. Twelve buyers over six days each fortnight, two on a Wednesday, two on a Friday and two on a Saturday. They each buy a kilo of each. We can get them to come at the times that suit you and can switch the days. We'll see what works.'

'How do I deal twice in an evening? Won't I need two bags? Won't that look suspicious?' Seb asked, looking confused.

'Fucking hell, there is a brain in there floating about,' Robert replied, laughing. 'You have one bag in another, same as when you collect the drugs. You have a bag to leave the gym with when Kyle or Dale have taken the bag with the drugs. That way, it doesn't look dodgy. So, you'll just have to take less hair gel and shit with you.'

Seb raised his eyebrows and lovingly stroked his hair, as if this was a compromise he wasn't prepared to sign up to. Robert rolled his eyes, and everyone else laughed.

'How am I going to get the drugs when you are locked up?' Seb asked.

'Probably in the same way,' Robert answered. 'I'm working on a plan to get the drugs to Caroline already cut. She'll then handle the bulk distribution for the courts, police stations and the office once we have worked out the amounts. I know what I do at the gym, but the rest is unknown territory for me, so we'll all be learning as we go. It's best to keep the deliveries separate to reduce the risk.'

'How do we see it working in the office?' Sandra questioned.

'As you know, I put a lot of clients your way. They are my associates, and even if they are not up for drugs offences, they are in the drugs world. If they are on bail, they'll either be collecting papers from court if they can't get to you, but if they can, they'll be coming in here. Make sure you print out their papers. We want this to look as legit as possible. However, inside the packages will also be the drugs. You can keep printing the same papers if you like. You know what clients are like always fucking losing them, so while their case is running, they'll be in several times. If they are in custody, we'll be sending the drugs into prison. Make sure it's marked Rule 39 and it won't be opened. I will sort out who we are sending them to in there.

'As far as the court is concerned,' he went on, 'Alex, William and Michael will give papers to those on bail. Not just those with hearings that day, but also those who can collect papers easier from the court than the office. You have those cards, so you get through security, no problem. You'll have the drugs, and they'll turn up with the cash. Now is prime time to cash in. You all know that fifty-three years were just given out a week ago to four major drug dealers round here. That means there is turf we can take. I've got the connections. I'm just ironing out a few of the minor details. In a couple of weeks, we'll be good to start.'

'We will also be delivering drugs to those attending the Crown Court in custody,' Caroline added. 'We can't in the mags, of course, because they are behind the glass screens. It is absolutely nonsensical that you have a partition separate you from a prisoner in the magistrates' court cells, but you sit next to the same person accused of the same crime at the police station, and when they are produced in the cells at the Crown Court. It's typical of this cock-arsed system.'

'A prime example of the system's madness,' interjected William.

'Too right,' responded Caroline. 'Again, all packages will be clearly marked Rule 39, so the prison staff won't be able to open them.'

'Once I know how much product we are going to shift regularly, I'll have it delivered to Caroline's. It'll be the same guy who delivers to the gym. He'll ring the doorbell like a delivery driver and if she's not in, he'll leave it in her safe place,' Robert explained.

Caroline added, 'That's my wheelie bin at the side of my house, so it's a good job it's not a Friday, bin day. That would be a disaster.' Everyone laughed. 'I'm always ordering stuff from Amazon, so the neighbours will just think it's yet another delivery,' she explained.

'You'll check it's there, Caroline, but leave it. Either Kyle or Dale will come and collect it later.'

'I'll be able to see them on my ring doorbell camera,' Caroline added.

'Good,' Robert responded. 'That way, you can keep tabs on them. Make sure they are fucking doing what they are supposed to. They are good lads, but supervision is necessary. They'll cut it at the same time as they are cutting the drugs delivered to the gym. They'll deliver it back disguised as delivery drivers again.'

'We often have the same delivery drivers in our area, so it won't be that strange,' Caroline commented.

'Why don't you just have all the drugs delivered to the one place?' Seb asked.

'To reduce the risk,' Robert responded. 'If for any reason something happens to one lot of drugs, we haven't lost it all. Remember, drug dealers ain't nice fucking people. The higher up the food chain, the less fucking nice they are. They won't like it if drugs get seized, whether they are paid for or not. They worry about snitching. We minimise the risk, and at least we can keep part of the operation going if we have to stop the other.'

'I'm worried about the drugs being delivered to your house, Caroline,' Michael said, with a concerned look on his face. 'I know we'll be in business with these people, but when all's said and done, they are dangerous individuals. It's very risky they know where you live.'

'I have thought about that, Michael, and I appreciate your concern. I do,' said Caroline, genuinely. She was not at all surprised it was Michael who was thinking of her. 'But let's be honest, if they want to do us harm, it isn't that difficult to find us, is it? They can find us here, for starters. It's only a question then of following us home. Plus, we can hardly have the drugs delivered here, directly opposite the cop shop. It's a risk with the gym being so close, but at least at face value, there's no direct connection with us. Here there's a bloody prominent sign over the door.'

'True,' Michael said, nodding his head. 'When you put it like that, I guess it makes sense.'

'How do I fit into all of this?' asked Ian.

'You'll be filling in where necessary. We'll need your help at the magistrates' court and the Crown Court when these guys are busy. This has lots of moving parts and with the unpredictability of our actual day job, and the running of courts, we need to make sure we don't have any gaps. I think if any clients can't get into court, maybe you could meet them at the pub down the road.'

The magistrates' court and Crown Court were directly across the road from each other, and just down the road was a pub. Lawyers often went there if they got the chance at lunchtime, although those days were far less frequent than they used to be. Clients also went there to celebrate a win or drown their sorrows if they didn't but had their freedom to do so. Caroline thought it would be a convenient place if a client was not allowed into court, which sometimes happened due to their behaviour or, if more likely, they were on a warrant and so were avoiding court altogether.

'Well, that sounds even better than Seb's deal,' Ian said, grinning. 'The pub works for me. A perk to this job at long last.'

'I thought you'd like that,' Caroline said, smiling at him.

'I think this is going to be an actual case of work experience,' said William seriously. 'We are each not going to know how it's going to work in practice until it gets going properly. We've got to have our wits about us though, otherwise this could go sideways incredibly quickly.' He looked at Seb directly while he said this.

'Don't worry about me,' Seb said. 'I'm on it like a car bonnet,' another one of his expressions that everyone hated. Harley woofed and the groan was unanimous.

CHAPTER NINE

PHILLIP

Caroline liked Phillip, the accountant, the minute Robert introduced them. She arrived at his office, which was about half an hour from her office, just as Robert arrived. Caroline had decided they should travel separately. The less they were seen together, the better. Robert was in their office quite a bit and attending courts to assist with the operations there. That was easily explainable if anyone asked. He did, after all, have a current case. However, explaining attending the accountants together was a different story.

'So how did you first meet Phillip?' Caroline asked, as they waited in a very modern reception area.

It couldn't be more different from my office, she ruminated.

An obvious sign that they were clearly better paid than criminal defence solicitors. Everywhere was glass, shiny stainless steel and black leather. They were sitting on a very soft, black leather sofa that hugged Caroline as she relaxed into it. In fact, she was certain if she allowed herself to, she'd be asleep in a few minutes. The reception desk was clear except for a shiny laptop. An attractive brunette in her thirties sat tapping away with incredibly long nails.

'I don't know how she fucking types with those,' admired Robert.

'Me neither,' said Caroline enviously. She'd had false nails for a couple of weddings, but they weren't practical. To be honest, she'd got bored while they were being done. Her idea would be to drop your fingers off at the nail salon, and your hair at the hairdressers, and just go back and collect them all when they were done. Other people found that sort of thing pampering, Caroline found it a total waste of time. She wasn't interested in small talk and magazines and tea. She just wanted to be done and out and on to the next thing. Perhaps, when she could live at a slower pace of life, she might enjoy such things.

Then perhaps not, she thought and laughed to herself.

'I met him through an acquaintance and it's one of the best fucking meetings I've ever had. He's one hundred per cent trustworthy, takes what's agreed and no more, and does everything he needs to with no fucking drama. I go online to the banks. I can see my cash and it's never been wrong. He knows he's on to a good thing and he doesn't want to upset it. He's connected and bloody good at what he does. But he's sensible. He sticks in his lane and plays the longer game.'

'Exactly what we need,' Caroline said approvingly. 'I will have enough less reliable links in the chain to keep my eye on, so it'll be good to just leave him to do what he does best.'

The telephone rang on a side table next to the reception desk. Why they needed the side table for the telephone was beyond Caroline. The reception desk was hardly cluttered. She thought about her own desk, piles of files, a laptop; she could lose a cup of coffee for days among all the detritus.

'Phillip will see you both now,' the brunette said, smiling at them both.

With that, she got up from her desk, and they followed her down a corridor to the right of reception, to the office at the end. She knocked and immediately opened the door. She then turned on her heels and said goodbye, leaving them to enter. Phillip got up from behind his equally immaculate polished wood desk and gestured to them to take a seat on one of the four comfy looking chairs spaced around a circular coffee table in front of his desk.

'Bit different to your office, eh, Caroline?' Robert joked.

'They are in different stratospheres,' Caroline agreed, and they all laughed.

'Mind you, it'd look a bit different if Harley wiped his nose on the chairs,' Robert said, grinning.

'Yes, he'd give them his unique stamp,' Caroline giggled. Phillip looked puzzled. 'Oh, he's my dog. He comes to work with me,' she explained.

'It's lovely to meet you, Caroline,' Phillip said, coming over and shaking her hand firmly.

Caroline liked a firm handshake. She felt it showed a person was in charge and confident. A limp handshake made her want to squirm. Phillips was a well-groomed man in his forties. His suit looked expensive, and his shoes were so shiny he could stand on the King's parade in them. He had dark hair, greying at the sides, which made him look distinguished. Lines that showed expression and a well-chiselled chin. Again, Caroline liked a strong chin, a sign of a powerful man who was in control.

'And Harley would be welcome anytime,' he added, smiling.

'It's lovely to meet you too, Phillip. I've heard excellent things about you from Robert,' she replied warmly, and sat down.

'Well, that's good to hear, but I should hope so. We go back quite a long way now and we've had a very healthy, profitable working relationship. I see no reason we cannot have the same,' he said, smiling at her.

'Music to my ears,' Caroline said genuinely. 'Robert says the set-up he has is very safe and so I would like the same, please. There are others on the team who want the same setting up for them too. I think Robert has given you the breakdown of who is getting what and if there is extra to be given to anyone, we will let you know.'

'Yes, I have everything here. I've printed a copy for you to cast your eyes over,' he said, as he handed it over to her. 'If you agree it's correct, I'll shred it immediately. I don't leave any paper anywhere about this. Everything is on a memory stick, which is encrypted. Nothing stored anywhere on a hard drive. You can't be too careful.'

'Yes, it's accurate, thank you,' Caroline said, handing it back to him.

He got up and went to the shredder next to his desk and shredded it immediately. Caroline knew they were going to get on famously. He worried about leaving a trail just as she did. He, too, was a professional with a hell of a lot to lose if anything went wrong. She felt confident that nothing would go wrong his end.

'So, as Robert will have told you, I take my fees and the cut for the casino. The rest is washed through the casino and put into the selected bank accounts. Only you, as an individual, have access to those. We can set them up online now. I don't know the passwords and passcodes, and I don't want to. That way, there can be no suggestion of any impropriety. I'm happy with what I make out of it and the more you make, the more I do. You have no connection to the casino, fewer threads and all that.'

'That works perfectly for me. You have no connection to my side either, so again, it reduces the risk.'

Caroline knew both of them could see that they were dealing with another professional party. They would each stick to their side, and neither would cause the other any problems.

If only the rest were like Phillip, Caroline thought to herself.

'How am I going to get the money to you?' Caroline enquired.

'I've been thinking about that. My view is I should take over partnership accounts from your current accountant. I'll match the price you pay now. That way, you are a legitimate client, and it will not be at all unusual for us to have an appointment regularly. If I am out and about near your office, I'll ring you and swing by. Otherwise, you can come here once a week. Package up the money, and if I'm in an appointment, you can leave it with my receptionist. I open all post so there will be no issue.'

'That sounds very sensible to me. I'll sign whatever you need me to today, and you can get Alex to do the same when you see him. I think he's booked in to see you tomorrow?'

'Yes, that's right.'

'Perfect. I'll give him the heads-up beforehand. Can you also assist the other staff we have if I get them to sort out appointments?'

'Absolutely. It's safer if one person deals with it all and as I'll have all the money in the offshore account I use, it's better for me to distribute it. The account belongs to a shell company hidden behind several others. It would take a forensic accountant a long time to trace any of it back to the casino and us.'

'Well. let's hope it never comes to that. I'll get them to contact you sooner rather than later so we can get everything set up and ready.'

Phillip nodded in agreement. 'Right, let's get these accounts set up,' he said to Caroline.

'You don't need me for that, do you?' Robert asked. He'd come along just to make sure Caroline was happy with Phillip, although he was sure she would be, and she clearly was. He'd also wanted to make sure she was happy with the figures he'd told to Phillip. Robert was OK at maths, but this was quite complicated and much larger amounts than he was used to dealing with. If there were any disputes, he wanted it sorting out while they were all there. Fortunately, things were going perfectly. Caroline and Phillip were both professional and organised, control freaks in their own domains to be honest. They were a match made in heaven for this.

'I don't need you, Robert, but thank you very much for coming over,' Phillip replied.

'Me neither, Robert. Thanks very much though, I am very happy with this side of things. Let's just hope we can get the rest up and running as easily.'

'Have faith, Caroline, have faith,' Robert said, getting up and grinning at them both.

'I do like Robert,' Phillip said, when he had left the room.

'Me too,' said Caroline. 'I've known him since he was a child.'

'I know he's a criminal, and so on the face of it, this is dangerous, but I've had absolutely no issues. It's been a relatively safe set-up,' Phillip said.

'There's always risk, though,' Caroline replied. 'Criminals are usually only loyal if they are frightened of you, and there are plenty of people in this chain Robert is frightened of, but it certainly isn't either of us,' Caroline continued. 'Some players in this will cut our throats literally if this goes wrong. I don't know them, but I obviously have a lot of knowledge of how these things work and the type of people involved.'

'I understand that, and I suppose I am a bit more detached from it than you. But Robert's on to a good thing and he can't continue to access the money easily without me, so we have no reason to hurt each other. My relationship with you will be the same. Robert needs you, don't forget; without you, this all goes down the pan when he goes to prison.'

'I think it's just my occupation means I don't trust anyone anymore. Over the years, I've seen and heard just about everything you could imagine. In fact, if I wrote a book, they'd put it in the fiction section.'

'I suppose that's true; I've never really thought about it. It must have affected your outlook on life.'

'Made me a cynical old cow, you mean?' Caroline said, laughing, and Phillip roared.

'No, I didn't mean that I can assure you,' he said. 'Now where's your ID?'

'Can I just ask you about cryptocurrency?'

'Sure, Robert said you weren't interested in that. Have you changed your mind?'

'No. I'm just a bit worried that I'm a dinosaur and maybe should move with the times,' she said, laughing again.

'You aren't very kind to yourself, are you?' Phillip said kindly. 'There are pros and cons, but the volatility will be too much for you, I think. You will want to know how much you've got to the nearest pence and that it's yours. Crypto, you can gain and lose multiple times a day. I think you will find that too unpredictable and provide you with another headache rather than a solution.'

'I thought that, but it's nice to have it confirmed, thank you.'

'Anytime, that's what I'm here for,' he said. Caroline felt the tiniest spark between them, that he was actually flirting.

She'd clocked the wedding band the minute they met, though. *No more complications,* she thought.

Caroline removed her passport, driving licence and utility bill from her handbag, and they got down to the serious task of sorting out the accounts. Phillip moved to his desk and tapped away on his laptop, and Caroline sat on one of the two very padded chairs on the other side. When appropriate, Phillip turned his laptop to her, and she entered the confidential details she needed to. He uploaded her documents through the relevant portals, and before long, she had three offshore accounts.

'Easy when you know how,' Caroline said.

'Like anything,' Phillip responded. 'Now if you can sign this document, I'll get Alex to sign tomorrow and then I'll send it to your current accountants. We'll get your accounts transferred to us, and when that's done, I'll be in touch. After that, I suggest you start doing the money drops. Let's get everything up and running the way it's going to be. We can iron out any glitches early then.'

'Great. That sets my mind at rest,' Caroline said. She felt herself physically relax. Her shoulders dropped, and the tension disappeared from her face. Caroline lived on her nerves a lot and was constantly stressed, but just for a moment, she felt calm.

'I'll let Robert know,' Phillip added. 'It's my idea, so if he doesn't like it, he can deal with me. He knows it's going to happen, but he might not want to give up the control just yet. Leave him to me.'

'Thanks. There's a lot for me to learn and do at the moment, so I'd like to get this part sorted and if Robert's on board, that helps.'

'Consider it done,' Phillip said confidently, and Caroline knew it would be.

CHAPTER TEN

SEB

Seb was already a member of the gym. Caroline had encouraged him to join after starting at Rigby Andrews & Co, explaining he had a much better chance of getting to the gym if it was close to work. It was a good gym. It was one of those twenty-four-hour ones, which meant he never had any excuse for not going, even when he'd been to the police station late at night. Not that he enjoyed going in the middle of the night; he'd moaned to Caroline, when he was absolutely knackered and still had about half an hour's drive home.

'You lightweight,' Caroline had retorted. 'You're a young pup, love,' she'd added. 'If you can't burn it at both ends now, you're never going to.'

She'd turned to Michael and said, 'Michael, they just don't make them like they used to.'

'No, they don't,' Michael had said in response. 'But the next generation will be even worse. With online shopping and working from home, they won't be able to move soon, or speak. All connection and communication will be through a keypad.'

'What a frightening concept,' Caroline had responded. 'Although we know already, they can't write.'

They'd all laughed at that, but no one had been able to argue with them. To be fair, even though Seb was lacking in stamina, Caroline didn't know where Michael got his energy from. He was as bright as a button first thing in the morning, late at night, in the middle of the night. It didn't seem to make a difference. He never said he needed a break to eat or to drink or to rest.

'Michael is a machine,' Seb said to himself as he got on the treadmill to do a five-kilometre run.

Robert was in the gym, too. They both knew each other would be there. That had been arranged. They'd agreed it would be around seven, but they hadn't made firm plans. Caroline didn't want it to look too orchestrated. Robert had been spending quite a lot of time at the office making sure things were running smoothly there, then at court. Although different people would be seeing them and so wouldn't be able to join any dots, she wanted to keep things as low profile as possible.

Robert had worked at and worked out at the gym for a long time, too, so there was no new coincidence there. They had come across each other in the gym, and Seb knew Robert was a client of the firm, although he'd never dealt with him directly. Robert knew Seb worked for Caroline, so they'd always acknowledged each other, but nothing more than that.

Tonight would be no different. Robert had explained to Seb exactly what he had to do to hand over the money and take possession of the drugs. He'd made the suppliers aware of the new arrangements and given a description of Seb. Robert had made it clear that he would be there if there were any problems. He'd be able to step in and sort them out. But if neither side contacted him, he wanted the handover to play out without him.

Robert saw the delivery man enter the gym and go into the changing room. He had a sixth sense about it now. Seb was oblivious. He was too engrossed in his workout, showing off lifting weights with a guy who looked like he got his muscles from steroids, rather than hours of pumping iron. Robert moved from the running machine, where he'd been trying to beat his personal record for ten kilometres without success. He was frustrated. He used to do it in under fifty minutes. Now he was lucky if he could get near fifty-two minutes. It didn't sound much difference but to a runner every second counts.

He passed near Seb and tried to catch his eye. He was unsuccessful. Robert didn't want to make it too obvious that he was trying to speak to Seb, so he carried on and went to the cross trainer, where he could see Seb and the other guy still chatting to each other, and Seb still lifting his weights.

After about five minutes, when Robert was ready to explode, Seb finally finished trying to make his body beautiful and got up from the weight bench. He looked around the gym and saw Robert glaring at him and tipping his head towards the changing rooms.

Fuck, thought Seb, knowing how pissed off Robert was.

He rushed to the changing room and saw the courier sitting on a bench with his back to him. He cast his eyes around the changing room and couldn't see anyone else. That didn't mean there wasn't anyone in one of the individual changing rooms. As he passed the courier to go his locker, the courier hissed, 'For fuck's sake man, don't fucking leave me sitting here like a fucking sitting duck. I messaged you, where the fuck have you been?'

'Sorry mate, I left my phone in the locker.'

'I ain't no fucking mate of yours and don't you forget it. What sort of fucking twat are you? Mobile in your locker. How the fuck am I supposed to contact you? This ain't gonna work. I ain't having you screw me.'

'Look …'

The changing room door banged open, and Robert came storming through. He did a cutting motion across his throat to silence the two of them as he systematically swept the changing room, checking all the cubicles. They were empty. Then he barrelled over to Seb and the courier, his face red with anger.

'What the fuck are you two still doing in here, having a fucking coffee morning?'

'It's this prick,' shouted the courier. 'Not fucking in here. Not watching. Not answering his fucking phone cos he's left it in his fucking locker.' Spittle was flying out of his mouth as he spoke. He was so worked up.

'Are you fucking winding me up?' Robert grabbed Seb by his t-shirt. 'I saw you out there acting the fucking big twat with those weights and that fucking dickhead on steroids. You gotta get your fucking shit together else you are off this, you fucking hear me?' His face was in Seb's face. Seb could feel the heat from the rage burning through Robert.

'I'm sorry I screwed up,' Seb said apologetically.

'Fat lot of fucking good that'll do us if we get nicked,' the courier snarled. 'I don't wanna deal with him. He's a cock and I ain't got time for that.'

'He is a cock,' Robert agreed, 'but he won't fuck it up again, will you?'

'No way, I'm on it,' Seb said to both of them. If looks could kill, he knew he'd be sprawled out on the floor by them both.

'I ain't fucking happy about this,' the courier said angrily, but calmer than he had been. 'We've had a good thing going and no problems. I report back about this. They'll pull the fucking plug.'

'No, they won't,' said Robert confidently. 'They know they are on to a fucking good thing with me. That's why we started this early, iron out any fucking teething problems.' As he said this, he looked at Seb in a way that let Seb know he was lucky his teeth weren't down the back of his throat. 'It won't fucking happen again. Now let's do the swap.'

Seb got his bag down from the locker and placed it next to the one on the bench belonging to the courier. He picked up the couriers and put it back in his locker. The courier took Seb's and got up.

'This is his one fucking chance,' he growled to Robert. As he left, he spat at Seb, 'Play with fire like that mate and you are gonna get fucking barbecued.'

'Well, that didn't go according to plan,' Seb said when the door closed after the courier left.

'Fucking understatement of the fucking decade,' Robert yelled and punched Seb hard in the face. He then grabbed him by the shoulders and shook him hard. 'Fuck up like that and you'll get us both fucking killed, do you understand? I'm not having you wreck what I've built up. Stop acting like a total fucking twat and do what you are supposed to properly. Caroline won't be able to save you from the people we are dealing with. Get that through your fucking thick head. We are dealing with the premier league of crims here, so stop playing fucking Sunday league.'

Seb was so surprised at being punched; he couldn't react. He knew he'd seriously screwed up and realised that his wit, charm and smile that normally endeared him to people might get him killed if he didn't get his act together.

'I won't let you down again Robert, I promise,' he said apologetically. Seb was extremely frightened by what Robert might do to him.

'You won't live to tell the fucking tale if you do,' said Robert as he slammed out of the changing room.

When Robert left the gym, he phoned Caroline on her burner.

'What's up?' she said when she answered.

'Your fucking trainee, that's what's up. What a fucking halfwit he is!'

'What's he done?' Caroline said, very concerned.

Robert explained to Caroline exactly what happened in the gym. Caroline started to laugh, which was not the reaction he was expecting. He thought she would be worried about them being caught and start over reacting.

'What the fuck you laughing for?' he asked, totally baffled.

'I wish I'd been there when you punched Seb,' Caroline said, between laughs. 'I can't tell you how many times I've wanted to do that. He's so fucking infuriating at times.'

'What the fuck you got him working for you, then?' Robert asked, also laughing now that he could see the funny side.

'Best there is out there. Youth of today, Robert. Country's gone to the dogs. I told you that.'

'It's more than gone to the fucking dogs. I'd rather have Harley at the gym sorting this than Seb,' Robert said. Although he was joking, there was a serious tone to his voice.

'So would I, Robert, so would I. That's why Harley and I are besties. He's totally reliable and his love is unconditional. He doesn't moan. He isn't entitled. He isn't lazy, and he isn't self-centred.'

'Tell him he's got to earn his keep. He's up next week,' Robert joked.

'I'll tell Seb you're seriously considering swapping them,' she replied, grinning.

Caroline considered ringing Seb after she'd finished her conversation with Robert but decided to wait. This needed to be addressed face to face. She wasn't going to let him off the hook over the phone. The next morning, he breezed into the office as if he didn't have a worry in the world. His carefree, couldn't give a shit, attitude drove her mad most of the time, but today she was incensed. Even the cut on his nose and black bruises under his eyes from Robert's punch didn't seem to have dampened his spirits.

'What the fuck do you think you are playing at?' she shouted at him the minute he set foot in her office.

'Robert spoke to you,' Seb said, and his face fell.

'You didn't think he would?'

'I hoped he wouldn't.'

'He wants you off the operation Seb, and I have to say I don't blame him. I feel the fucking same. Life is not all about you, your wants, your needs. You are part of a team, so start fucking acting like it. He actually said Harley would do a better job, and I agree with him. A trained bloody orangutan would do a better fucking job.'

Harley stood next to Seb waiting for the obligatory biscuit. He looked at Seb as if to say, 'I could do a better job, but I don't want it unless it involves balls and biscuits.'

'I'm sorry I let you down,' Seb whispered meekly, while feeding and stroking Harley, grateful for the distraction. Caroline could see he was genuinely sorry, but she wasn't letting him off the hook that easily.

'That'll be no fucking comfort when I'm in a prison cell or, worse still, dead,' she retorted, glaring at him.

'I know I get it. I really do,' Seb said earnestly.

Caroline believed he'd been frightened by Robert and the courier and perhaps did now realise what he'd signed up to. His entrance had clearly been bravado and nothing more.

'You aren't there to train at the time the courier is due. It's your cover. Train before and after but be aware of what you're doing. I always say to you that you'll be struck off before they put you on the roll, but that's the least of your worries now. Take this seriously or you'll be dead before you qualify.'

She let that hang in the air and then got up and left the office. Harley followed her. Conversation over. He knew where he stood, and she knew Robert wouldn't let him screw things up again.

Caroline reported back to Robert that she thought Seb had learned his lesson.

Robert wasn't so sure and certainly wasn't as prepared as she was to forgive and forget and give him a second chance. Things were very curt between them, but there was no relapse in his behaviour. He certainly never forgot his phone again when he went into the gym. Seb got into a proper routine, exchanging the drugs with the courier for the money. They never spoke again, and it suited them both. Seb was frightened of him and just wanted the transaction over as soon as possible. He also got the handoff of the drugs to the dealers down to a fine art. Robert watched him and he was polished, quick, with minimal eye contact. If you didn't know what was happening, you wouldn't see it.

After eight weeks, he met with Caroline and Seb in the office.

'He's on it now,' Robert said about Seb to Caroline. 'I've watched him meet the courier several times now and do the deals, and there's no issue. He's quick and careful now that his mind is on the fucking job. I think I can back off from the gym now and leave him to it, if you are happy with that. I'll still go to the gym to train and work but I won't time it for the meets. If I'm there, I'm there, but he needs to be there on his own now.'

'Well, well, well,' Caroline said. 'You've come a long way since day one. Graduation time. How do you feel about that, Seb?'

'I'm good about it. I know what I'm doing. It's easy now. I'm in the zone.'

'Shouldn't have fucking taken as long as it did,' Robert commented. 'It was the only part of the operation that was up and running properly and you almost managed to take the whole fucking thing out. But we are where we need to be, and you need to be doing it on your own for a while before I'm locked up. You gotta have your wits about you and report back if there are any problems. Don't cover them up. Otherwise, you won't have to worry who's coming with the knife for your back. You'll see me coming right for your throat.'

Seb nodded sheepishly; his bravado gone. Caroline had no doubt Robert would deliver on his promise if he was pushed, and she could see that Seb knew it too.

CHAPTER ELEVEN

ALEX

Things got off to a flying start at court. Robert attended the Crown Court, not because he was on the list, but because he was collecting his papers. At least, that is what he told the security staff when they searched him. The problem, on the face of it, could be coming into court with a lot of money. However, this was easily overcome. Robert proved it the first time he tried. Nothing was found on his person. He was subject to the metal detector, a full wand and pat down search by a burly security guard, so didn't want to risk anyone finding it. It would immediately raise red flags.

His bag was searched by the security guards, but they just poked through it, not a proper search. The lining at the bottom of Robert's bag wasn't as intact as it appeared, but no one noticed. Within a couple of minutes, he was through into the body of the courthouse with £1,200. No one was any the wiser.

If they could keep to dealing like this, he thought to himself, *no one would have a bloody clue what was going on.*

He went upstairs to where the courtrooms and client interview rooms were and waited, as arranged with Alex, outside court four. The benches were wooden and designed to give defendants and their families somewhere to perch, rather than make themselves comfortable. After about twenty minutes of waiting, Alex emerged from court and Robert had to stifle a laugh. His gown was askew, revealing his waistcoat, which was undone halfway down. The bottom two buttons were nowhere to be seen.

Typical fucking Alex, Robert thought.

Alex motioned with his head for Robert to follow him into an interview room across the corridor. Robert followed.

'Hi Robert,' he said grinning, 'you OK?'

'Me arse is bloody numb,' Robert replied. 'I'd forgotten how bloody uncomfortable those sodding benches are.'

'Probably part of the plan to stop people coming back,' Alex laughed.

'Too fucking tight to put some padding on them more like. You need to go on a diet mate. I see you're busting out of your waistcoat,' Robert commented.

''I know. God knows where the buttons are.'

'You wouldn't bloody sew them back on anyway,' Robert retorted.

'No, I wouldn't. You're right,' Alex chuckled. 'At least I've got cufflinks on today though,' he showed Robert his cuffs. 'Even worse than that, I forgot my bloody jacket today. The judge asked me if I was entering a pool tournament.'

'No one would ever believe what you do for a living, Alex,' Robert said, howling. 'You're bloody good at your job but putting our lives in your hands is as important as putting our lives in the hands of a surgeon. If my surgeon turned up looking like you, I'd fucking run fucking fast.' They both laughed.

'I'm hoping when this new set-up pays off, I'll have time to go to the gym and run again. I keep trying to get healthy and then I just can't fit it in with work. I'm doing intermittent fasting, but by the time I get home I'm so knackered I just eat crap to keep going. Good job I can have caffeine. I wouldn't be able to function without my million cups of coffee a day.'

'Well, those days are numbered if this all goes well,' Robert pointed out. 'The world will be your oyster. Don't understand that, but it's what they say, isn't it?' he asked.

'It is, whoever they are. Anyway, how did it go getting in here today?' Alex asked.

'Easy as,' Robert said, proudly. 'They don't fucking search properly at all. Had a little poke around in the bag, but nothing major. Didn't spot a thing. I'll get the word out. This is the best way. Most defendants come in with a bag in case they get sent down, so it doesn't raise any eyebrows. What about you, any problems with the drugs?'

Alex had brought some in today, as a trial run, disguised as papers for Robert. He handed over the package labelled "Robert Smith Case Papers".

Robert opened his bag and showed Alex the join in the lining allowing access to the hidden compartment below. He removed a package containing the money. It was labelled Alex Fraser, Rigby Andrews & Co. It had been Robert's idea to pass the money in this way. Then, if Alex misplaced it, as he was likely to do, hopefully no one would open it, they would just return it to him.

'Fucking comes to something when the client's having to think for the fucking lawyer,' Robert had said, laughing to Caroline. However, they both knew that Alex was the most likely to mess this up, and they had to do everything they could to prevent that. It wouldn't be deliberate on his part, but at some point, as sure as night followed day, it was inevitably going to happen.

Caroline knew it was very useful having Robert on the outside doing the first dummy run, and making sure things were up and running properly, long before he found himself back in custody. He telephoned her to report that all had gone like 'fucking clockwork' getting the money in and the drugs out at the Crown Court. She pondered how he had fed them numerous clients over the years, and she had often wondered how he knew them all. Although he was involved in crime from time to time, he wasn't exactly a major player, she'd thought. Robert wasn't one of those clients that seemed to be re-offending all the time, often having more than one file on the go, "the revolving door client" as they tended to be referred to.

How wrong could she have been? Robert was just sensible

not to get caught for the big stuff. That is what had impressed her despite his hot-headedness, made her think they could pull this off. It was quite clear now that Robert was extremely well connected indeed. Not only in the drugs world, but in the criminal underworld. The two often went hand in hand, but not always. This was especially so with the level of dealer that Robert was. They often chose not to get their hands dirty and mix with the minions at the bottom of the food chain. Not so with Robert. He'd grown up with a lot of them and, being local, was well known. Robert had used his connections wisely to his advantage and had done the same for them as a firm. He'd put a lot of clients their way and now would continue to do that. They would be getting the funding for the cases through legal aid, but that was small fry in comparison to the money they would be making this way.

Sometimes the stars aligned, the gods smiled, and things fell into place. Robert had expanded his operation by taking over the turf of a major rival when the key players were sent to prison. Fortuitously, this happened at the same time as she had dreamed up the expansion plan, and they'd all got on board. Robert didn't give the gang time to regroup, but contacted the dealers that were left directly. He found out how much they were selling and what their purchase price was. Robert had now organised it so that they could move the same amount through the courts as they could at the gym. The delivery was made to Caroline's and the same deal had been negotiated with Dale and Kyle for cutting and returning.

However, it couldn't all be shifted in such a large volume. That kind of amount often couldn't be easily hidden in a file or a bundle of client's papers. It wasn't so bad for those attending on bail or coming to court to collect papers. But it was far too much to hand over to a prisoner. While serious cases often had a high page count and so the packages were quite large, the drugs had to be well hidden among them. As a result, they'd worked out that a nine bar was the right amount to hand over to those in the cells.

Caroline had to give Robert credit where it was due, he'd

thought things through very carefully. He had planned and plotted meticulously and, fortunately, one of those that had been pinched in the most recent drugs arrests was a good friend of his. Jason rang Robert from prison using an illegal mobile and they cooked up the plot between them. They'd send the drugs in through the cells at the court with prisoners they could trust. They'd get them to Jason, and he'd distribute them his end.

'Is this safe?' Caroline had asked when he'd told her.

'Nothing's fucking safe in this world, Caroline,' he'd replied. 'It's as safe as it can be until I get in there. Jason's lost everything. He needs to rebuild. His partner Chloe will meet Ian in the Half Moon. The drugs'll go through court, but the money won't. I've known him since I was a kid. He's alright, and he's got a long time to do. We know where he is if he fucks up, and he knows that. He won't want to cross us.'

'What's he getting out of it?' she questioned.

'Thirty per cent,' Robert replied. 'Had to make it attractive enough to him while making a fair bit for us. Don't forget it's double bubble. By the time I get in there, he'll probably have been shipped out or be on his way, cos he's serving such a long sentence, so it'll fit in with me taking over the op.'

'How much does he think he can do?'

'I think we send in a nine bar of each a week and see how he gets on. I'm sure he'll build it up quicker than that, but I don't want him to get too cocky or desperate. Less is more.'

'I totally agree,' Caroline responded quickly. 'I don't know him and that makes me nervous.'

'Everything makes you nervous, Caroline,' Robert chuckled. 'I know him. That's what counts. I'm also getting him to send you an authority to take over his appeal. He doesn't want to appeal. He's no chance on conviction or sentence and he knows it. But then he's on your books and we can send drugs in through the post if he can move more. Only so many papers can go through the cells without the cell staff becoming suspicious.'

'Absolutely. And with more and more clients appearing on video links for hearings, it's not as easy as it would have been a few years ago. Why don't we just send all the drugs into him?'

'Keep him on his fucking toes,' Robert replied, as if the answer was obvious. 'We don't want to make things too simple for him. It's all about control. We are in the driving seat, he isn't. We need to keep it that way and he needs it made fucking clear to him.'

This was no small operation and required a lot of last-minute arrangements as court lists changed suddenly. This was especially so in the Crown Court. If cases overran, then clients were bumped from the list without warning. Some got very upset at this. It was understandable, as the cases were more serious than in the magistrates, but the magistrates' cases were more likely to go ahead on the date fixed. For those who were genuinely interested and concerned about their case and were working, it was understandably incredibly frustrating. However, in Caroline's experience, it was not usually those clients that shouted about it. It was, of course, the ones that weren't working and had no plans other than to stay in bed all day who became aggressive. They were often screaming down the phone at Sandra, 'that they had better fucking things to do than wait and see if the court case was on or not.'

The plan developed in practice at the Crown Court over the next several weeks after the first dummy run between Robert and Alex. Robert contacted Caroline each evening to find out who was in court the next day, already knowing who was supposed to be in. If the client had been bumped from the list but still needed to collect their drugs, Alex would take their file with their papers, and they would still attend. That way, he could hand over the drugs and they could hand over the money. Robert was dealing with a handful of people he knew well who he could trust to give him the names of those in court that they wanted to deal on their behalf.

Caroline didn't know whether any of the clients were, in fact, the players he directly dealt with, and she didn't ask. That was his side of things. He'd set up a good network at the gym, so she had to trust this would work equally well. And so far, so good. It was riskier because there were a number of different people dealing with Alex at court. More people could expose them, but she had to trust that those handling them could, in fact, handle them if the need arose. Robert had assured her that this was the case when she'd asked him.

'Oh yes,' he'd said with the utmost confidence. 'The lot I've chosen are loyal but right nasty bastards. You wouldn't want to fucking cross them. Yer life wouldn't be worth fucking living. They'll keep them in fucking line, word won't get out.'

Caroline made sure the drugs were packaged up for the client with the client's details on and gave them to Alex. Sometimes he would make it back to the office to collect the next day's files, papers and drugs, but very often he didn't, and would then collect them first thing in the morning.

Their client base was increasing at court as these people were asking for the firm to represent them and the drugs operation was expanding nicely. Alex gave Caroline the cash he collected. She was the thin controller of the operation. She liked being the controller of this one much better.

It surprised Caroline that Alex didn't question what he was getting. He didn't appear to have joined all the dots as to how much the whole operation must be making, and what his cut was from it. She was grateful for that and just kept quiet.

With the unpredictable nature of the job, every day presented problems. About three weeks after starting up, Caroline phoned Robert to tell him that Tyler hadn't been produced at court as they'd expected. He'd apparently been sick and so his hearing had been adjourned.

'I know,' said Robert. 'I've already had Jason on the phone fucking moaning that he's got buyers and no product.'

'What did you say to him?' Caroline asked.

'To cool his fucking jets. I'd talk to you and find out when the case had gone off to. If it's not too long away, we'll try again. If it's a way off, we'll send the drugs in.'

'How did he take that?'

'He's no fucking choice, has he? He's in no fucking position to get them himself, is he? I said to him some is going in via the post. Some through the cells. Spreading the fucking risk is the only way to go, and he's either in, or he's fucking out, but he don't need to tell me how to run the fucking ship. He soon shut the fuck up.'

Caroline was pretty sure he would have done if Robert was like that with him, but again it was potentially a loose end, and she really didn't like those.

On another occasion, about three weeks later, Caroline received an urgent email from Alex.

'I won't make it down to the cells in time to see Frank,' he'd typed. 'This sentence is dragging on forever and he'll get taken back to prison before I get there.'

'I thought you were going down to see him at lunchtime,' Caroline typed back, frantically.

'I didn't get a chance. My case in court one didn't finish until one-thirty and then I had to see this sentence guy.'

Lawyers are crap at judging time, Caroline thought. They said things would take ten minutes when invariably they would take at least an hour. Alex was one of the worst for that. Time seemed more elastic to him than most.

'I'll try to get one of the guys to come over from the mags,' Caroline typed back, frenziedly. 'Ian's at the police station, so I can't get him to come over.'

Caroline rang William, knowing that he was the only one of the two of them that would answer his phone. It rang and rang and then went to voicemail. Of course, she didn't leave one. She was in the process of typing an email to him when an email arrived from him in her inbox.

'You OK? I'm on my feet in court, can't answer,' it read.

'Need you or Michael to get over to the CCT asap to deliver papers to Frank in the cells. Alex stuck in court, and they'll take him back if we don't get over there sharpish,' she typed back desperately.

'I think Michael has finished,' came William's reply.

'Yes, but I'll never get hold of him,' Caroline said to herself out loud, panicking. Sure enough, she tried his number and was told his phone was off. 'No fucking surprise there,' she muttered angrily.

She loved Michael, but he could be so infuriating when he didn't have his mobile phone on. It was no good emailing him either. He didn't read those. Michael was a proper dinosaur. He was happy with the time he lived in, and didn't want to progress. There was something to be said for that she had often thought. Most change wasn't always the positive move the powers that be would have you believe. But at times like now, when she needed to get hold of him quickly, she wished he'd moved on from snail mail.

Caroline rang the usher's desk at the magistrates' court. This was the desk where all defendants checked in when they were arriving on bail to let the court know they had attended.

'Hi Helen,' Caroline chimed cheerily when she answered the phone, recognising her voice. 'Is Michael still there? I really need to talk to him.'

'Not got his mobile on then?' Helen laughed.

'The day I get him on that, I think I'll have a heart attack,' Caroline replied, trying to be friendly. What she wanted was for Helen to get on with finding Michael as soon as possible.

Helen howled. 'I saw him a couple of minutes ago. Hang on, I'll see if I can grab him,' and Caroline heard the clunk of the phone receiver being put down on the desk.

She found herself drumming her fingers on the desk and tapping her foot nervously while she waited. It seemed forever until the phone was picked up and Michael's cheery singsong voice said, 'Hi Caroline, do you need me?'

Even though Michael was so frustrating at times, it was impossible to be cross with him. She knew he knew it too.

'Alex is stuck in court, and he won't have time to drop the papers to Frank in the cells before he gets taken back to prison. Can you go over to the Crown Court asap, grab the papers from him in court and go down and hand them over?' Caroline found she was breathless and realised for the whole time she had been waiting for Michael to come on the phone she had been holding her breath.

'Of course, I can,' Michael said, as if he didn't have a care in the world. 'I'll go straight over now.'

'I'll ring the cells. Hopefully, he'll still be there by the time you get there.'

'No worries. On my way.'

As soon as she had finished speaking to Michael, Caroline dialled the cells at the Crown Court.

'Hi Sam,' she said, as soon as the call was answered, recognising the cell officer's voice immediately. 'It's Caroline.'

'Hi Caroline, how are you?' Sam asked gruffly.

'Oh, you know,' she answered, 'same old, same old. And you?'

'No lottery win here sadly, so same shit different day. Not helped today by Alex, I have to say.'

'Oh no, why?' Caroline questioned.

'Said he'd be down with Frank's papers, but we haven't seen hide nor hair of him. I asked for a tannoy to be put out for him and still he's not been down. Of course, he's told Frank that he's bringing them down and Frank's been kicking off for the last hour. We've got a bus coming for him and the others in five minutes and he's threatening to kick off if we try to put him on it. Says he's not going without his papers. Job's difficult enough without this kind of shit,' Sam said grumpily.

'Ah well, I can help you there,' replied Caroline brightly.

Thank goodness they could resolve this. She'd have to have a word with Alex. They couldn't be upsetting the cell staff, they relied on them for access to the clients and they could make life extremely difficult for them if they wanted to. Also, they didn't want Frank shouting his mouth off in case he said something he shouldn't.

'Alex emailed me to say he's stuck in court ...'

'Bloody typical,' Sam interrupted. 'Lawyers love the sound of their own voices. Go on and on when they don't need to. I crack up when I'm in court and they give time estimates for cases. Might as well stick your finger in the air and pluck the first figure that comes to mind.' He carried on grumbling, moaning and complaining.

'Yes, but I've got Michael coming over from the mags. He's getting the papers from Alex, and he'll be with you, I would think, in a minute or two.'

'Well, I have to say I am grateful for that,' Sam said, his tone immediately more cheerful. 'Michael is the perfect person to calm Frank down, too. Everyone loves him, you know. He's everyone's grandad.'

'I know,' and Caroline knew then that was exactly why Michael always had been and continued to be such an asset. Everyone loved him. He was kind to everyone while quietly manipulating them without anyone ever realising. No one would ever believe he could ever be involved in something like this.

'Got to go,' Sam said. 'He's here now. Thanks for sorting, I do appreciate it,' and with that, the call ended.

Caroline heaved a tremendous sigh of relief, smiling to herself.

CHAPTER TWELVE

WILLIAM AND MICHAEL

William, with a commanding presence, instantly made clients feel as if this man had everything under control. His knowledge of the law was second to none. In fact, many prosecutors, court clerks and other defence solicitors regularly picked his brains. When he spoke in court, the magistrates and judges listened. It didn't always go the way his clients would like. He wasn't a magician, after all. Sometimes he couldn't take away how strong the case was against them, but if there was a legal loophole, he'd find it. Robert was enjoying being at court with him and Michael, getting the operation up and running. He wished he didn't have his own case looming over him. It would have been nicer to be in court, not knowing he'd be a defendant again soon. But that was life.

'What are you smiling at, Robert?' William asked.

'I was just thinking how different you are to Alex,' Robert chuckled. 'You are what I think most people would imagine a solicitor to be. He is most people's worst fucking nightmares. You're arrested. You appear in court and you lawyer turns up without your file, half his clothes hanging off, and the other half held together with bulldog clips.'

'I know what you mean,' William laughed. 'But appearances can be deceptive. He's a damn good lawyer. It takes actual balls to do what he does in the Crown Court every day.' William clearly admired Alex. 'Also, don't forget that chaos doesn't apply to his cases. He's always well prepared for those. His opposition will assume the dishevelled way he presents will be reflected in his performance in court. He lulls them into a false sense of security. How wrong they are.'

'Yes, I suppose in some ways he's a fucking master of disguise,' Robert said.

'Well, I wouldn't go that far,' William guffawed. 'I don't think he can help the way he is. It just so happens that he's bloody good, so he can get away with it. How do you think he'll get on with this new line of work?'

'I don't have the confidence in him I have in you,' Robert said quickly. 'With you and with Michael, I know the drugs and money are safe. They'll get to the right fucking people. With Alex I worry he's going to fucking leave them behind, not even fucking realise he's left them, and it'll go horribly fucking wrong. I tried to persuade Caroline we should keep him out of it. But he's her business partner. She was never going to do that,' Robert confided genuinely.

'To be honest, I wouldn't have been surprised if she had tried to keep him out of it. Although, I am not sure I could have gone along with it if that were the case. I know she despairs of him daily. We look in a file and there are the notes of another client filed on there, instead of what you need. If he stands still, he leaves his stuff there, rather than taking it with him. Or maybe it abandons him. There's always files and papers lying about, and you think where have they come from? Then you know Alex is around.'

'That's my big fucking worry, William. He's always leaving fucking stuff lying around. That's why we are fucking packaging the stuff the way we are. If he leaves drugs around, hopefully, someone will see the package addressed to the client coming from us and hand it back to us. If he leaves the money, again it's packaged to him, so it should make its way to him, rather than falling into the wrong fucking hands. Even if he doesn't fucking lose it, he's bound to leave his case open and have something on show. Or take a package out of a file in front of everyone. It's as safe as Caroline and

I can make it while including a fucking nitwit in our op.'

'It's been a long time since I heard someone being called a nitwit,' William said, laughing.

'I wanted to say something much more impolite but didn't feel I could in your company. You being posh and him being your boss,' Robert replied, laughing too.

Robert went to find Michael in court. Michael was in court four doing a trial. Court hadn't started yet. There was just Michael and the prosecutor, a young lady called Sarah, Robert found out from overhearing the conversation between them. When he walked into court, they both turned round.

'Court hasn't started yet,' the lady, now known to him as Sarah, said.

'It's fine, Sarah,' Michael replied. 'He's a client of our firm. I need to speak to him in a minute. Just wait at the back, would you, Robert? I'll only be a minute or two.'

'Sure thing,' said Robert, taking a seat. He was pleased to see Michael in action without it being anything to do with him.

'So, you are happy with all of those admissions I've drafted then?' Michael enquired of Sarah.

'Sure am, Michael. Thanks so much for doing that for us. I haven't got the time this morning. I've two other trials I haven't even looked at yet. Just aren't enough hours in the day.'

'I know that feeling,' said Michael, and he turned and smiled at Robert.

What have you done, you sly old dog? Robert thought to himself. He couldn't put his finger on it, but there was something in Michael's smile that said *Gottcha.*

Michael had signed the document, and Sarah was now signing it, too.

'I'll get the usher to copy this for us, the clerk and the mags. I'll go and have a quick chat with the client and Robert,' Michael said, looking at his watch.

It was just gone nine-thirty in the morning. Court didn't officially start until ten. If you wanted to get anything done at ten, though, you had to be there much earlier to chat with the opposition beforehand. Robert knew that from experience and knew that everyone who worked for Caroline got to court well before it started to begin the day's haggling.

'It'll give you a chance to make a start on the rest of your day,' he said, gathering his papers.

'Thanks Michael, can't wait for this day to be over already,' Sarah said, head buried in the next file.

'What have you done?' Robert whispered to Michael as soon as they left the courtroom and were in the corridor outside.

'I don't know what you mean,' Michael said, smiling coyly.

'You've pulled a fucking flanker, I can tell.'

'You're very good at reading a situation, aren't you?' Michael said.

'Most of the time except when I lose me head,' Robert replied, and Michael nodded in agreement. 'So, what have you done? Come on, I'm fucking dying with anticipation here?'

While they were talking, they were walking, and so were now entering the interview room where William was reading something on his laptop. It was the same room he and Robert had been talking in earlier.

'You didn't get far,' Robert commented to William.

'Just been sent papers on a case that are over three hundred pages. It's going to take me a while to get my head around these,' William said, looking up from his screen.

'Well, take a break while Michael fills us in on his devious doings,' Robert said. William looked intrigued.

'Come on then Michael, spill the beans,' William encouraged.

'Well,' said Michael, looking thoroughly pleased with himself. 'Sarah's prosecuting in court four …'

'Don't tell me,' William interrupted. 'She's having a terrible day and hasn't read half of her files.'

'How did you guess?' Michael replied, grinning.

Sarah was well known among all the court staff. It was fair to say that prosecutors had a heavy workload, but Sarah had a reputation for being lazy. She left everything to the last minute and was then always stressed and moaning.

'Anyway, as you quite rightly guessed, yes, she is having her usual sort of day. So, I offered to draft some s10 admissions for our trial this morning,' Michael went on.

'Right,' said William. 'And why do I get the feeling that she's going to regret letting "Mr Nice" take charge of that this morning?'

'Because she's just signed an admission to say that they cannot prove the ownership of the item in question. She's not going to be able to prove her theft case, is she?' Michael laughed.

'You sly old fox,' William said, full of admiration. 'Only you'd ever get away with that. No one would ever believe that nice old Michael would try to get one over on them. The rest of us have every word scrutinised, but not you. I bet she barely read it.'

'I just watched the fucking smiling assassin at work, and it was magical,' Robert said wholeheartedly. 'You are dead fucking right. She barely read the bloody thing. She just heaved a sigh of relief that she hadn't had to fucking draft them, and she could move on to her next case. I suppose at least she'll get to her other cases quicker, eh,' and they all chuckled.

'OK, while it's wonderful watching you two work, we have got other things we need to do,' Robert said, bringing the focus of the room back to the reason the three of them were together. 'You guys have it easier over here because at least we are not dealing with anyone in the cells. Caroline will tell you each day if there is anyone you should be expecting. Like today, you'll have the drugs in your bags. Good job you don't get searched given you won't give up your fucking carrier bag, Michael. Bit difficult to conceal items in there.'

'Nothing wrong with my carrier bag. You know, it's a bag for life, and I'm getting my money's worth,' he said, and they all burst out laughing.

'I bet it thinks it's drawn the really short straw,' William said, still laughing. 'Having to work with you at your age. It thought it would be long retired by now.'

'It's no good moaning about being a poorly paid criminal solicitor, you know, and then turning up with a flash bag. This bag represents what we are, the poverty-stricken end of the profession. Clients know me as the solicitor with the carrier bag. I've built up a good following of clients with my reputation,' Michael said proudly.

'Well, you'll be able to afford Louis Vuitton soon,' Robert said.

'Louis who?' Michael asked, and they all laughed again.

'How did you get the money in today?' asked Michael.

'Same way I did in the Crown Court. These security guards have no bloody idea how to do a proper search. They can't be fucking bothered. They have a little poke about in your bag with no idea there's a false bottom. Money's safely in here.' Robert opened the bag and showed them.

'Perfect,' replied Michael. 'Here's my share of the papers for you,' and he handed over his envelope.

'And here's mine,' said William, taking an identical envelope from one of the folders on the table beside his laptop.

'And that's all there is to it,' Robert said, sitting back in the chair. They were uncomfortable, hard plastic and bolted to the floor. They never used to be when he was first in court, but he assumed it was because too many of them had been thrown in the past. Sign of the times, he'd commented to Caroline the first time he had attended court after this new change had happened.

'I nearly broke my arm,' she'd replied to him. 'The first time I sat on them after they'd been done. I didn't know they'd been bolted and tried to move it.'

'It's a lot simpler than I first imagined,' William commented. 'In fact, it seems too easy.'

'You lot are never fucking happy,' Robert laughed. 'You say

how hard you work to earn a living, and I agree you fucking do. Now you are moaning it's too fucking easy. There's no pleasing some people.'

'I agree, we are a negative bunch,' William replied. 'I think we are just so used to things going wrong that we almost expect it. When it doesn't, we are waiting for it to go wrong.'

'Well, we don't want this going fucking wrong, otherwise we'll all be in another room together, but you won't like where it fucking is,' Robert warned. 'It's supposed to be easy, no one drawing attention to anything. Me and Caroline have put a lot of thought into how this is all going to run, so we're not expecting any fucking problems, except when people don't turn up on time. You know as well as I do crims ain't the best fucking timekeepers.'

'Yes, we won't be expecting anyone in the mornings,' Michael said, laughing. 'They'll have overslept, missed the bus, forgotten their meds, the car will have broken down or any of the hundreds of excuses I've heard over the years.'

'Caroline will tell you who to expect. She'll give you the package and when they turn up, they'll give you theirs. Easy as. If they don't turn up, let her know. Ring on your burners don't email. The less trail, the better. If there's a change of plan she knows about, like they are going to meet Ian at the pub instead, she'll let you know. You'll have to take the drugs to him at lunchtime. Otherwise, gentleman, this is as fucking tough as it gets. Welcome to easy street where we can all make lots of easy fucking money.'

'Here, here,' William and Michael said simultaneously, grinning like Cheshire cats.

CHAPTER THIRTEEN

IAN

'It's funny how life changes direction when you least expect it,' Ian said to Robert, handing him a pint.

He had just been to the bar of the Half Moon and bought a pint of IPA for Robert, and half a Guinness for himself. They were sitting in the furthest corner from the bar, at a table at the back of the pub for four that had become their regular spot. It had been a brilliant idea of Caroline's to use this pub to meet all those they needed to. In fact, they were going to be using it to meet far more than they initially intended to.

The pub was on the corner of a busy junction. About a hundred metres down the road from the magistrates' court, and directly opposite the Crown Court. It couldn't have been positioned better if they'd built it themselves, Caroline had commented when discussing the logistics. In the past, they had reminisced, it was busy at lunchtime with solicitors and barristers, if they got a chance to grab lunch. More often these days, they grabbed a sandwich in the town centre, or took their own lunch into court. Digital working didn't seem to have provided more free time, sadly. If anything, it pervaded every working hour.

After court, they'd sometimes gather there, celebrating wins, or commiserating a loss. Again, this was far less than it had been twenty years ago. It seemed that lives were more frenetic, rushing from place to place. Racing home after court to prepare for the next day, or off to the police station for another case. There was no time to reset, or even just pause.

This is what Ian was moaning to Robert about, repeating the conversation he'd had with Caroline, and he added, 'That's why this seemed such a good idea to me. I just gotta find some time for myself to do whatever the hell it is I might want to do when I'm not working all the time. Trouble is, I'm not even sure what that is. It's been so long since it happened,' he said, laughing sadly.

'Well, that'll be a lovely journey to go on then,' Robert said. 'Who knows where the fuck it'll take you?'

'Off grid, that's for sure,' Ian replied. 'I'm not having a mobile, a smart watch, a tablet, a computer. Absolutely nada,' he responded emphatically. 'When all this stuff first came in, they said going digital will free us so much time. No paper, things'll be faster. Are they? Are they fuck? Typing ain't in my skill set, so it all takes so fucking long. That's if you can get a Wi-Fi connection. Everything takes longer, and we all just seem to be working 24/7. When I first started, there were no mobiles. If you weren't in, the police couldn't get hold of you. You had time off and the world still turned. Along comes the mobile phone, and now anytime, anywhere, people can get hold of you. They seem to think you are there at their beck and call all the time,' he grumbled.

'You can turn the fucking thing off, though,' Robert said. 'It's a control thing, you know. All you lot are doing is going along with it without fucking questioning it.'

'True. Michael gets away with turning his off all the time. He's such a nice guy, you know, but inside he's bloody sharp. He pretends he's too old for the tech, but I reckon he doesn't want it,' Ian replied.

'Oh, he's the brightest of you lot. Make no mistake about that,' Robert said, laughing. 'He can learn anything he fucking wants if he puts his mind to it. Michael can see exactly what this fucking tech is all about and he doesn't want it. He'd have made a fantastic fucking crime boss, you know. No one would ever believe he's involved, he's so pleasant and sweet. Everyone thinks he's the nice old guy conforming and helping, but he's a fucking smiling assassin, you know. He lures you in. You think he's playing the game, but trust me, he's playing his fucking own.'

'I know, you are dead right. Caroline was telling me the other day he won a trial because he got the prosecution to agree a fact that fatally undermined their own case, so they couldn't prove it. Had to drop it. They'd never have fallen for it from anyone else.'

'That's what I fucking mean, smiling assassin. He pretends he's old doesn't know what he's doing. I've seen him distract the prosecution by pretending he can't get his computer working. They help and before they know it, they've agreed to fucking bail on a case they weren't intending to. I've been watching him; I was there the other day when he was dealing with that case Caroline was telling you about. He's a fucking master.'

'I'd love to be like that, and I'd love to be as laid-back as he is. It's just not in me,' Ian said enviously.

'You'll have to practise your yoga and meditation and get more fucking Zen like as part of your reinvention,' Robert chuckled.

'Can't see it myself,' Ian smiled. 'So let me check I've got this right. On a Monday and Friday, I'm to be here early afternoon. Anyone who hasn't been able to get into court and pick their drugs up and hand over the money will deal with me. Caroline will let me know who that is, and I'll sort out getting the drugs from court. On a Wednesday, I'll be in here to collect the cash for what's being sent into prison. Have I got that right?'

'Yep, that's right and there's to be no fucking deviation from that,' Robert said firmly. 'We're running the fucking show so gotta be tough from the off. Remember, they're all criminals and will try to fucking turn us over if they can. Not fucking gonna happen. Gotta be more ruthless than they are. Be sure the guys we getting the stuff from fucking are. Chain only as good as the weakest link and it fucking ain't gonna be any of us. Ain't gonna be too many people either. We ain't street dealing. Too many fucking comings and goings. Too much fucking risk and not enough cash to make it worth it. We are much higher up the chain than that. We are dealing with those who will then be doing big street deals to others, who'll be dealing individual wraps. Don't want to go any fucking lower than that. A street user might rat you out. Be a fucking fool, but might to save their own skin as not too invested and not dealing with the big guns. The guys we dealing to got a lot to fucking lose and answer to some fucking nasty people. They defo aint gonna rat us out, and that's the way we want it to be.'

'Too right,' Ian agreed. 'I definitely don't want the risk of a withdrawing heroin or crack addict knowing I'm involved. They might not even spill the beans for a deal. It could just come out when they are withdrawing, shivering and shaking, not knowing what the hell they are saying. I want to be involved with those who have as much to lose as me. So, I'll know who to expect from court, but what about the drugs going in to prison? Who will I be meeting about that?'

'That's going to be whoever Caroline tells you at the minute. Depends who we are sending the drugs in to and who they send on their behalf. While I'm not looking forward to it, that part will run better when I'm in. I'll be able to set up a network in there, and limit who is coming on the outside to drop the money off. The bigger the transactions and the fewer people involved, the easier it is from our point of view.'

'And you said to just have the drugs in a carrier bag?' Ian enquired.

'Yep, no one suspects a carrier bag. We all fucking use 'em. We all put all sorts of crap in 'em,' Robert replied. 'Michael's made a bloody career with one. No one will think twice about it, and that's what we want. Sit here and get your laptop out and do some work. Surf the net, whatever the fucking hell you want. You'll blend right in.'

Ian looked round and saw that Robert was right. There were several people hooked up to the pub's Wi-Fi. A man in a suit clearly working, a young woman with pink hair in her early twenties, he had no idea whether she was working or not, and several others of all ages on tablets or laptops. There were four or five groups – he didn't know whether they were work related or social meetings – and six or seven older men reading papers. He'd have no trouble blending in.

'You'll know who to expect,' Robert continued. 'You have your bag down at the side of you, like you have now. They'll sit down opposite you, like I am now, with their bag. You've got the drugs, they've got the cash. They'll pass a few words with you, then get up and leave. You'll be left with a bag. They'll take a bag. No one will notice the swap.'

'How do I know the amounts are going to be right?' Ian asked.

'Same way they know the drugs will be the right amount. Trust,' Robert said, as if the answer was obvious. 'They fucking rip us, off they get their throat slit; we rip them off, same happens. You've joined a whole different fucking culture mate, and that's how it works, but it works.'

He continued, 'That's why I've never been caught. Feds got no idea what I'm about. Honour among crims is very important. The higher up you go, the greater it is, cos the fucking risks are so much greater. It only works cos we all know our place, and what we gotta do, and what happens when we don't do it. Big rewards but huge fucking risks if it goes wrong, and if it does, big punishment. Keeps everyone in line.'

'It's discipline like the army,' Ian commented.

'Yep exactly,' Robert replied coldly. 'Step outta line and you ain't fucking coming back from it.'

CHAPTER FOURTEEN

THE OFFICE

Robert could not stop laughing. 'Stop laughing at me, Robert,' said Sandra, giggling herself.

'You are like a one-man comedy band, you,' Robert retorted.

He was sitting on one side of Sandra's desk, and she was sitting on the other. Caroline was sitting at the end. The fourth edge butted up against the wall. Robert was sitting on the side where clients sat, a point that had not escaped him. This was the position he had occupied every evening this week. It was Friday, and there was always a feel-good factor in the office on a Friday, Sandra had told him earlier. The relief the weekend was finally upon them. He could feel it now.

Spending so much time recently with all of them, both individually and collectively, in the office and at court, had enabled him to understand what a tough job they did. Caroline described herself as constantly spinning plates, and she wasn't wrong. How she remembered what everyone was doing and the details of so many cases were beyond him. She had skills beyond anyone he'd ever seen as far as multitasking went. Now, she was running two ships side by side, and seemed to be taking it in her stride. He also saw how close they were, a real family, with an "us against the world" attitude. That's what made them so good at their legitimate and illegitimate work, and he enjoyed being a part of it.

'It's you making me laugh, Sandra,' Robert said, still chuckling. 'I've told you three times that the name on those drugs is to be

Tony Collins, and three times you've come up with a totally different bloody name. You'll be trying to send them to Joan Collins in a minute.'

'Or Phil Collins,' she retorted quick-wittedly.

'Well, hopefully we'll have as much money as both of them soon,' Caroline said, joining in.

'At least you know if we get caught it won't be me that grasses you up, cos I'll never get your names right,' Sandra said, and they all cracked up laughing again.

'Woof,' joined in Harley.

'Well, I'd never forget your name, H,' Sandra said affectionately rubbing his tummy. 'But I'd never grass you up either, you can be sure of that,' she added firmly.

'Right, let me check that,' Caroline said, taking charge.

Sandra passed her the package, and Caroline was relieved to see it clearly said "Tony Collins papers from Rigby Andrews & Co hand delivered at court Rule 39". The Rule 39 was stamped on, indicating to the prison staff that they couldn't open the papers; they were privileged communication between the client and the solicitor.

'Perfect,' she said, then added, 'at last,' and they all laughed again. 'I'll put them on Alex's pile as he's going to hand them to him at court on Monday when he's produced.'

'He's not taking them home, is he?' Robert questioned.

'No, he's bloody not,' Caroline said immediately. 'Christ knows what he'd do with them between now and Monday. He'd misplace them, that's for sure. No, he's coming in here on his way to court on Monday and collecting them.'

'Here's the next one,' Seb said, passing Caroline a package. He was sitting at the other desk in reception and had been on the phone when they'd been messing about earlier. Caroline knew he had been trying hard not to laugh, as she could see his shoulders shaking.

'Jesus Christ,' Caroline exclaimed. 'You two really are the

dynamic duo. There's Sandra changing the bloody names, and you writing? Well, I don't even know you can actually call that writing, it's scrawling, but I'm not sure what the hell it says.' She turned the package so that Robert and Sandra could see, and they both fell about laughing again.

'For fuck's sake,' Robert gasped between laughs. 'I thought I'd have a bit to teach you guys, you know, learning the ropes of being crims, but not how to fucking write. My writing is absolute dogshit, but it's fucking better than that. How the bloody hell did you get a degree?'

'Computers, mate,' Seb replied, grinning.

'Caroline, wherever you got him from, see if they'll take him back,' Robert said, winking at her. 'I know you have a soft spot for waifs and strays, but they are supposed to be the clients.'

It was true. There were some clients over the years that Caroline had become attached to, she thought, reminiscing. She had always appreciated that most people were only three mortgage payments or rent payments away from homelessness, and that it was a struggle for many. However, there were those that never had any chance of getting their own place and relied on friends or family. Very often, they didn't have the sort of friends or family who would help them out. If anything, they made life more difficult.

One of her homeless clients used to meet her on the doorstep as soon as she arrived at work. Sleeping rough was very tough, especially in the winter, when it was cold and wet. He would come in to make her a hot drink, and she always allowed him to make them both one. He would hang around the office looking for odd jobs to do. She let him stay for a while each day, making all the staff a drink and giving him the chance to warm up a bit. Caroline brought him some warm clothing and would fill a thermos flask for him each evening, so that he could have hot drinks overnight. She brought him food, and he'd make soup in the microwave. He was an "old school" client, grateful for whatever anyone could do for him. Sadly, he died from a drug overdose and that had hit Caroline hard.

Caroline returned to the cheerful mood in the room, retorting, 'Robert, they wouldn't take him back, would they? They were rubbing their hands the day we got landed with him. Do it again, Seb,' she said. 'Alex has got to hand that over to Marshall Thompson. It's bad enough it's Alex wandering around with a package of drugs, but when he can't read who the bloody hell he's supposed to be giving it to, it's a recipe for disaster. Do you want to get struck off and sent to prison before you even get on the Roll?'

'No, I don't,' said Seb. 'It's not that bad,' he added, taking the package back and looking at it.

'Well, you need a fucking trip to the optician's asap then, me old fruit,' said Robert, laughing. 'Cos that's the worst excuse for fucking handwriting I've ever seen, and I've been in prison with some right divs. I've got me fair share of prescriptions from doctors, and I ain't ever seen anything like that.'

'Well,' said Seb, feigning that he was offended. 'I'll try to make it a bit clearer.'

'A lot clearer,' said Caroline. 'Write in capitals, for goodness' sake.'

'I told you his degree came free with a box of Frosties,' Sandra quipped, and they all laughed again.

Harley, who'd returned to his bed and was watching them closely, looked at Seb, and then turned and woofed at Robert as if to say, 'I could have done better than that.'

'I think he's saying he could have done better, and he would be happy to be paid in tennis balls,' said Robert, and everyone howled.

'He loves putting his paw prints all over paperwork,' said Sandra. 'He'll go out in the garden, get his paws muddy and then come back in deliberately looking for paper to walk over. He grins at you while he's doing it.'

'What about that file I had to produce at the audit?' Caroline reminded them and explained for Robert's benefit. 'It was covered in paw prints, and when the auditor asked about it, I told him it had Harley's seal of approval. Fortunately, the auditor had a sense of humour.'

'Harley is our secret weapon for audits. No auditor can resist him,' Sandra said proudly.

'Woof, woof,' said Harley, looking very pleased with himself. His tongued lolled to the side of his mouth as he grinned.

'Except the time he rolled in mud in the garden when it was raining. He then ran upstairs before we could catch him, and jumped on the auditor's lap, licking his face,' howled Sandra.

'Yes, that was pushing things,' Caroline agreed, laughing too.

'Probably best he doesn't add to our envelope issues at the moment then,' Robert said, chuckling. 'This one is for my mate inside,' he added, showing Caroline the package he was working on. The name and prison number were clearly written, the prison address, and Rule 39 professionally stamped. He got a dog biscuit and fed it to Harley, who looked at him appreciatively, but as if to say he was being a bit stingy, surely it wouldn't hurt to have another one. Robert grinned at him and relented.

'Brilliant,' said Caroline. 'How professional does that look, eh, Seb? Oh, it looks like it's coming from a solicitor's office, just like it should do, and he doesn't even work here.'

'Teacher's pet,' joked Seb.

'Mind you, Robert, you say I'm a soft touch with Harley, but I don't think four biscuits are necessary, do you?' she said, with her arms on her hips pretending to be cross.

'Now look what you've done, you've got me into trouble,' Robert said, glancing at Harley and winking.

He looked back as if to say, 'too late mate, I've had the biscuits so I'm happy.'

'And here's mine for Michael to hand over at the mags on Monday,' Caroline added. Hers, of course, was nicely done and easy to read. As a reward, Harley stood up and came over to her, wiping his nose on the back of her legs, as he often liked to do. 'I'm not your tissue, Harley,' Caroline laughed.

'That's your punishment for stopping the biscuit supply,' Sandra said wryly, and they all giggled.

'Did Connor come in for his papers today?' Robert asked Sandra.

'No, he didn't. He rang about three or four times to say he was running late but he'd get here, but he never showed. I tried ringing him just before we closed, but it went straight to voicemail. I didn't bother leaving him a message.'

'Well, that's not going to go down well,' Robert exclaimed. 'That means that silly twat is wandering around with a lot of someone else's money and fuck all to show for it. No doubt I'll be getting a call soon asking if he showed. He better lie low until Monday else he's gonna get a fucking kicking. Money'll be lost, those drugs not being sold this weekend, and important people ain't gonna be happy. I wouldn't wanna be in his fucking shoes, that's for sure.'

Suddenly, there was a loud banging on the door. Then a voice shouted, 'You still open? I need me papers for the weekend. Let me in, I beg you,' the voice pleaded.

Harley let off a volley of barks that was so loud he surprised himself. He looked around as if to say, 'where did that noise come from?'

'For fuck's sake,' Caroline exclaimed. 'It's dickheads like this being involved that'll drop us in it,' she continued, as she hurried to the door and opened it.

Connor practically fell through the door into her arms. 'Caroline, Caroline,' he said, 'thank fuck you're still here. I'd be a fucking dead man if you'd gone home.'

'Get off, Connor,' Caroline said, pushing him back, as she turned to walk back down the corridor, Connor following. 'I could kill you myself, you daft prat.'

'Why? What have I done?' he asked.

'If you seriously don't know,' Robert shouted, 'I'll fucking kill you right here right now.' He'd got up from the desk and was standing blocking the doorway between reception and the corridor. 'Nice garden outside. Harley wouldn't mind if we dug him a nice big hole and threw you in it.'

'Woof, woof, woof,' said Harley, who was beside Caroline, having followed her to the door when the banging started.

'See, he says you're a useless fucking prick and we should get on with it,' Robert continued. 'It's seven pm on a Friday night. We are opposite the pig pen. I know they are as thick as shit, but even they are gonna think it's a bit fucking odd for a client to be so desperate for his fucking papers at this time on a fucking Friday.'

'Yeah, but it ain't my papers I want, is it?' Connor said.

'I fucking know that. You fucking know that. But we don't want them to fucking know that do we?'

'Oh yeah,' Connor said slowly, the penny finally dropping. 'I see what you mean, sorry.'

'Be a bit fucking late for sorry if we're all banged up together, won't it?' Robert growled. He was leaning down right in Connor's face. 'And trust me if I'm fucking banged up cos of you, you're gonna wish I had fucking killed you and buried you in the garden.'

Caroline had never seen Robert so angry. In fact, she'd never seen him like this. She'd imagined what he would be like when he got angry, and this was pretty much an accurate reflection. One thing was for sure, she didn't want to cross Robert if she could help it, but she was glad he was a part of the team. She was extremely angry with Connor but didn't feel that she'd be able to get the point across quite as well as Robert was doing. There was no way Connor would ever do that again.

'OK Robert,' she said more calmly than she felt. 'He's got the message. Let's just cool our jets a minute.'

'You better fucking have,' Robert said, pointing and glaring at Connor as he took his seat again.

Harley thought the tension had defused sufficiently in the room to approach Connor and look at him. Connor looked at Caroline who smiled and nodded towards the biscuit tin. Connor took one out and gave it to Harley who took it gladly. Connor patted him on the head.

'At least he's forgiven me,' Connor said to Caroline.

'He's easily bribed,' she answered, looking at Harley and shaking her head, pretending he was naughty. Harley didn't care, he'd had his biscuit and the look on his face told her so.

'Why are you so late?' Sandra asked Connor. 'You kept ringing to say you were on your way but would be a bit late. Then you never turned up. I rang you, but it went straight to answerphone, and then here you are hours after you first said you were on your way.'

'I just had things to do, and they took longer than I thought,' Connor said sheepishly.

'Well, nothing's more important than getting here when you are supposed to,' Robert retorted angrily. 'Do it again and I'll make sure you are not a fucking part of this, and that those who need to know the fucking reason why.'

'You wouldn't,' Connor said, looking scared. 'Would you?'

'Don't fucking try me,' Robert spat. 'Cos, I don't think it would work out too well for you.'

Sandra gave the package to Connor, and he took out the money from his rucksack and handed it over. 'To be fair,' Sandra said trying to ease the tension, 'it is properly packaged and looks better than what Seb turned out.'

'Don't need to fucking count it, do we?' Robert asked.

'I'm a twat, not suicidal,' Connor said back.

'Well, turn up on fucking time. Otherwise, you'll be meeting your fucking maker quicker than you want,' Robert warned.

'Sorry to mess you about, Sandra,' Connor said apologetically. 'And sorry to you too, Caroline. I wouldn't do anything to hurt you, you know that.'

'I know you wouldn't do anything on purpose, Connor,' Caroline said. 'But behaviour like that could get us all in serious trouble. Don't do it again.'

'I won't, I promise,' he said meekly, and headed for the door.

'Do you think we ought to stop using him?' Caroline asked Robert when Connor had left.

'Nah, he's a fucking dick, but he's learned his lesson now. He won't do it again, so we're probably better off sticking with the devil we know.'

'We don't need shit like that, though. My heart was pounding out of my chest by the time I opened the door.'

'I know. At least we're nearly finished. I'm going to the pub for a drink after this,' Robert said.

'I'm having a nice bath and a glass of wine,' replied Caroline. 'Or maybe the whole bottle.'

Robert opened the package that Connor had handed over and counted the money. As he had said, it was exactly the right amount. He was daft, but not that daft.

'Let's put the packages and money in the safe,' Caroline said, and she and Robert gathered them up.

The safe was four feet tall and was in the corner of her office. It had stored a lot of contract documents before they'd gone digital with them. That was one of the benefits of computers and the digital age Caroline had thought, when they first decided to go along with Robert and join his operation. Until then, the safe had been virtually empty, a sign of the pre-digital era. Fireproof and waterproof. It had cost a lot of money when she bought it, over fifteen years ago. However, there were a lot of documents held in it in the past that would have been impossible to recreate, so it had been worth it. Now it was proving its value again, for a different reason. The drugs could be safely left in the office, along with the money.

Caroline placed everything in different piles for who needed it, to ensure they didn't get muddled up.

'I'll send the package on Monday to the prison, guaranteed next day's delivery,' she said over her shoulder to Robert.

'That'll be fine,' Robert replied. 'I'll let him know it's due Tuesday.'

Caroline knew Robert was watching her entering the code to

the safe. He wanted to make sure if anything happened to her, he could get to the drugs and money. Even though he couldn't access the office, she had no doubt that he'd break in if anything happened to her, or if he thought she'd crossed him in any way. What he didn't know was that she would change the code again on Monday. She changed it every few days to make sure she was the only one that knew it. It was all about control, and Caroline wanted to make sure that she retained as much of it as she possibly could.

CHAPTER FIFTEEN

THE DOG WALKERS

Caroline found dog walkers were good friends and her sort of people. They didn't want anything other than to chat with you, and for you to take an interest in their dog. That Caroline could manage easily. She loved all dogs, although of course none of them were as special as her Harley. The dog walkers didn't want to come round to your house or invade your personal space. They were happy to be kept at arm's length, but just wanted to see you regularly on the circuit walk round the estate and have a catch-up. Caroline often felt drawn to them because they all treated their dogs as children, and all seemed to prefer animals to people, as she did.

She realised over the years that she was, in fact, a bit of a loner. Caroline was happy with her own company, and Harley's, of course. She didn't seek solace or companionship from others. Caroline had friends, but as she often reflected, she wasn't a good friend. It was them that messaged her or rang her. Caroline rarely, if ever, initiated the contact. She assumed it was her job, listening to people and their troubles all day. She simply didn't bother when she was at home.

Deep down, she knew that this was just an excuse. Truth be told, she didn't need anyone, and each relationship for her had a purpose. She cared deeply about her staff at work; but that was work. She didn't socialise with them out of work. She had two close friends. One from her school years, and one from university. She saw them infrequently. Both were married with children and so their lives had gone in totally different directions. They'd made the effort over the years to include her, but a five-year old's birthday party had never been the highlight of her pretty empty social calendar.

Her sideline idea crystallised when she was reflecting on representing Paula and Joe's son, Tom. They were obviously worried about him and what would happen to him, but didn't seem so bothered that he was in trouble in the first place. She thought that they would be mortified. They always gave the impression of being a strait-laced, middle-class couple. However, they hadn't been surprised that it was drug related, which gave her the inkling they knew more about what he had been involved in than they were letting on. They just didn't know exactly what he'd been caught for.

One day, they were standing in the pocket park catching up. The three dogs were chasing after their balls and each other's when it suited them. They were talking about Tom's case. Caroline joked that solicitors should be the orchestrators of drug operations; they knew all the pitfalls and wouldn't get caught. She'd expected them both to laugh and say that would never happen. Surprisingly, Joe questioned how she would do it, if it were her, hypothetically, of course. It caught Caroline off guard. She hadn't expected to be asked more about it. Of course, she didn't want to let on that she was involved in anything untoward, but she had set out her idea of the poo bins.

'I would set up an operation round here for dog walkers involving the poo bins. No one would ever suspect dog walkers; they are such a trustworthy breed of people. Nobody likes poo bins. That's what makes them such a good idea. You put the drugs in a poo bag and hang it from a hook just inside the poo bin. I don't know if you've ever looked in them, but when you lift the lid, inside the bin is the plastic bag to hold all the rubbish, but there's a metal rim round it. I'd attach a hook to that.

'I come out with Harley at pretty much the same time each night. I'd have a drop-off night for each poo bin. That way I wouldn't have too much on me at one time and people wouldn't collect on the same night. This would prevent it from looking too suspicious to others that might see multiple dog walkers when they are out. The dog walkers would know what night I was dropping their drugs and what time. A few minutes beforehand, they'd leave the money in a poo bag on the hook. I'd fish that out and replace it with the drugs. No one watches anyone around a poo bin. They assume they know what you are doing, and everyone hates poo.

'Most people do two circuits of the pocket park. We all seem to go virtually the same route. So, when the person came back round, they would take out the drugs. They would sell them and keep all the profit. I would already have made on what I sold it for. Everyone would be a winner. No one would make a fortune overnight, but no one would be wandering around with huge amounts of drugs or cash on them in areas they couldn't explain, drawing attention to themselves. Low risk. An easily managed operation, but a very good return.'

While Caroline had been telling them her idea, she could see Joe had hardly drawn breath. He hadn't taken his eyes off her the entire time. In fact, he didn't seem to have even blinked. At that point, Harley ran back to her, not with his ball in his mouth. Bailey was chasing him with Harley's ball. They had swapped. Harley looked happier about that deal than poor old Bailey.

'Anyway,' Caroline continued, 'I better get back and carry on reading the papers of someone who really has made a bloody mess of things, to see if there's anything I can do to dig them out of the hole they are in. Sadly, I don't think so.'

They exchanged pleasantries and Caroline continued on with Harley, who still had Bailey's ball. He hadn't been willing to give it up and Paula had said it was fine, he could keep it. Bailey had Harley's and a ball's a ball, right?

'Well, a ball's not a ball to you, is it, H?' she said as she carried on. 'You wouldn't have let me walk away if you wanted yours back, and it's not like you to swap like that. What are you up to?' Harley was looking very chuffed with himself. Caroline assumed, given that he was the older dog, he was just pleased that he'd got it off Bailey and at all costs wasn't about to let him have it back.

'Joe was very interested in my plan,' Caroline told Harley when they got back to the house and were in the hallway. Caroline took off her shoes and coat, Harley flopped on the floor. 'If I'm honest, he caught me out. I wouldn't have quite told him it all like that if I'd thought about it,' she continued. 'I'm glad you came back to me and distracted me with the ball situation. Still, he doesn't know what's going on. He'll just think it's all in my imagination.'

A couple of days later, Caroline and Harley were in the pocket park playing ball and Paula and Joe and the two black labs appeared. Caroline was throwing the ball with the ball catcher as far as she could. Harley seemed to have more energy than normal, and she certainly didn't. It didn't take long for Joe to bring the conversation back round to the poo bin drug operation.

'Are you serious about this?' he asked.

'It was just something my imagination conjured up,' Caroline replied warily. 'It comes with the territory for defence solicitors. I would imagine the same can be said of the police. You see clients being caught on CCTV, with DNA, phone evidence, etc. and you think what a moron, you should have seen that coming, I wouldn't make the same mistakes. That's all. And a bit of wishful thinking about more money for all the hours I put in.'

Harley returned with his ball, and Caroline picked it up with the catcher and threw it again for him. All three dogs chased after it. *Carnage,* Caroline thought.

'We're incredibly interested if you want it to be more than a pipe dream,' Joe persisted. 'Tom has caused a lot of debt for us. He owed money to some extremely nasty people, and we've had to re-mortgage the house to pay them off. Now, with the rise in interest rates, we are struggling to pay it off. The extra cash would be incredibly helpful for us. He has customers but no ability to get the product. Seems ironic to be using the same means to get us out of the mess that's got us into it, but we can't see any other way and your plan seems simple and as safe as it gets. No connection with each other's houses. No connection by phone or computer. Nothing to easily catch us out. Especially this time of year. We are all wearing gloves, even better.'

'Oh OK. Look, I don't want you getting the wrong end of the stick here. I was telling a story. I wasn't saying what is happening or what could happen. It's not something I've ever thought of in that way,' Caroline said emphatically. Of course, that wasn't strictly true, but she didn't want to agree to it without thinking it through very carefully. Especially as Tom had got himself into debt and owed money to people. That was a potentially dangerous cul-de-sac she didn't like the sound of.

'We are not saying you are,' Paula cut in. 'We are just saying we think it's an extremely good idea and if you want to get it up and running, please count us in. We weren't involved with what Tom was doing. We knew what was going on, of course, but we'd be doing this, we'd be doing the deals. It would be his connections, that's all. We wouldn't allow him anywhere near it. He's got us into a heap of trouble. We won't give him the opportunity to get us in to anymore.'

Caroline believed them. She could see how desperate they were, and desperate people do desperate things, especially for their children.

'Look,' she said. 'I'll think about it. I know people, of course, but I don't deal with them in that way. It wouldn't be something I could set up overnight and also, we'd need more people involved to make it worth my while.'

Although Caroline had the other operation, she wasn't going to start something like this to make a few extra quid. It simply wasn't worth the risk and the hassle.

'I think Anthony would be interested,' Joe piped up.

'What makes you say that?' Caroline asked.

She knew Anthony well but wouldn't have thought he'd be a candidate at all. Anthony was in his mid-sixties, on his own, with the very pretty but extremely spoilt beagle, Millie. Harley could be demanding when he wanted to be, but he didn't hold a candle to Millie.

Harley would sniff her, but then look at Caroline as if to say, 'way too high maintenance for me with her ridiculous range of pretty collars and in winter coats and jumpers to match. What does she think she looks like?' Millie had Anthony firmly wrapped around her paw and both of them knew it.

'He's bored and the money. That's the simple answer. He's retired and doesn't know what to do with himself. He didn't retire out of choice. I don't think he has the money to do that if I'm honest, reading between the lines. But I think his firm forced him out, wanted to make way for younger, cheaper blood,' Joe divulged.

'Well, his firm are idiots,' Caroline responded. 'The younger, cheaper version will be off sick every five minutes and won't have the dedication to their job that I'm sure Anthony did. I knew he had recently retired, but I didn't know the circumstances of it. I'd love to be retired, so many things I want to do that I haven't got time to do, but if you haven't planned for it, I bet it takes some adjusting.'

'Absolutely, and he isn't there yet, I can tell you,' Joe said vehemently. 'Do you want me to sound him out?'

'You can do but be careful. We could get done for a conspiracy without actually doing anything if anyone reported this plan if it gets much further,' Caroline warned.

'I will, I promise, but we've got to ask people if we want them to join us,' he said objectively. 'Who are you thinking of?'

'Christine might be a possibility,' Caroline suggested.

'Are you sure?' Paula replied. 'I wouldn't have thought that at all. She's a very prim and proper sort, isn't she? She's a teacher, am I right?'

'Yes, you are, but isn't that the brilliant thing about this idea?

You wouldn't suspect any of us. You two come across as prim and proper and very middle class, but you are interested,' Caroline retorted.

'Yes, I suppose you are right,' Paula said, laughing.

'Touché. Do you want to speak to her then?' Joe encouraged.

'Yes, I can do. Harley loves Clive, so when I see her, we always end up having quite a chat.'

Clive was Christine's elderly golden retriever and was such a gentle soul. Harley and Clive had played for hours over the years, both slower now than they first were. However, both still loved rolling in mud and fox poo if they got the chance before Caroline and Christine tried, usually unsuccessfully, to drag them away.

'Anyone else?' Joe was clearly on a roll now, enjoying this.

'I think we tap those up first and see how we get on,' Caroline advised. 'Plus, Harley isn't looking so happy now that Barney has his ball. He didn't seem to mind at first. I've been watching him. Now his hackles are up and yes, the barking has started. "Mum, retrieve my ball," he's saying. Last time he was happy to swap, but today he's not giving his up. OK, today's Wednesday. If we haven't seen each other by Monday for a catch-up, then shall we say we'll be here at 7:30 to update each other?'

'Yes,' Paula and Joe agreed in unison.

As it happened, they didn't need to wait until Monday, bumping into each other on Saturday evening.

'Exciting lives we lead even on a Saturday,' Joe said by way of a greeting.

'Exactly,' replied Caroline.

'So?' said Joe.

'So what?' said Caroline coyly.

'Did you speak to Christine?'

'Did you speak to Anthony?' asked Caroline. She didn't want to say anything until Joe told her. She wanted to make sure they were fully invested before she disclosed anymore of her hand.

'Yes, and he's in. He didn't take any persuading at all, did he, Paula?' he said to his wife.

'None at all,' she added, nodding her head in agreement. 'He thinks it's a great idea., I think he was quite envious he hadn't come up with it himself.'

'Who would he deal them to?' Caroline asked. 'He isn't the type to be hanging around with drug users,' she pondered.

'Now you are making judgement calls,' Paula laughed. 'However, you're right, he doesn't, but his nephew, his sister's boy, does. He's a total dropout, drives Anthony mad. We wonder if he's thinking at least it'll give him an income instead of sponging off his mum, Anthony's sister, all the time. He was saying she works two jobs to keep a roof over their heads and he's still in bed at three in the afternoon.'

'More fool her,' Caroline responded, tutting.

'I know, the youth of today are useless, but it's hard when you're the parent, we should know,' Paula said.

'What about Christine then?' Joe said, itching to know.

'As I thought, she's like me, totally disillusioned. It's hard work being a teacher these days. The kids are aggressive. You can't touch them, and you rarely get any backing from their parents. She wants out and will do what it takes.'

'Fantastic. What about getting hold of the drugs?' Joe was pushing. Caroline could tell he was very keen to get this up and running as soon as possible.

'I might have found a source,' Caroline said, playing her cards close. 'We need the drugs cutting. I'm not doing that, so it takes an extra element to the chain. I'm working on it.'

Caroline didn't want to let on that she was already involved with anyone. Everything needed to be kept separate and on a need-to-know to reduce the risk. She also didn't want anyone getting wind that there was more money to be made. They seemed keen, but everyone needed to be kept in their individual role or it would get very messy.

'OK, who else then?' Joe said, determined to drive the conversation forward.

'I think Julie-Ann might be a possibility,' Caroline volunteered.

'I agree,' said Paula. 'I saw her yesterday, and she's having a very hard time at the moment.'

Julie-Ann was a lovely person, one of the friendliest, bubbliest people you could meet. She'd always got a joke to crack and a funny story to tell. She was the first to ask how you were, taking a genuine interest and concern in others' lives, when she didn't have it easy herself. Julie-Ann was a single parent to two small girls and was always beating herself up that she wasn't doing a good job. She put so much pressure on herself all the time, when everyone knew she did all she could for her girls. She balanced raising them on her own with a part-time job. The girls' father wasn't on the scene, had no contact with them and didn't pay any maintenance. The Child Support Agency had had no luck trying to trace him and so she soldiered on alone. It was such a shame. This could significantly help them.

Caroline normally saw her at the weekends with the girls and their needy French bulldog, Lola. She was a total diva, and they all pandered to her. It usually took a while for Julie-Ann to complete the circuit because when Lola planted her feet and refused to move, that was it. She was going nowhere. She just looked at Julie-Ann as if to say, 'no thanks, I'm not feeling it today.'

'I think she'll be worried about the risks with the girls, but she needs the money,' Caroline added.

She'd have to keep an eye on Julie-Ann, though, if she agreed. With her lack of confidence in herself, it could make her anxiety worse. Not what they wanted if they were to keep this under the radar.

'Fine, you speak to her then,' Joe delegated.

'Woah there, Joe. This is my plan, not yours,' Caroline said, reining him in.

'Of course. Didn't mean to overstep. We just desperately need the cash,' he said apologetically.

'I understand, but we've got to get this running properly, otherwise you'll make bugger all and end up in prison,' she chastised.

'Yes, Joe,' said Paula sharply. 'Stop trying to take over. Leave it to the professional.'

'Well, I wouldn't go that far,' said Caroline, winking at her. 'The last person I was thinking of is Marie. What do you think?'

'Bloody perfect,' Joe exclaimed. 'No one will ever suspect her. She's got to be well in her seventies. Pottering along on her scooter with that dog who seems to spend more time in the basket than walking,' he said, laughing.

'Oswald is so handsome,' Paula said.

'But he can be so lazy,' replied Joe. 'He's supposed to be a lively dog, but at times he makes Julie-Ann's Lola look active.' They all laughed.

'Yes, he can be the laziest cockapoo I've ever met,' agreed Caroline. 'But at other times, he runs around with Harley like a mad puppy. It's because Marie pops him in the basket when he asks. Or he hops on the scooter itself when it pleases him. Chauffeur driven, he is, and it's made him very entitled.'

They all laughed again. Joe said, 'You know Marie calls him Mr I Want.'

'That's about right,' Caroline added. 'Mr I Want and Mr I Get.'

'I think she'll be up for it. She's got that lazy grandson of hers living with her. Honestly, at her age she doesn't need that good-for-nothing layabout,' Paula explained.

'No, she doesn't,' agreed Caroline. 'There seems to be a bit of a theme here, doesn't there? The older generation having to support the youngsters who can't be bothered, when it should be the other way round.'

'Christ, I hadn't thought of it like that, but you're right,' Joe exclaimed. 'What is this world coming to?'

CHAPTER SIXTEEN

THE VIDEO LINK

'Hi, Robert,' Caroline said, as soon as the link connected, and he appeared on the screen in front of her. He looked bulkier than he had when she had last seen him a few weeks ago. He was clearly working out inside, even more than he had on the outside. 'You are looking well,' she added.

'Cheers,' he replied, clearly pleased at her noticing. 'Gotta keep in shape. Never know when you'll need to take care of yourself in here,' he explained.

'They'd have to be one screwed up bastard to mess with you, Robert. Surely everyone knows you by name and reputation, even if they don't know you personally,' Caroline responded, with a tone of surprise.

'That's what I'm counting on, Caroline,' Robert retorted, smiling at her. 'Lots of locals in here, so word will have spread. But you can never be too careful. Drop your guard and you're a dead man.'

The matter-of-fact way he said this made her shiver. 'Sorry if I came across harshly on the phone,' Caroline said genuinely. 'I know you were clearly excited to tell me something, but calls are recorded, you know that. We just can't risk anything. We've been so careful up till now, and things have been running well, even with Alex and Seb in the mix. But it only takes loose lips on one occasion to sink ships.'

'You did fuck me off a bit,' Robert responded seriously. Then he grinned. 'But I'm over it and besides, you're right, of course. You fucking always are. That's why I picked you. So, I can't be mad when you're doing what you should be.' He winked at her.

'So come on then,' she said impatiently as she winked back at him. She was relieved he wasn't cross with her. That would just be another headache she didn't need. 'Yesterday, you couldn't keep your trap shut. Now you are just sitting there grinning like a Cheshire cat.'

Robert guffawed. 'Women!' he said. 'There's no pleasing you.'

Caroline was relieved to see that he was coping well in custody. Although he had been full of bravado, she knew he truly didn't want to go back inside. Very few people did, unless they were homeless. At least that way they were guaranteed free bed and board, and hot meals. This time was different to the other times, though, for Robert. He'd built something up on the outside that he was a part of. He'd thoroughly enjoyed being part of the team in the practice, expanding the empire. She'd been worried that he might unravel emotionally when he went in, but he'd still got enough control over the operation from in there to keep him stable, hopefully.

'Also, why didn't you phone me from your burner phone to mine yesterday? Why ring the office phone?' Caroline questioned.

'I'm still a client,' Robert said, sounding a little hurt. 'I'm still allowed to phone the office, ain't I?'

'Of course you are,' Caroline replied quickly, not wanting to upset him. 'I was just surprised, that's all. Every other day you've been ringing me from the burner.'

'Well,' Robert said, laughing, 'I did an Alex. I dropped the fucking phone down the bog. It's alright, a little soggy, but it's drying out nicely. Got me mate who works in the kitchen to get me some rice in a bowl.'

'Jesus Christ,' Caroline exclaimed. 'Isn't one clown in our circus quite enough?' and they both laughed.

Harley, who was in his usual place, tucked under the desk

on his bed, reacted to Caroline's laughing by lifting his head and placing it on her feet. He snuggled his body into her legs.

'So,' Robert began. 'It looks as if things are going to work out real well in here. Me dad's been in touch. He's back in prison in Manchester. Got out after he'd done his sentence. Parole board kept him in a couple of years longer, so it was fucking eighteen years after he first got banged up. It's too fucking long, Caroline, when you've got nothing on the outside. The world moves on so fucking fast and you're just not a part of it. He fell in with a nasty lot and got involved in an armed robbery. That's him back in for life now. No fucking chance of parole.' Robert looked genuinely sad about the situation.

'I'm so sorry, Robert,' Caroline said gently. Robert was obviously very sad about this. He reminded her of the lost little boy she had met at the police station all those years ago. 'I didn't know, and I didn't realise you had contact with him.'

'It's not been good contact, to be honest,' Robert said sadly. 'A message here or there. But he didn't want to meet me when he was out. He got out when I was twenty-four. Now I'm thirty-five, so there was plenty of time. Said he'd got nothing to add to my life, and he'd drag me down. I was dead sad at the time. You know how much he meant to me, still does, but I guess he was right. I have screwed up, but nowhere near as bad as him. He's been back in nine months. I didn't know myself till I got back in here.' Robert looked as if he was in deep thought. 'Still,' he said more brightly, 'no point dwelling on what might have been. Every cloud has a silver lining and we've been in contact. He's happy to be part of the op and have drugs sent to him to distribute. Stable long-term situation, he ain't going nowhere.'

'Jesus, Robert,' Caroline shouted. 'I thought we all agreed. No one told anyone outside of the team about the operation. Family included. It was you who made that clear at the meeting. Then here you are looping in your dad, who you barely know, let's be honest, and who has nothing to lose. That's a real potential loose cannon.'

Caroline was so angry with Robert she was physically shaking. 'You could have put everything, and all of us, in real danger. Why did you have to open your bloody mouth?'

This was exactly what Caroline had been afraid of. Robert was unpredictable, especially when stressed, and prison was an extremely stressful environment. It always was going to be the most dangerous part. On the outside, she had much better control over him.

'Keep yer fucking wig on,' Robert yelled back at her. 'We might not have the best father–son relationship, but we love each other, and deep down, that's all that fucking matters. He's got nothing to gain either from blabbing. No way he's getting out, whatever he tells, so he's no reason to fuck this up. He's bored in prison. This will help, and give him some power over the younger lads, which won't do him any harm. It's another prison. A whole new network. Bigger dough means a faster fucking payout all round.'

The shouting had upset Harley. He was standing up, with his head in Caroline's lap.

'It's alright lad,' she whispered, stroking his head. He looked at her intently with his big brown eyes. 'Nothing to worry about. Mummy's OK.'

Harley didn't look convinced, and remained eyes locked with her for a few more moments, as she carried on stroking at him. She could feel her heartbeat slowing, her blood pressure coming down. Harley could obviously feel it too and licked her hand before returning to his spot under the desk.

Animals are amazing, she thought. *Harley can tell every emotion and knows exactly how to help; shame people aren't like that!*

'I can see that,' she said tersely. 'But it magnifies the risk immensely. I don't know your father personally. I have no connection with any prison in Manchester.' Caroline could see lots of ways this could go sideways and fast.

'It'll be fine,' Robert jumped in. 'He's going to write to you, so you've got his prison number and details, and ask you to review his case. He'll send you an authority, and you can get access to the papers. You can then send him letters and papers and the drugs. You won't be reviewing his case, he knows that. Fucking Mickey Mouse could review it, or the good Lord himself. No way, no chance is he going anywhere, and he knows it. All it does is give you a reason to set up a file and be sending him papers. All tidy your end.'

'I don't like it,' Caroline said. She was less angry than she was initially, but she was far from happy.

'You only don't like it because you don't feel in control of it,' Robert said gently. 'But you are. He knows the score, and he'll fit in fine.'

Caroline knew Robert was right about the control. That's why she'd ended up running the business, she knew, although she didn't like to admit it. It was because she didn't trust anyone else to do it properly. She was, when all said and done, a control freak.

'There's something else,' Robert went on.

'Are you trying to give me a heart attack or what?' Caroline exclaimed.

'No, and this is not something I went looking for. It's kind of fallen in our laps.'

'Before my heart actually leaps out of my chest, do you think you could wind it up and get on with it?' Caroline said breathlessly.

'It's OK, Caroline. You have gone very pale, are you alright?' he asked, clearly worried.

'I'm fine.' Caroline said, fanning herself as she felt a little hot. 'Or at least I will be if you tell me.'

Harley reappeared from under the desk, sensing that Caroline was tensed and stressed. She stroked him and he sat at the side of her, putting his head in her lap. She cradled his head.

'A screw called Dave came to see me in my cell yesterday. That's what made me ring you,' Robert explained. 'I think you know him. He said he knows you and the firm cos he books all of your prison visits and links.'

Caroline knew him on that basis. He was always very friendly and incredibly helpful. He would always try to squeeze them in if he possibly could.

'Yes, I know him,' said Caroline guardedly. 'He seems like a really helpful guy.'

'He could be even more helpful,' Robert went on. 'He has an idea about the drugs, I think. Didn't say it in so many words. But said he'd like an opportunity to earn extra cash and his wife works on the women's side. I think you know her too, as she does the visits and links for them.'

'Is it Louise?' Caroline asked.

'Yes, that's right,' Robert answered.

'She's always really helpful, too,' Caroline added. 'But I'm extremely worried about how Dave knows anything. We've been so careful.'

'I don't think he knows what's going on,' Robert said calmly. 'I think he just knows that I'm connected in here. So, in his mind, that means I'm connected to drugs. Even if I'm not the supplier, he assumes I'll be in the know. He's clearly suggesting he can move any drugs from this side to the women's side through his wife. You'll be proud of me. I kept my trap shut and never let on. Never said I could help. Just said I'd keep me ear to the ground and tip him the wink if I heard.' Caroline could tell by his tone of voice he was trying to reassure her. Robert continued, 'Could be lucrative, though. Question is, do we want to loop them in, or not?'

Caroline rubbed her face. 'This is like an octopus growing too many arms and legs,' she said. 'On the one hand, it offers expansion, and of course, more money. But the actual concern is supervision, keeping these arms and legs under control. The more people, the more chance of it going wrong. Someone catches wind of something. Someone overhears something. Someone blabs. Bringing in the guards like that, you don't think they are trying to set us up, do you?'

'Defo not,' Robert said, firmly. 'Dave ain't like that. He ain't one of the nasty bastard screws and he ain't one of the ones who's nice to your face, and a total fucking cock behind your back. He's just a straight up nice guy, doing his job. Dave doesn't judge us. He treats everyone well. You ask anyone in here. He's their favourite screw. He watches out for everyone. Tries to make sure everyone's coping and doing as alright as you can in this fucking place. I would guess his wife is the same. What do you think from your dealings with them?'

'They've always been great. Like you say, they go out of their way to help. I know Louise is always saying what a tough job it is. Not just from the prisoner point of view. She said you'd expect that to be the worst bit, but it isn't. It's the totally unreasonable demands from the management. Too few staff with too much to do, and crap pay. Pretty much like my job, to be honest. I think that's why we get along so well. We cheer each other up with our moaning,' Caroline said, laughing. 'We're always taking about the lottery and how mad these people are who say it wouldn't change them, and they would still go to work. Not us, we say. Wouldn't see us for dust! I hadn't made the connection between her and Dave, though. Guess it's just never come up.'

'Well, what do you think?' Robert asked. 'Cash is king, after all.' He was clearly enthusiastic about expanding this side of the operation.

'Well, I suppose Dave might be able to help you distribute easier on the men's side. If Louise could sort even half the amount you are doing on the men's side, it's got to be worth it. As long as they can be trusted to absolutely keep it to the two of them. No cutting in any of their mates they feel sorry for. We don't want so many people involved, it's just harder work managing it all, but by the time we've paid them, we are making next to sod all out of it.'

Robert couldn't fault Caroline's logic. She was always so practical, but he felt he stretched her capabilities in ways that were good for them both.

'Gotcha,' he responded. 'And I think we pay them a percentage of what they get rid of. I've got a pukka arrangement dealing on my wing and getting the drugs to one of the other wings through a pal I meet working in the laundry. I also meet another pal at the gym. He sorts out another wing. It costs us next to nothing. They just get a bit for free. However, there are a couple of places it's more difficult for me to get to. We'll see if Dave can help with that. He's not getting a share of what I can do myself. Course his missus opens up a whole new income stream, so if that works, that's proper expansion for us. How about we offer them twenty-five per cent and see what they say?'

Robert sat back in his chair like he was the CEO of a big company making a major business deal. It made her smile. 'Whatcha smiling at?' he asked her.

'You,' she replied. 'Alan Sugar eat your heart out. You're loving growing this from in there, aren't you?'

'Sure, I fucking am,' he grinned, opening his arms wide, as if to show her the size of his empire. 'I'm part of something. I started it. Now I'm growing it and even this setback ain't turning out to be a fucking setback. In fact, it could turn out to be a bloody good move in the long run.'

'Quite a drastic move,' Caroline replied. 'Not one you need to repeat. But I agree, it might prove to be a positive thing to iron out any issues in there. You can make sure everything runs like clockwork for when you leave.'

'That ain't happening for a while,' Robert said. 'Things will be well under control long before then.' He seemed very confident in himself.

'We've just got to be careful. Just because something is a good idea doesn't mean that we need to do it all at once. Too much, and we'll make a mistake. It won't take much for this to all go badly wrong.'

This was always a worry at the back of Caroline's mind and added to her sleepless nights. She didn't want them to get greedy and to over-commit. To go too big and risk what was already proving to be a good thing.

'You are a born worrier,' Robert interrupted her thoughts. 'I bet you are one of those people who worry when they don't have anything to worry about,' he teased.

'Good job one of us worries, Robert,' she responded. 'And doing my job, I've never been in a position to have nothing to worry about. We want an empire we can control, not that is controlling us. Or worse still, is totally out of control. I have no desire to join you in the other half of that place.'

'I know,' he said sympathetically. 'I'm not laughing at you. You know that. We got this, though. The risk is spread. Different parts, not on the face of it, connected. I'm running the prison part. You're running the outside, but we help each other. I help you with names for the outside. You help me by getting the drugs in here. We ain't going to get this wrong. I ain't gonna let you down. You've been the one consistent good thing in my fucking life.' He stopped as his voice cracked a little.

'Jesus, Robert. You'll have me in tears in the minute, you daft git. Speak to Dave and let me know on my burner what he says. I'll wait to hear from your dad, and we'll start small there. I'm far more anxious about that.'

'OK,' Robert replied. 'Is everything else going alright out there?'

'So far, so good,' Caroline responded. 'But I'm not counting my chickens until this plot has properly hatched, and I'm sitting on a beach sipping a cocktail with this all a distant memory.'

'You will girl, sat next to Harley, with his diamond-encrusted collar,' he said, laughing.

'You think you are joking, don't you?' she teased. 'But more likely a diamond-encrusted ball,' and they both laughed.

Harley raised his head from her lap as if to confirm the position, but to indicate he'd need several.

The time was up on the link, so they said their goodbyes. Caroline said she'd book another link for them to update each other in a week or so. She sat back in her chair afterwards, replaying the conversation in her mind. The Manchester angle kept coming to the front of her mind like an awkward itch that no matter how hard she tried to scratch, didn't go away. She couldn't make herself feel better about the situation and she really wished Robert hadn't said anything to his dad.

'No point crying over spilt milk,' she said to herself. 'Just going to have to make the best of it. I need to make the cash faster and get out quicker.' The pep talk didn't reassure her, however much she tried to tell herself things were under control. That she had things under control. Even stroking and kissing Harley, her routine coping mechanism, didn't quell the churning in her stomach or the sense of bile rising from her stomach and up her throat.

CHAPTER SEVENTEEN

LOUISE AND DAVE

Robert was in the gym, working out hard. It was the one time in the prison where he could forget where he was, concentrating hard on lifting his weights. For that small window of time, his life was much the same as it was on the outside.

'Any news?' Dave enquired.

'What you doing in here?' Robert asked.

Dave wasn't the screw in charge of the gym. He hoped he wasn't deliberately seeking him out before things had even started between them. Discretion was key. Enthusiasm was welcome, but not if unnecessary risks were being taken. In a prison, unnecessary contact was such a risk.

'Don't worry, I'm supervising the gym today. Trev's gone home sick. Although, why anyone would think I'm the person to work in here, Christ knows. I wouldn't even know how to use half of this equipment,' he said, laughing.

'About as useful as a fucking chocolate teapot,' Robert agreed, laughing, too. 'As it happens, I do have news, but not here. Too many eyes and ears. They might not be the brightest fucking bulbs, but we don't want anyone picking up on anything.'

'Righto,' Dave said, nodding his head. 'I'll come by your cell later. Now get back at it. You ain't broken a sweat yet.'

'Fuck off,' replied Robert, chuckling.

Dave arrived at Robert's cell later that afternoon. Robert was on his bunk, reading a book.

'Christ,' Dave exclaimed, as his face broke into a smile. 'Didn't know you could f'ing read.'

'Yer cheeky bastard,' Robert replied, good humouredly. 'Granted, it's not fucking Shakespeare or Dickens, but it's a proper book. And I'll have you know, I've read a few of them in me time now,' he said, chucking it in Dave's direction.

'Missed,' Dave said, winking.

'Trust me, if I wanted to hit you, I wouldn't have fucking missed,' Robert retorted.

'I'm damn sure you wouldn't, and it would probably be a better weapon than this,' Dave responded, picking the book up and handing it back to Robert.

'Too fucking right,' Robert said and gestured for Dave to push the cell door closed. Dave did. 'Right, you sure you still want in on anything I can hook you up with?' he said, looking Dave straight in the eyes.

'You know I do. Louise too,' Dave said earnestly.

Almost desperately, Robert thought.

'OK. Well, this is what I can do for you. I get drugs coming into the prison. They come in through my post. That's why I ask you to get it to me as soon as, and you do, so that needs to fucking carry on. I deal with those drugs. Nothing to do with you and you get nothing for helping me with that part. You've been doing it so far and that's how others get paid. I'll get extra if you get it to a pal of mine on C Wing. I'm struggling to get drugs over there. No fuckers are reliable enough. You get it to my pal in his cell. That's all you gotta do. He'll take care of it from there. You need to speak to your missus to see what she can do her end, cos that'll affect how much comes in. I'll give you her stuff and you get it to her.'

Dave's face showed no reaction to what Robert was telling him. It was obvious it what he was expecting.

'Easy for me to get to C Wing. I'm over there most days at

dinnertime, so I can do that. Give me that name and I'll make arrangements with him on how best to sort it. With Louise, I'll make sure I'm outside in the exercise yard at the same time as she is on the women's side. There are some holes in the separating wall. I noticed them a few months back and wondered what sort of stuff has gone back and forth. Now I can make use of them. We'll have to be quick and careful and get our timings organised, but I can do that.'

'Be careful about messages on yer phones,' Robert warned. 'This thing goes sideways; we don't want any more evidence than there has to be.'

'Good point,' Dave said. 'I'll ring her on the internal phone. I do a lot anyway for work and also for personal stuff, so no one will take much notice.'

'Walls have ears, mate; walls have fucking ears. So just keep it short and be aware who's around you when you're doing the swap in the yard.'

'Relax mate. I've got this covered. I won't let you down. Can't let me old man down,' Dave said sadly.

'And don't get distracted and have any drugs on yer when yer leave, else when you're searched, you're fucked.'

'Jesus, Robert,' Dave exclaimed. 'What sort of thick bastard do you take me for?'

'It's easily done,' Robert warned sternly. 'You gotta have your fucking wits about you all the time. You're not used to this. Something might kick off and distract you and then you forget. And if the shit hits, don't be sending any my way. You wanted in. You know the fucking risks.'

'I won't get distracted. Believe you me, I know how fucking dangerous this is. It goes tits up for me and Louise, and we both end up in here. Prison ain't a good life for a screw as a screw, but as a prisoner, you know exactly what'll happen to us. It's the seg unit or we take our lives in our hands every day we're in. Also, me dad'll be totally buggered, so trust me, they'll be no fuck-ups on our end.'

'Just don't want it to go wrong. I'm only a small part of a much bigger fucking machine, and they are a much nastier fucking bunch than me. We lose their drugs, and feds start sniffing about, and you'll be too fucking frightened to shut your eyes and sleep ever again.' As he said this, Robert made a cutting motion horizontally across his throat with his right hand.

'I hear you, mate. I don't wanna cross you, let alone anyone else. I've seen the type. I know it's dangerous, but I got no other way of raising the cash, so I gotta take the chance and get this right. By the way, what sort of cash are we talking about here?'

'Took you long enough to ask,' Robert said, laughing. 'Thought you were going to do it for free.'

'Fuck off,' Dave replied. 'Just wanna make sure I know what I've gotta do first. Now I wanna know how much I'm gonna get for risking me neck.'

'Twenty-five per cent of everything we make on your part. I think we can shift an ounce of each per week on C Wing, if we play our cards right. That's £4,400, so you get £1,100. Then it's whatever Louise can shift on the ladies' side. I don't know what sort of players are already on it over there, but it could be a large amount of cash.'

'Well, she can at least do the same as me, I would hope. I've got one wing, she's got the whole prison, so £2,200 per week's not a bad aim to start.'

Robert could see that Dave was spinning the figures in his head. Understandably, that's what everyone did. No one was in it for anything other than the cash. Dave was obviously delighted with the numbers. Robert knew he'd easily be able to sort his dad's fees out, and start putting some money away for him and Louise so they could get out and have a better future for themselves. He knew their two girls were off their hands now, but the university fees had crippled him. Dave had confided in Robert they had no savings, and credit card bills of, he would guess, around £30,000. He'd explained he tried not to add them up too often as the figures frightened him. Dave and Louise still had about five years left on the mortgage, having borrowed against it over the years. Robert knew this money could make a dent in their debts quickly and enable them to start to build a nest egg.

Robert understood that even though it was only a fraction of what the overall operation was making, it was a lot of money to Dave. There was also the possibility of a lot more money being earned if Louise could make a success on the other side. However, that was the unknown, and Robert was a bit worried about that. He didn't know Louise or the women she'd be involved with.

Christ, you're turning into Caroline, he thought, and smiled to himself. *Trying to control everything. Relax, it'll be fine.*

But try as he might, Robert couldn't quell the unease in the pit of his stomach.

'So, you'll give me the drugs I've gotta get to C Wing and the drugs to pass to Louise. How do I get my money?' Dave asked.

'Think I'm gonna rip you off?' Robert joked.

'Course not, but you ain't gonna be dishing out large amounts of dough in here, are ya?' Dave replied. 'Nor do I want it. Don't forget we get searched in and out. How'd I explain coming in with a tenner and going out with a few hundred? That'd raise some eyebrows pretty sharpish.'

'I'll give you the number of my accountant. Tell him your part of this and I sent ya. He'll set you up with whatever you need, offshore account, Bitcoin, whatever works best for you. I'll let him know what your cut is.'

'Cool,' Dave said. 'Don't know the first thing about Bitcoin, but might have to drag my dinosaur arse into the twenty-first century, eh?' he said, and they both laughed.

Then Robert got serious again. 'Don't put pressure on Louise to make as much as you, Dave. Your cut almost pays for your dad. Hers is a bonus. Tits up means nothing for no one, and we don't fucking want that. Don't forget, I'm doing the rest in this gaff, and you've got one wing. And I've got you the contact. You're home and dry. Her side isn't going to be as fucking easy as that. She's gotta understand that, or she'll approach the wrong fucking person. Then we're blown. Or worse for her, she could get hurt, and I mean real fucking bad. Drug dealers ain't nice people, Dave. Don't ever fucking underestimate them.'

'I hear you, Robert, and I'll make it clear to Louise. If she can help, that's great, but if she can't, she just needs to keep stum. Thanks for cutting us in on this, mate. I can't thank you enough. It is such a relief to have a way to help Dad.'

'I ain't your fucking mate, Dave,' Robert warned. 'Fucking remember that. Drug dealers don't have mates. We got a working relationship now and, hopefully, it works, for all our sakes. But make no mistake, you fuck up, you're going down. You ain't fucking taking me with you, you got that?'

'Loud and clear, mate, loud and clear.'

'So did you speak to him then?' were the first words out of Louise's mouth as she flopped into the passenger seat of the car in the staff car park of the prison.

'Hello darling, lovely to see you too,' Dave said, laughing. 'Have you had a good day?'

'Hi love,' Louise said wearily. 'It's been a totally shit day as usual and I'm hoping you are going to put me out of my misery. I don't think I can take much more. We are so short staffed. We're having to lock the girls up more than normal. They don't like it, and to be fair, I can't say I blame them. But then they kick off, and we've to try to deal with it without the bodies we need. I got clocked by one of them on the back of my head this afternoon. I've got a cracking headache.'

Dave looked over at Louise. She looked exhausted. The job they did was tough physically and mentally every day. You had to be on your guard always. Most of the inmates were criminals, after all. But they were also human, and some of them were quite nice. He knew neither of them felt like they got to do a good job, and they certainly didn't get the pay and conditions they deserved for a job that, at times, was downright dangerous.

It hadn't been an easy decision to approach Robert, but they'd both felt that they had no choice. They were at the end of their tethers. When he came back into custody, they saw it as a sign. Dave and Louise didn't always talk shop, but it was difficult not to when it was such a big part of both of their lives. Over the years, Dave had mentioned Robert when he was back inside. They had just clicked, and Dave had told Louise that if they had met in a different way, he felt sure they would have shared a pint or two.

Although he had never been in for serious drug offences, Dave had a gut feeling that Robert was connected to the drug world. Of course, inmates knew each other if they came from the same area. The criminal underworld in some places was a relatively small, tight-knit community. Everyone knew of each other. However, with Robert, it had felt more than that. They seemed to look up to him as if he was a big fish. Far bigger than the stuff he'd been in for, which didn't seem drug or gang related.

When he'd returned this time, he seemed to be even more active among the other prisoners. Nothing Dave could put his finger on. He just appeared to be connected to some other inmates who were in for drug-related offending. Admittedly, Robert knew others who were not in for such offending, but Dave had suspected that if Robert wasn't the orchestrator, he was involved, or getting some kind of kickback, and maybe could get Dave in on the action.

Louise and Dave weighed up the pros and cons, going backwards and forwards, and round and round in circles, it felt at times. Once Dave made the enquiry of Robert, he was crossing a line. Robert would know he was potentially dirty, and that could be dangerous. Robert could abuse it. Or he may have read Robert totally wrong and make an enemy of him. While Dave liked him, he wouldn't want to be on the wrong side of him. As a screw, you didn't want to be on the wrong side of any prisoner. They could all be dangerous in their own way, but it did come with the job at times. However, here he'd be actively putting himself in the firing line, and if he'd misjudged it, Robert could make his life very difficult indeed.

Dave didn't think he had, though. So, the biggest risk was being in bed with a prisoner. They didn't always get it right, which was obvious by the fact they were in custody. Therefore, Louise and Dave had worried that if it went wrong, and Robert got found out, they too would be found out and be in real trouble. Worse than that, though, Robert would have it over them that they were bent, and he might try to abuse that by wanting more out of them.

Dave had said to Louise that he didn't think Robert would do that. They'd be in it together, and they'd all want it to work, so why would Robert risk that? His greatest fear was if they screwed it up, and Robert came after him, and presumably even worse people that he was working for. That did frighten the pair of them, and for a few days Louise kept saying that it was 'too risky, a ridiculous idea'. However, the mounting bills, and the threat of not being able to afford the care fees, kept bringing them back to this as their only solution. Hence, the conversations that Dave had had with Robert, bringing them to this moment.

Dave set out for Louise exactly what he would be doing, and what Robert had suggested she could do, and the money that they could make.

'Wow,' she said excitedly. 'This is good money for us, without too much risk, I think. He's obviously getting the drugs in OK; we don't need to worry about any of that. I was worried about that, thinking he might want us to get them into the prison. I didn't want to be involved in that. Far too high risk with searches etc. This, though, could work well. We don't have drugs in or out. What about the money, though? How's that going to work?'

Dave explained what Robert had told him about the accountant. 'You and Bitcoin,' Louise howled. 'The kids would be impressed by their tech dad, if that ever happens.'

'They sure would,' Dave agreed, grinning. 'They aren't to know nothing about this, though. No one is. Not sure crypto is the way to go, though. It can be a bit volatile. We need our money. We are happy with what we'll be getting, and we don't want to lose any of it. As long as it can't be traced easily, I'm not worried. We'll see what the accountant comes up with. I'll give him a bell tomorrow. You've gotta be real careful, though, Louise. I'm in an easy position, I'm passing to Robert's mate. Risks, of course, but as low as it goes. You've gotta make contacts, and that won't be so easy. You gotta be sure who you choose. Robert's worried this is where it might go wrong.'

'Oh, so the woman's the weakest link, is she?' Louise said, huffing, clearly taking offence at the suggestion.

'No way, honey,' Dave said, patting her arm. 'It's just you've got the more difficult part. We can almost sort Dad with my bit, and you can build your side up gradually for us. Just don't want you to feel under any pressure to earn as much. We don't want to be too greedy. Slowly, slowly, catchy monkey, and all that.'

'I know, love. I'm not a bloody fool, you know. But you'll see, I'll build up an empire before you know it,' she said, winking at him.

CHAPTER EIGHTEEN

THE MANCHESTER OPERATION

A couple of weeks after the video link with Robert, Caroline opened the post, as she did every day, and sighed. There, as Robert had promised, was the authority from his dad, Richard, to take over his case. Caroline took it out into reception where Sandra was alone, other than Harley on his bed under her desk chomping on a bone. She showed it to her.

'Here's the authority from Robert's dad to get access to his case.'

'I'm surprised it took that long,' Sandra said.

'Me too. The post must be incredibly slow in there. I've been expecting it every day since Robert told me about it, but I haven't wanted to chase him about it.'

'You aren't happy with this, are you?' Sandra quizzed Caroline.

'No, I'm not. What we are doing is dangerous enough, but weighing it all up is well worth the risk. We've got things running as well as we can, and we have enough to worry about – Alex, for example – without this. I don't know the prison. I don't know his dad. There are just too many variables that we can't know and control. We are making enough money, and I am worried this is us stretching ourselves, getting greedy, and that it'll go wrong.'

'I don't like it when you are worried,' Sandra said, looking concerned. 'I mean, you worry all the time about the firm and audits, but I know you are well prepared and in control. So, I worry about you being so stressed, but I don't worry about what you are worrying about, if that makes sense. With this, though, you are very unhappy about it, and I can see why. What does Alex say? I haven't seen him for ages. He does still work here, doesn't he?' she added, laughing.

'Yes, I can assure you he does. Haven't you noticed the continual trail of destruction? Papers, ties, a shirt or two, even a couple of shoelaces I noticed yesterday. I have no idea what's happened to the shoes they are supposed to be partnered with,' Caroline said, giggling.

'Oh, yes, I suppose if he'd left, the cleaner would think he'd been sacked through lack of work,' Sandra quipped.

'Too right. Alex has been coming in extra early and heading off to court early. It's not worth him coming in when he finishes court, so he goes home to prep.'

'You trust him with money overnight?'

'No way. I stop at his house on the way home if he's got money on him, or we'll never see it again. It'll be forever hidden under a mountain of Alex junk,' Caroline said, gesticulating a mountain with her hands.

'Very smart,' Sandra said approvingly. 'So what did he say? You have told him, I assume?'

'Yes, I told him and, as expected, he was very flippant. Said we'll be billionaires, not millionaires, and to stop worrying. It's all going swimmingly well, and Robert will have it under control.'

'Typical Alex response,' Sandra said.

Sandra was nobody's fool, Caroline thought to herself. She knew the dynamics of the office and the partnership. Alex was a great lawyer, but if it was left to him to run the business, they'd all be out of a job. He was far too laid-back and disorganised to run his own life, let alone the infrastructure that ran the lives of so many people.

'Look Caroline, we'll follow you whatever you want to do, whatever you think is best. But if you are unsure about it, if your gut is telling you it's wrong, my advice, for what it's worth, is to follow your gut.'

'Robert will be furious if I back out of this part, though. He's such an integral part of this, Sandra, I can't afford for him to really go rogue and start working against us. This sort of off-the-wall behaviour is bad enough.'

'You don't think he would try to hurt us, do you?' questioned Sandra, her eyebrows rising into her hairline.

'I honestly don't know, Sandra,' Caroline replied quietly. 'He's a criminal at the end of the day and they do bloody silly things at times, as we well know. If he thinks I don't trust his judgement, who knows what he's really capable of?'

'Decisions made in haste are repented at leisure. That's what my mum used to say,' Sandra added.

'I think I'll test the waters. We'll send a small amount to see what happens. If I'm not one hundred per cent happy after that, I'll pull the plug with Robert. At least I'll have some evidence of why I'm not happy. I might trust my gut, but I don't think he will.'

'Well, he should. He picked you for you, and your gut is a large part of the decisions you make, and who you are.'

'Yes, but then it took me to being a criminal solicitor and look how well that's gone over the years,' Caroline said, laughing loudly.

'It's been bloody hard work, Caroline. There's no denying that. But you are extremely good at it, so maybe it's the way things were meant to be.'

'Well, let's hope that success in this venture is written in the stars too,' Caroline retorted.

Later that day, Caroline emailed the authority from Richard to his previous solicitors, asking for them to send his full file of papers, and grant her access to the digital case system. This was the system used in court to allow all relevant parties to gain access to the case papers.

'Sometimes technology has its advantages,' Caroline said to Sandra, later on that afternoon.

'Why? Have you just had notification you've won the Euro millions?' Sandra enquired eagerly.

'I should be so lucky,' Caroline sang the lyrics. 'Mind you, it probably helps if you actually do them. No, those solicitors that represented Robert's dad have been quick off the mark. They've emailed me their digital file and granted me access to his case. I'll print some of this stuff off, and when Robert rings, I'll discuss with him how much we are sending. I'm definitely going to get him to keep it to the minimum, though. A trial run of getting the correspondence through the system. They'll be more suspicious in HMP Manchester. It's a max security prison and they don't know us from Adam. So, I think we just send a ten-pound wrap. If we do get found out, it's going to be easier to say a client must have left it and it got muddled up with the post, rather than a bigger amount.'

'I agree. If you are going to send any at all, send the smallest amount. If it's found, it's still a serious offence to try to talk our way out of,' Sandra said gravely.

'Do you know what? I think I'm going to send some of these papers and no drugs. If Richard gets the papers OK, and they don't look tampered with, we'll try a small amount. More haste, less speed, I think is the motto here.'

'I think you are fucking panicking over nothing, Caroline,' Robert said angrily, when he phoned her later that afternoon from his cell, using his dried-out burner.

'I'm not, Robert, really, I'm not. Peterborough see post from us all the time. They know us. I have never sent a letter to HMP Manchester in my career. I think Richard needs to let the screws know he's got a new team on board, and we let some letters go through. Let's test the waters, then they get used to us, and possibly less suspicious. I know prisons have drug dogs checking normal post for inmates. I don't know whether it applies to legal correspondence in max security prisons or not, but I don't want to find out the wrong way. Otherwise, I'll be seeing the inside of a similar institution, and I'm not taking that sort of risk. There's no rush. Let him know what we are doing and make it clear it's not him we don't trust. It's the system we are checking out.'

'Well, he's getting drugs in from a source at the moment, isn't he? It won't be the legal route, so they can't be that fucking on the ball there, can they?'

'You can't assume that, Robert. You don't know who knows who and who's doing a favour for who. I don't know what the rush is. You're making good money out of what we've got going. If you're trying to impress your dad, I get it. But surely, he'll be more impressed by our vigilance and organisation, rather than going off half-cocked. And don't forget, he's nothing to lose, but we all have, including you. It took a long time to get that authority from him. It clearly doesn't work in there the same way as it does where you are, and the way we are used to.'

'OK, OK. Have it your fucking way. I'll tell him the revised plan when he rings me later. How many sets of papers do you want to send through before you're happy?'

'I'm going to send four lots on random days over the next month. In one of them I'm sending a ten-pound wrap ...'

'A ten-pound wrap?' Robert scoffed. 'What the fuck is that all about?'

'Because if it gets found, it'll be easier to try to bluff our way out of that. We can say a client left it in the office. It got caught up with the post on Sandra's desk. We are terribly sorry, and all that, rather than a bigger lump. We could still land in the shit, but, hopefully, it wouldn't alert anyone to what else is going on,' Caroline said determinedly. 'I'm really not happy about doing this, Robert, so this is the concession I'm prepared to make. But if you and your dad don't agree to it, I'm not doing it. It's that simple.'

'Who said you could call the fucking shots?' Robert challenged angrily.

'Me,' Caroline growled, equally angrily. 'I'm on the outside keeping all the wheels turning. You wanted me involved because I have the organisational capability. Well, this is one of the things about me you might not like, but you can't have part. It's all or nothing. I gave in to your Dave and Louise idea because although it makes me a bit nervous, I can see the advantages of it. This is far riskier, and I'm not going to be pushed or bullied into it, Robert.'

There was a standoff. Nothing was said, each waiting to see if the other said something. Caroline didn't intend to; she'd made her point, and it was for Robert to decide how he was going to deal with that. The minutes passed, and the silence continued. Caroline stared at him on the screen, not blinking.

Eventually it was broken by Robert snarling, 'Alright. I'm not fucking happy, but if this is the way it's got to be, then I've no fucking choice, have I?'

'No, not on this you haven't.'

'Just don't fucking push it, Caroline. Just cos I'm in here, doesn't mean I'm not a fucking part of this.'

'I'm not pushing anything, Robert, other than trying to stop you from pushing our luck too far. Damn right you're a part of this, an integral part. Therefore, if it goes fucking wrong, the shit's coming down on you by the ton, too. It isn't all coming in my direction. I'm trying to avoid that happening. I want tons of cash instead.'

'I'll tell Richard.' Robert's words suggested compliance, but his demeanour conveyed anything but. Caroline could see from the jut of his chin and the look in his eyes.

'Tell him to be honest if anything looks tampered with, though, Robert. I know you don't think this is a good idea, but you've got to sell it to him. There's no point otherwise. We don't know what he's got set up in there. He might have made promises to all sorts of people. I don't want him keeping quiet. If something looks off, he needs to tell us. You've got a future, he hasn't. That changes a man's perspective, you know.'

'OK, OK. I'll tell him.'

As soon as the call ended, Caroline left her desk and went through Sandra's office out of the rear door to the garden. It was a small walled garden, no grass, just paving and gravel. However, it was perfect for Harley to roam around and chase his ball. That's exactly what he was doing now, while Sandra was having a cigarette break. The rules in the office were simple. If you were having a break and Harley was in the office, you had to throw the ball for him in the garden. Everyone knew the rule and Harley made sure that no one forgot it. If he didn't think you'd been out for a break regularly enough, he would appear and drop his ball at your feet. Then he just stared at you and then the ball until you got the message.

Fortunately for Harley, everyone in the office smoked, except for Seb, the gym freak, and Caroline, his mum. It wasn't an issue with Caroline. She'd go into the garden with him and throw the ball, but Harley often looked at Seb longingly, begging him to go into the garden. No one could resist his pleading eyes, and so Seb would go out, even when it was raining, although he'd deny it if he was ever asked about it. Caroline often thought to herself she wished she had whatever power it was that Harley possessed, because he could get Seb to do more for him than she ever could.

'Are you OK?' Sandra asked, throwing the ball for Harley again, who went sliding through the gravel to get it.

'Just spoken to Robert.'

'And?'

'He wasn't happy, and I'm worried he won't pass the message on to his dad. Or if he does, it'll be half-heartedly, and his dad won't take it seriously. Or his dad will just say all is good when it isn't. Who knows what situation he's in?'

'If it feels wrong, it's wrong, Caroline. Don't be bullied into this.'

'I won't. Let's see how it goes sending the papers and we'll take it from there.'

Sandra finished her cigarette, and they both went back in. Caroline printed off about fifty pages of Richard's case papers and they packaged them up carefully, using extra tape, and clearly marking the solicitor's rule. Sandra went straight to the post office and sent it by guaranteed next day's delivery.

'Well, we can't do more than that,' she said on her return. 'You'll have to see what happens and try not to worry about it in the meantime.'

When she got home, Caroline poured herself a large glass of red wine, an Argentinian Malbec. She felt in need of something with some real body to it.

This is not good, she thought to herself. *Drinking during the week is a slippery slope.*

Caroline liked a glass of wine and often drank at home alone, the nature of living by herself. However, she was very careful to only drink at weekends, well aware it could become a real habit if she wasn't careful. She knew this was a sign of how uneasy she was feeling about the situation with Robert.

Caroline knew the dynamics would change between Robert and her when he was serving, and that he wouldn't like her being in control. However, the way he had spoken to her, not so much what he said, but the tone, unnerved her. She didn't think he'd deliberately drop any of them in it. It wasn't in his interests to, but she was worried that he might try to hurt her if he didn't get what he wanted out of it. Maybe as a way of trying to keep her in line, almost coerce her into doing what he wanted.

Don't be bloody silly, she tried to persuade herself. *It's Robert. He's a hothead, but he's not a calculated psychopath. You are getting yourself in a state over nothing. Relax, finish your wine, and take Harley out.*

She did just that, but even when she was getting ready for bed, she was aware of the uneasy feeling in the pit of her stomach. Her dinner hadn't settled and felt like it was swishing in a washing machine. She couldn't shake the feeling off that a line had been crossed today, and there was no going back from it.

Robert was furious when the telephone call ended. *She's being fucking paranoid,* he thought to himself. *No reason my dad can't do what I'm doing in here. Give him something to live for and make us all a large stash in the process.*

He went to the gym to try to vent some of his anger and frustration. It didn't work. He returned to his cell an hour and a half later, just as livid as he had been when he left.

'Fucking woman telling me what to do,' he grunted out loud to himself in the mirror above his sink. 'Can't be fucking having this, Robert. Got to get a fucking grip on this situation. You're the fucking boss. You're the man and they all gotta fucking know it.'

At seven that evening, he rang his dad, as agreed, and told him what Caroline was doing. He knew she wouldn't be happy with how he told him, but tough fucking shit, that's all she was getting.

'She's got her fucking knickers in a right fucking knot because the firm isn't known in there and she doesn't know you,' he said to Richard angrily.

'What's her fucking problem?' Richard said, equally annoyed. 'Rule 39's Rule 39. It doesn't fucking matter which fucking firm it is. They can't open it, and that's that.'

'Don't I fucking know it? Fucking told her the same, but she can't get it through her fucking head,' Robert spat. The rage he felt earlier when speaking to Caroline was boiling up inside him.

'I was relying on you, Rob,' Richard said. 'Got debts in here that need paying, son. You said you'd help me.'

'I am Dad, I am. Let's get these packages through to you and then hopefully the silly fucking bitch'll calm down and we'll be rocking and rolling. In the meantime, I can get cash for you, if that'll help. I can get my accountant to call whoever you need.'

'That might work to tide me over, if you can. I'll speak my end and find out who is best to deal with.'

'Let me know, Dad. I told you I'll fucking take care of this, and I will.'

'You gotta get her under fucking control, Robert. This is your set-up, not hers. She ain't the fucking boss,' Richard said, goading Robert.

'No, she fucking ain't.'

Robert was absolutely furious when the call finished. This was now going to cost him some of his cash to sort out the fuck-up Caroline was making by being such a stupid fucking cow. Well, this was a situation that he would not allow to continue. He'd have to take care of this somehow. She was making him look weak and out of control. In front of his dad, too. He'd have to make it clear to her, and everyone else that wasn't the fucking case at all.

CHAPTER NINETEEN

PROGRESS

'It's all running perfectly,' Caroline said to herself. As usual, she was sitting in her office, with Harley keeping her feet warm. It was another grey day outside her window. She recalled a comment from her mum.

'The trouble with England is all the seasons look the same. It just gets a colder or warmer grey day. Unless you are outside, you have no idea what month it is.'

So true mum, she thought. *That's why I'm making the big bucks now. Me and Harley are going to live somewhere sunny by the sea.*

She didn't allow herself to daydream and be content for too long, though, before the nagging doubt returned. *It's all running too well.*

'Don't be ridiculous,' Sandra had said when she voiced her concern earlier. 'It's running exactly as it should with you at the helm.'

Caroline was busy running the operation and the practice, but in any moments of quiet she had, there was a worrying thought at the back of her head that wouldn't stop. It was like an itch that she couldn't scratch.

Seb was doing well at the gym. Robert's punch had done its job and there had been no further issues. He took delivery of the drugs and made payment like clockwork and distributed the drugs on the days set. The only hiccup was yesterday, when one of the buyers was sick, but someone had attended and passed on a note to

Seb, rearranging the pickup.

Seb informed Caroline as soon as he arrived in the office that morning. Caroline made sure to destroy the note. She didn't trust him to do that. She'd set fire to it in the bin.

Seb watched her doing it. She knew he was thinking she was so anal; she could tell by the way he looked at her.

'What are you grinning at, Caroline?' he asked, confusion in his voice.

'I was thinking back to one solicitor who used to work here, called James. He's long retired now. It was in the days when you could smoke in the office; he smoked a pipe. He was working in the office I was in and was smoking away. He then emptied his pipe and went off to court. About half an hour later, I could smell smoke. I glanced over to where he had been sitting and saw the bin was on fire. After putting it out, I rang him and asked him why he didn't like me. He was ever so puzzled on the other end until I told him he'd tried to kill me,' she said, laughing. Seb was now laughing at the story. 'He was so upset and apologetic. I, on the other hand, just couldn't stop laughing.

'We were also at court together one day. This was in the days when you could smoke everywhere in the court building except the courtrooms. Solicitors would leave their lit-up cigarettes on the dado rail outside, burning away, while they dealt with their cases in court. They'd then come out and smoke the remainder. How the building didn't burn down, I'll never know.'

'And you say millennials are reckless,' interjected Seb, his eyes wide with disbelief.

'It gets worse,' Caroline added, still laughing. 'James had been smoking in the foyer when his case was called on, so put his pipe in his pocket and went into court. It was halfway through the case, and he stood up to speak to the magistrates. I had to hiss at him that his pocket was on fire.' Seb was howling with laughter now. 'Those were the good old days,' Caroline mused.

'Sound bloody dangerous to me,' Seb grinned. 'No wonder

they banned smoking in public places. He was a one-man accidental arsonist. He makes me look reliable.'

'I wouldn't go that far, and Harley certainly wouldn't agree. He adored James and James loved Harley, too. We went to court one day and opened our case to get our files out. In the case was a ball. Harley had put it in. James was so upset that Harley might be missing his ball, he phoned Sandra to make sure he was alright. Of course he was. Harley had no shortage of balls, but the look he gave James when he returned it when we got back to the office was as if James had stolen it.'

'Harley is such a manipulator,' Seb said.

'Oh yes, he kept looking at James and James kept feeding him biscuits. After each one, Harley eyeballed him as if to say you haven't repaid your debt yet!'

'Anyway, see,' said Seb, laughing and returning the conversation to the present. 'Everyone laughed at me when I was asking Robert all those questions. He said no one had ever been sick and here we are.'

'Good job he's not here to see you gloating,' Caroline replied with a smile. 'Otherwise, he'd be wiping that smirk off your face with his fist.'

'Don't tell him when you next speak to him,' Seb said, smiling, but seriously. 'He might send someone else to do it for him and I think there would be a queue,' he conceded, grinning.

'I might just volunteer myself,' Caroline half-joked.

Caroline couldn't resist it when Robert phoned her later that day.

'Seb was full of himself today,' she said, giggling.

'No change there then,' Robert retorted.

'True, well, fuller of himself than normal, shall we say.'

'Why? What's up with the little prick?'

'One of the buyers was sick yesterday, couldn't collect. Seb was handed a note at the gym with alternative arrangements. He couldn't stop going on about how you ribbed him at the meeting when he asked about sickness.'

'If I recall the conversation correctly, he was asking about the fucking supplier being sick, not a fucking buyer. So, he's got half a fucking story. He's far too much like Alex for my liking. Has he always been like this? Or are they spending too much time together and it's rubbing off?'

Caroline was laughing loudly when she said, 'No, sadly they are peas in a pod without trying or encouragement.'

'Not a fucking good look,' Robert replied. 'Mind you, at least he's doing what he should be, and he's in the right fucking place at the right time. Unlike Alex. I know courts can overrun, but, Jesus, he seems to make it a daily fucking mission to keep as many people waiting as fucking possible.'

'Sadly, I don't think it's in any way intentional. Disaster just seems to follow him. Still, for the most part, he's OK. At least he's getting the right packages to the right people, and Ian is a great help at the pub when we need him.'

'Don't count yer chickens, Caroline,' Robert warned. 'With Alex about, trouble's never too fucking far away.'

'And I thought I was the negative one,' Caroline exclaimed.

'Maybe I've just gone from a fucking optimist to a realist,' Robert laughed. 'And tell Seb to stay in his fucking lane or I'll knock him back into it. Don't want him thinking he's fucking cleverer than he is, do we?'

'No danger of that. He asked me not to tell you. He's worried you'll try to knock his block off again.'

'Well, maybe he's not such a thick twat after all.'

Caroline continued her ruminations later in the day when she and Harley were at home. They were snuggled up together on the sofa, Harley with his head in her lap snoring. *Robert is right,* she thought. *The only serious problem we have is courts overrunning.*

This was continually a problem in the Crown Court, but only presented a problem in the magistrates' court when William or Michael were doing trials. Otherwise, the hearings, unless they were exceptionally long bail applications or sentence hearings, were pretty swift. That afternoon, William told her he was constantly amazed clients could get themselves to court on time when it suited them. Those that seemed to have problems getting out of bed in the morning and always made excuses for being late, the bus was late, their lift was late, their granny was sick, all managed to get themselves in the right place at the right time when there was drugs or money involved.

He'd also expressed surprise that the money was never short. 'I thought I'd seen it all,' he said to Caroline, returning a package of money he'd collected. 'Clients are always saying they haven't got money for the bus fare, but we've never been short-changed.'

'We aren't dealing with that level of client, William. The ones collecting the drugs or bringing the money aren't the users struggling to get together the money for their wrap and trying to get it on tick. These are higher up the food chain. In any event, they wouldn't dare. It's not us they are frightened of, far from it. It's those above us. I don't think any of them think you are seriously going to wipe the floor with them. But we are quite different from Robert, and I think he's mild compared to those above him. He seems respectfully frightened of them. So, I have no doubt if we report back higher up that there's an issue, someone's going to get hurt badly, or maybe worse.'

'What a terrible thought,' William said, shuddering. 'I guess I am still a bit naïve.'

'Nothing wrong with that, as long as we are squeaky clean. No one will show any interest in us if we are doing what we should, when we should, and don't step out of line. They know Robert is sound and trust that anyone connected with his op is too. Unless we give them a reason to come looking, we should be fine. That's the message Robert has passed on to his foot soldiers, and that's why we don't have any real problems.'

'I doubt he passed the message on like that, though,' William said, laughing.

'No. I expect it had a lot of expletives, threats and cutting motions. He'd want to be in no doubt that they all got the message.'

'Well, he's very effective. I have to say that. He even got Seb in line,' William chuckled, and so did Caroline.

'I know and I thought that was mission impossible,' she added, and they both started singing the theme tune.

Patience was another thing that all the advocates had commented on with those collecting or handing over money at court. Anyone who dealt with criminal clients knew that they were perpetually late, operating only on a time that suited them. But if they were kept waiting for more than a nanosecond, they were shouting and screaming at Sandra, who, of course, had absolutely no control over the workings at the courts. Whenever she tried to explain this, it usually resulted in a torrent of abuse and nasty comments about paying her fucking wages. Not so when money or drugs were to exchange hands. Tempers didn't fray, and patience was in abundance.

Michael's client today sat through one of his trials waiting to collect his drugs, as he was late. Allegedly, he'd had a flat tyre. 'That old chestnut,' Michael had said, and he relayed to Caroline the client had smiled wryly. He had, however, witnessed the wizard in action creating a defence out of nowhere and been thoroughly impressed by it, he'd told Michael. When Michael returned to the office, he'd relished telling Caroline.

'Best afternoon out I've had in ages. How the fuck did you come up with that?' the client said, amazement in his voice.

Michael just smiled and said, 'You need to get out more, son.'

'I want you doing my trial,' he'd said, only to be told by Michael that he didn't go to the Crown Court. 'Well, you should,' the client said.

Michael laughed, saying it was too late to teach this old dog new tricks to which the client had said, 'Fuck off, you're brighter than most twenty-year-olds'. Michael was clearly delighted at this, enjoying telling the story.

Michael was such an asset. But it only worked in this operation, Caroline knew, because William ensured she didn't have to chase either of them down. He constantly updated her by email as to who had turned up and his and Michael's whereabouts. It would seem innocuous to anyone who didn't know what was going on, but saved her from having the panic of trying to locate Michael. His phones continued to gather dust at the bottom of his carrier bag.

Caroline smiled to herself as she changed the channel on her TV absentmindedly. She wasn't watching anything, too busy in her own head. Earlier, she commented to William that he made a brilliant PA, to which she received a two-finger gesture and the sarcastic comment, jokingly, that he should be paid more. He was, and he knew it, winking as he said it. Michael wasn't taking a share and William got a bit extra for his babysitting duties. Caroline was pleased to pay him; it was one less headache for her, and there were plenty of them.

Caroline reflected she had done her best to increase the payments made at the pub and drugs were being handed over by Ian, too. Alex had commented on this, but Caroline had told him the clients preferred to go to the pub, rather than the court, unless they were in court. While that might have been true – after all, who wants to go to court when they don't have to? – it wasn't an accurate reflection of what had taken place. The clients, or their representatives, would go wherever they needed to when there were drugs or money involved. They didn't question Caroline's engineering towards the pub rather than the court. It gave her more peace of mind that Alex's exposure, and so the risk of exposing them, was reduced to the bare minimum, without him being suspicious that he was being cut out altogether.

Alex didn't know it, but the turning point for Caroline was a particularly stressful day a month ago. Most days were stressful, but this one was horrendous. Thinking about it now made her palms sweat and her heartbeat quicken. Without realising, she had started stroking Harley with more force. It woke him from his slumber, and he looked at her quizzically.

'Sorry Harley,' she said apologetically. 'Didn't mean to wake you. I was just getting stressed thinking about Alex,' she added, kissing him on the top of his head.

Harley looked at her as if to say, 'what's new? That idiot is always stressing you out.' With that, he returned to his original position, nuzzling into her left thigh.

It wasn't just what had happened, it was the way he dealt with her, and the blasé attitude he had to it all that had made her take stock and change tack.

She knew from Alex's point of view it had been no issue. He was on the way to court when he had a car accident. Nothing major. He drove into a pole and damaged the front end of his car. That had made him late, and he was never early for court at the best of times. Caroline knew he hoped he was going to have a rare day in the office, but they had a lot of prisoners held for court, so he went to the magistrates' court to help William and Michael.

He hadn't been there ten minutes when it was necessary for Caroline to ring him. He'd missed two cases out of the Crown Court diary and the Crown Court had phoned the office chasing his whereabouts. The job was difficult enough without making life worse by internal issues, she'd said to him during the call. Caroline knew instantly from his tone that he thought she was overreacting. She knew he referred to her as "Miss Perfect" sarcastically behind her back, and the way he spoke conveyed that opinion. He failed to appreciate what was blindingly obvious to her. How could she run things if she didn't know what she was running?

His anger and frustration had subsided later that day when he told her the rest of his adventures. As he was running across the road from one court to the other, he realised he didn't have the appropriate shirt on. In the magistrates' court, a solicitor wore a normal shirt with a tie. In the Crown Court the attire was a collarless shirt, bands over the top, then the gown.

Sipping her cup of tea, Caroline replayed the conversation he'd had with her.

'There I am running down the road shouting fuck, fuck, fuck, breathlessly though, cos I'm out of shape,' Alex said. He was laughing so much he was having trouble speaking. 'I haven't got the right collar on. I've never been so pleased to see Aldi in my life, you know, the one next to the pub.'

Caroline nodded in agreement, but said nothing, concerned as to how badly this story was going to end.

'I ducked in there to buy a pair of scissors. As I'm running out of the store, I ripped the scissors from their packaging. Stood outside, I'm trying to cut the collar off as best I can. I chucked the collar and the scissors in the litter bin outside. All I could think of was I can't be done for possession of an offensive weapon. I did then smile to myself, thinking about what I could be caught in possession of most days at the Crown Court.'

'What would anyone have thought if they'd looked at the shop CCTV?' Caroline said, shaking her head but smiling at the same time. She was still cross with Alex over the way he spoke to her earlier, but she couldn't help but find the story amusing.

'God knows, and it gets worse. As I was racing across the road, coat flailing as I hadn't bothered to do it up, towing my suitcase behind me, one of the wheels came off. I just lost it. I burst out laughing and started singing out loud, "three wheels on my wagon, but I'll keep rolling along." I passed a homeless man sitting on a sleeping bag outside the perimeter wall of the Crown Court. He looked at me as if I was stark staring bonkers. That had just made me laugh more.'

Caroline realised if it was only to be the wheels on his case and not the wheels of the whole operation that were to come off, she needed to limit Alex's involvement. She had laughed with him at his story while inwardly panicking that if he was this unprepared for his normal job, she couldn't have him playing a major role like he had been. It was only a matter of time before disaster struck. She would get more drugs and money flowing via Ian at the pub. Alex would never notice.

He is definitely the weakest link in our chain, Caroline thought to herself, which was saying something when competing with the likes of Seb.

Ian was the polar opposite. A completely reliable character, and as solid in this venture as he was as a police station rep. He blended in well in the pub, sitting there on his laptop with his pint, looking totally innocuous. He tapped away. "Two fingers Terry" he called himself, with his earbuds in listening to his favourite tunes or a podcast. Anyone watching observed the occasional person stopping to say a few words to him. It wasn't just the clients, or their associates, attending the organised meetings. Regulars he saw in there each time he visited came over to exchange a few pleasantries, or have a moan about the weather, or the latest ridiculous political decision. He blended in with the surroundings. Nothing looked at all suspicious, and no one noticed the exchange of the carrier bags.

Ian hadn't questioned the increase in role, either. Caroline was sure he had guessed why it was happening. Everyone knew what Alex was like, and she knew Ian was like her. He would feel happier to be more secure and in control. In addition, it had saved him scurrying over to the Crown Court when Alex had kept clients waiting too long, and they came to find him at the pub. Or when they had been arrested and so didn't make it to their court hearing and later came to sort things out. It occasionally happened with clients in the magistrates' court but Michael and William, well no that wasn't right, Michael was worse at communicating than Alex and that was saying something, William made sure that Ian knew if there was an issue and sorted out getting the drugs to Ian to pass on.

Caroline had no desire to cut Alex out of the money. He wouldn't agree to that and would pose too much of a risk that he might drop them in it. However, damage limitation, in what was a very risky enterprise, was for Alex to have as little involvement as possible.

Sending drugs to the prison was far easier since Robert went into custody, as they had expected. All the drugs were sent to him. There was no need to send them in via the cells or to others in custody. Continuing to mull things over, calmer now, Caroline felt this had significantly reduced the risk. It had lowered the numbers involved in the operation and the fewer the better as far as she was concerned. It also helped to have Dave ensuring the drugs got through as quickly as possible. Robert got a lot of correspondence, but no one at the prison ever questioned the amount of legal communication. Caroline didn't worry herself too much about that. It was their local remand prison, and a lot of legitimate post was sent to the prison every day for a range of inmates. Unless someone was specifically monitoring communication from the firm, or communication to Robert, they wouldn't pick up on it. Legal communication was rarely monitored unless a specific reason arose. All she had to do was keep her fingers and toes crossed it didn't happen while Robert was incarcerated. Caroline found that she had crossed her fingers and toes without realising while thinking about this.

Get a grip, girl, she thought to herself. *Stop thinking, get outside your own head.* Try as she might, she couldn't. Caroline carried on with her analysis of the entire operation. Harley was oblivious to it all, snoring away beside her.

Those coming to the office managed to get in on time, most of the time. Of course, they were still the main criminals and had not had personality transplants, so they were often late, or didn't turn up on the day they were supposed to. However, much to her relief, there had been no repeat of Connor's hammering on the door in the evening fiasco. The ring doorbell she had installed at the office, which was connected to her mobile, had given her no cause for concern.

This was why she was so concerned about the Manchester operation. Caroline clenched her fists as she felt her stomach churn even thinking about it. The prison side had been the most dangerous while Robert was on the outside. Relying on sending drugs in via the Crown Court cells by prisoners, and to prisoners in the prison. There were so many ways it could have gone terribly wrong if any of them had been searched and not been able to keep their mouths shut. Now they were just sending the drugs to Robert, and so the biggest risks had been eliminated, except Alex, of course, but he was at least more contained. Here was Robert, creating risks where they simply didn't need them. They were making enough money.

Caroline knew this was the main itch that she couldn't scratch. The main cause of her restless nights. Robert wasn't thinking clearly enough about this. He clearly felt indebted to his dad, and that seemed to outweigh the size of the risk he was prepared to take. Ever since this had become a "thing", she'd had a pain in the pit of her stomach and increasing heartburn. Her gut was telling her it was wrong. She knew she needed to take Sandra's advice and listen to it.

'Kyle and Dale are very loyal and reliable foot soldiers, exactly as Robert said they would be,' Caroline said out loud, when she got round to thinking about that part of the operation. Harley didn't stir. He was used to her mutterings.

Robert's incarceration made no difference to their roles. They did exactly as instructed and never deviated from what was expected of them. They didn't seek to move further up the food chain, so didn't challenge what they had been asked to do. They didn't seek more money, didn't improvise, they just got on with it. Caroline admired them immensely and thought about how useful they could have been if they had decided to use their skills in a different field.

Neither of them missed collecting the drugs from Seb at the

gym and delivering them back. They arrived at the gym at a similar time to Seb, but never at the same time. They did their workout, Seb did his. They exchanged pleasantries as all gym members did to others that attended regularly and so they became familiar. A nod and a hello. The odd comment about what they were concentrating on that session. What equipment they were using, what weights they were lifting. The usual gym nonsense that anyone listening in would expect from people who train around the same time and so see each other most weeks.

The three of them trained for a similar length of time, and so were in the changing rooms together. Again, the odd comment was passed, but nothing more. With identical bags, it was easy to pick the other up without anyone realising. Their stuff from the gym was in a carrier bag ready to be added to their sports bags, so no one noticed they were, in fact, not the bags they came in with. The magician's sleight of hand was invisible to others concentrating on themselves and paying very little attention to the gym banter and the others present in the changing rooms.

Kyle and Dale were equally reliable at Caroline's house. The delivery of the drugs to her wheelie bin was by the courier who she never saw. He arrived within the window she was expecting. She could see him on her ring doorbell, passing the door and going to the wheelie. In the middle of the night, Kyle or Dale, whoever's turn it was, came and collected the drugs. They did it in the middle of the night, as this was the part that was the most suspicious if anyone saw. Taking something out of the bin was far more difficult to explain than putting something in it. Caroline put her ring doorbell on silent so that it did not disturb her, although more times than not she was awake. She knew, in fact, that it was more for Harley's benefit than hers. If she didn't hear them, she checked the footage the following morning. As regular as clockwork, there they were.

Caroline chuckled as she thought about her neighbour. He was a friendly but retired, nosy gentleman. He commented to her about the regular deliveries to her wheelie bin. Fortunately, he didn't seem to realise that some of the deliveries were at the same time each week or by the same people. Nor was he awake and aware of Kyle and Dale removing items from her bin. Otherwise, that would have triggered alarm bells for him. Caroline had a lot of genuine deliveries, too. Like many busy working people, she ordered a lot from online sites. The delivery drivers for the delivery firms seemed to be the same ones. They obviously got the same people each time on their route.

'Ahhh, I have all my deliveries put in there,' she told him when he mentioned it to her. 'I got an extra bin, so my rubbish goes in one and the deliveries in another. It was worth paying for the extra bin to do it. It means I don't mistakenly put my packages out with the rubbish,' she added, laughing.

'That wouldn't be good would it,' the neighbour agreed, laughing too. 'That's a clever idea.'

'I want them all to go in the bin,' she added. 'I'm often at work and they got into the habit of just leaving them on the doorstep. Living at the end, I think I'm more vulnerable to someone just walking up and taking them.'

'Absolutely,' he agreed. 'It's very Americanised, isn't it? We'll be getting our newspapers thrown on the lawn next,' he added.

'That's if you get them delivered at all. I don't bother myself, but my dad is always moaning about it. The paperboy is either so late the news is out of date, or he doesn't turn up at all.'

'That's very true. It's not like it used to be,' he said whimsically, and Caroline could tell he was travelling back in time in his own mind.

'I also like them put in my bin even if I am here,' Caroline continued her explanation. 'The doorbell sets Harley off barking, and they deliver so late now, don't they? I'm often heading for bed. So, it just makes sense all round. It's nothing I can't live without until the next day.'

'Very sensible,' he said, nodding his head approvingly. 'I don't have many deliveries myself. I'm not into this tech. But I see the drivers round here very late. I wouldn't want to answer the door at that time of night. This is a nice area, but you can't be too careful, can you?'

'No, you can't,' said Caroline, wondering what on earth he would make of it if he knew the truth about her and the purpose of the deliveries.

It's a shame I don't see Phillip a bit more, Caroline pondered. *Then maybe it's not. Life is complicated enough, without anything developing there.*

'Got tabs on yourself, girl,' she said out loud. 'He wouldn't be interested in you. Get a grip.'

Of course, nothing had gone wrong with Phillip. "Mr Reliable" had proven to be just that. He had visited the office once or twice when passing. Otherwise, she'd taken the money to his office. He'd commented kindly about their different working environments, as she and Robert had identified when they went to his office.

'But Harley more than makes up for that,' he'd said affectionately, rubbing Harley's head and ears.

Harley had looked at Caroline as if to say, 'he's nice,' and Caroline had laughed to herself. Sandra said the same. Caroline made it clear it wasn't an option. The money was in her accounts as she expected, and that was where her relationship with Phillip ended.

Caroline looked at her watch and was startled at how late it was.

'I have been totally lost in my own thoughts, Harley,' she said, disturbing him. 'Time for bed.'

As she got into bed, she was still thinking about it all. Given the number of moving parts and the fact that many of the parts were criminals, Caroline was surprised it was plain sailing at the moment. Or as much as it was ever going to be with Robert, Alex and Seb involved too. That's what made her uneasy. She couldn't decide whether it was because, like Julie-Ann, she too lived on her nerves. She was so used to things going wrong and worrying, it made her anxious when things ran smoothly. Or whether the adage was right, 'if it seems too good to be true, it is.'

In the middle of the night, Caroline woke with a start. Her heart was pounding, and her mouth was dry. Her hair was stuck to her head with sweat, as were her pyjamas. She knew she had been dreaming about Alex, or rather having a nightmare. Trying her breathing exercises to calm herself down, she tried to recall what the dream had been about. She knew as far as Alex was concerned, he had thought he had things down to a fine art at the Crown Court. He, like Robert, couldn't understand what she got "her knickers in such a knot over" as he had said to her on more than one occasion. He was constantly criticising her for being too stressed and worried, either about the practice itself and cases and running the contract, or this operation and making sure everyone was doing everything they should be. She had always micromanaged and with this, she was even worse. How could she not be? The risks were so much higher. He told her he could understand her fears to some degree, but they were all taking a risk. If you dwelt on it all the time, it would just consume you. What he failed to appreciate was that his laid-back, laissez-faire attitude made it worse.

Caroline got up to get a drink of water, disturbing Harley in the process. He opened one eye to see what she was doing.

'Sorry lad, didn't mean to wake you. I had a nightmare about Alex.'

Harley looked at her as if to say, 'what do you expect? He's a buffoon.' With that, he wriggled, and Caroline knew she'd conceded a little more of her space on the bed.

As hard as she tried, she couldn't remember the detail of the nightmare. She had an unsettled feeling in her stomach and a tingling in her spine. All of her senses told her something was wrong with Alex's part. She couldn't think what. She'd sidelined his role as much as she could. The feeling didn't subside, and as Caroline got back into bed, she knew she wouldn't be able to go back to sleep. It was going to be a long day.

CHAPTER TWENTY

ALEX'S BAD WEEK

Later that day, the reason for the constant knot in Caroline's stomach became clear. Alex seemed to have completely unravelled. He was far more chaotic and disorganised than normal, not that Caroline had thought that was possible. He left a client file in an interview room with drugs in it. The first Caroline knew was when she received a phone call to the office from a barrister who'd found the file and realised it belonged to the firm. Thank goodness the name of the firm was stamped clearly on the outside of the file, so he hadn't needed to look inside. This was an extra precaution Caroline had insisted on when they first embarked on this project. At the time, Alex had said she was making an unnecessary additional administrative burden, criticising her for her micromanaging. When she got hold of him on the phone, she tore a strip off him.

'Have you forgotten something?' she yelled as soon as he answered his mobile.

'No,' Alex said indignantly. His first line of defence being attack.

Not the right play. Caroline was incensed.

'Not missing a file by any chance?' she continued angrily.

'Oh fuck,' Alex replied. Carline knew from his tone of voice that he didn't remember leaving a file, but knew he had, otherwise they wouldn't be having this conversation.

'An amiable man named Daniel just telephoned telling me you

have left a file in one of the consultation rooms. He's put it in the corner of the robing room where you leave your gown. He said he was pleased we have the name of the company clearly emblazoned on the front, so he knew who it belonged to. I thought, thank fuck we do, because there might be something in the file that is going to get us into serious trouble.' Caroline was screaming at him now.

Her face was red, and she was physically shaking, as she had been when she had first received the call from Daniel. Harley jumped out from under the desk at the raised voices and scrambled into her lap, shaking. She hugged him, trying to reassure him, but she couldn't quell her anger. If the situation hadn't been so serious and stressful, she would have seen the funny side. Harley wasn't a lap dog and practically smothered her.

'Is there drugs or money in that file?' she growled.

She was met by silence on the other end of the line. She guessed Alex was opening and closing his mouth without saying anything, goldfish like, knowing what a potentially catastrophic position he had put them in. She'd seen him do it before when she'd confronted him, but never about anything as serious as this.

'Alex, silence is not going to get you out of this!' she yelled. 'Answer me. You are always saying I'm paranoid, I should relax, take a chill pill. This is the reason why I don't, and I can't. You are the reason. You make Seb look organised and in control, and that's saying something.'

'I'm so sorry,' Alex stammered. 'I was in such a rush. There was a tannoy for me to get into court. I shot out of the conference room and forgot that file.'

'Well, I don't think that's going to cut it if anyone finds out what's in these files, Alex,' Caroline shouted. 'You have got to have your brain in gear. I'm not going to prison because of you. Now what was in that file?'

Caroline felt the heat of her anger rising through her body in waves. She thought it was a good thing they were not in the same room. She might actually do him some serious physical harm.

'Drugs,' he replied quietly.

Caroline gasped.

'Brett didn't attend court today, so I didn't get to give them to him. I don't know why he didn't turn up,' Alex mumbled on.

'Money would have been bad enough to explain, but how the fuck would we have got out of this if Daniel had opened the file?' Caroline was beside herself with anger and fear.

'It was packaged up carefully so hopefully he wouldn't have noticed anything was wrong.'

'That's a fucking risk I'm not prepared to take Alex. If anyone felt the package, they might suspect something was wrong. I'm not going down because you are a bumbling oaf, Alex, I can assure you of that. Get your head on straight because if this happens again, I'm going to make sure your head is not on your shoulders and Christ knows what Robert will do to you.' Caroline was screaming at him again now. She could feel Harley quivering as he licked her face, trying to calm her down.

'Don't tell him, Caroline,' Alex begged. Even though Robert was in custody, they both knew he had a long reach.

'The way I'm feeling at the moment, Alex, don't push it. If this ever happens again, I'll feed you to the wolves myself, and I won't think twice about it.'

'It won't happen again, I promise,' Alex said, almost in tears.

'It better not,' Caroline retorted, totally unconvinced and still furious. Harley was still shaking on her lap as the conversation ended. She buried her head in his fur, trying to reassure him and calm her own frazzled nerves at the same time. Her heart was pounding so much she could hardly get her breath.

He'll be the death of me, she thought.

Later that same week, Caroline was in the garden having a break, throwing the ball for Harley. It was late afternoon, and it had been an unusually lovely day. The sun was shining, and it was quite warm, not that she had enjoyed much of it. She tilted her face towards the sky, feeling the tickle of the warmth of the sun on her cheeks. Her eyes were closed, and she felt the calmness and the stillness of the moment. It didn't last for long. Harley was before her, barking as he had placed his ball at her feet for her to throw again, aghast that she had the audacity to ignore him.

'Alright cheeky,' she said to him. He did not look amused, moving his head from her to the ball on the floor as if she was a moron. It was obvious where the ball was, and it needed throwing now. She bent to the floor, picked it up and threw it. He bounded up the stairs onto the gravel after it. He skidded to a stop where the ball was, gravel flying in all directions.

'It's a good job we didn't spend a lot of money on this garden, Harley,' she said to him, giggling. 'You have many skills, but landscaping isn't one of them.'

Harley returned the ball to her feet and looked at her as if to say, 'I have no idea what landscaping is, and I'm not sure it is anything I would want to be involved in, anyway. Especially if it interferes with my ball-playing time.'

Her mobile phone rudely interrupted the quality time she was having with Harley. Caroline answered it and it was Ian.

'Hi Ian, is everything OK?' she asked. He often rang her between cases at the police station. Or when he was on his way to or from the pub or to court to assist one of the advocates. So, his call was not unusual.

'No, and you won't be either, when I fill you in,' he replied angrily.

Caroline felt her stomach drop as if it was sitting on her hips. It was churning in a whirlpool-like fashion, and she felt dizzy and sick. She reached out to the low wall at the bottom of the steps in the garden to steady herself.

'You there?' Ian asked.

'Yes,' she said. She closed her eyes, leaning to the left side against the wall, trying to get the nausea to subside. 'What is it?'

'I have come to the Crown Court to collect the papers for Kris.

He was arrested this morning so didn't make it to court and his case was adjourned. It was a crock of shit what he was in for, and he was released and obviously wanted his stuff. I agreed with him I'd get the papers from the court. He didn't want to come in when he didn't have to and I don't blame him, to be honest. He's waiting for me in the pub.'

'OK, that all sounds fine, so I'm guessing that's not the point of the story,' Caroline said, as he seemed to have paused without telling her what was going on.

'You don't sound good Caroline, are you alright?'

'I was before you rang. Now I feel sick, but it's no good not telling me, so spit it out.' She bent forward with her eyes still shut, certain that in a moment her undigested lunch would be spilling all over the paving.

'I'm so sorry that I'm the one that's making you feel like that.' Ian was genuinely concerned.

He knew Caroline worked very long hours, was always stressed, and always looked ill. She looked like she needed a month in the sun being properly fed. Fat chance for any of them unless this paid off, and that was looking less likely with situations like this.

'I get the feeling that it's not your fault Ian, you're just the messenger. Whether I like it or not, I need to hear what you have to say, so get on with it. The delay isn't making me feel any better,' Caroline said, swallowing the bile that was rising in her throat. She didn't want to be sick on the phone to Ian.

'I went into the advocates' room to collect his file. There is Alex's case in the middle of the table by the window, open for all to see what's inside. It's a good job the packages are all so well done up, but it looks a bit odd. There's about six of them, some with drugs and some with money, I assume. I didn't take too much notice. I grabbed Kris's papers and zipped up the case and stood it in the corner where it looks far less conspicuous.'

'For Christ's sake, what the hell is he playing at?' Caroline was now swaying. The nausea hit her in enormous waves. 'I'm sorry Ian, I'll ring you back in a minute.' She abruptly ended the call and then promptly threw up all over the slabs.

Harley, who had come to sit by her while she was on the phone, was clearly concerned about the way she was. Now he started barking frantically. With her eyes still closed, Caroline reached out her right arm to stroke his back.

'Don't worry, Harley. Mummy's OK,' she whispered, feeling anything but.

The barking brought Sandra out of the reception door that led to the garden. When she saw Caroline, she came running over.

'Caroline, are you alright? Clearly a stupid question. What's the matter?' She came up the side of the steps that Caroline was perched on, avoiding the sick. She crouched in front of her, and stroked her hair as her head was bent between her knees. Harley was still barking frenziedly.

With her other hand, Sandra stroked his head. 'It's alright, H,' she said soothingly. 'Mummy's a bit sick, but she'll be fine.'

Harley stopped barking as she stroked him, but looked at her as if to say he wasn't convinced.

Caroline raised her head slowly. She looked at Sandra, who moved her hand from Caroline's head to her right hand and took it. She held on to it and looked Caroline straight in the eyes.

'What's going on?' she said firmly. 'You were perfectly alright, well as alright as you ever are, when you came out here. Now your lunch is on the floor.' The stare told Caroline she wasn't going to get away with not telling her.

'We need to go inside; I can't tell you out here,' she mumbled.

'OK,' Sandra replied, worry and fear in her voice. It was obvious what it was about if they couldn't talk in the garden. 'Will you be able to get up?'

'I think so. I need to clear this sick up.'

'I'll do that in a minute. Don't worry about that. Let's get you in.'

Caroline braced herself on the wall and tried to stand. Sandra had her hands on her shoulders to help her.

'How are you feeling?' Sandra enquired once she was vertical.

'My legs don't feel as if they are mine,' Caroline replied weakly. 'They feel very wobbly.'

'Slowly does it please,' Sandra insisted.

'I don't think I could run if my life depended on it,' Caroline said, looking at her with a weak smile.

With Sandra's help, Caroline dragged herself along the paving into the office. She slumped down in the first chair in reception, her head back in her hands. She had a pounding headache; her head was spinning, and the nausea had subsided a bit but hadn't left her.

Harley bounded in and started nuzzling, trying to get his head into her lap. She raised her head a little to let him and then put her head on top of his, stroking his back.

Sandra went to the kitchen to fill a bucket with water. She went outside to swill the paving, taking three buckets in total to disperse the unhappy contents of Caroline's stomach.

'Right,' she said when she returned and sat down in her chair. 'Fill me in.'

At that moment, Caroline's phone rang. She pulled it out of her pocket without raising her head. Sandra came over and took it from her.

'It's Ian,' she told Caroline. 'I'll get it for you.' With that, she answered the phone.

'Caroline, are you OK?' came the worried voice on the other end. 'You were going to ring me back, but you didn't.'

'It's Sandra, Ian, not Caroline,' Sandra said. 'Caroline's been sick. What's going on?'

'Oh no, poor Caroline,' Ian said in a worried tone.

'Don't worry Ian, she'll be OK. Harley and I are looking after her. Tell me what is going on.'

Ian filled Sandra in on the conversation he'd had with

Caroline. Apart from a few swear words, Sandra said very little, letting Ian tell the story.

'Well, thank God you went in there, Ian,' she said, relieved that no one had discovered what was going on. She was clearly angry at such a close call. 'Were there many people in the robing room?'

'Not too many because it's quite late in the day now. But obviously I have no idea how long the case has been open like that.'

'Knowing Alex, most of the day,' Sandra replied.

'Are you still there?' Sandra asked Ian.

'Yes, but I have to go as Kris is waiting.'

'Any idea where Alex is?'

'No. I literally went into the robing room, saw what I saw, grabbed the papers, zipped up the case and then came to an interview room to tell Caroline straight away.'

'OK well, you've done all you can for now …'

'Ask him to go back to the robing room and get the case, please,' Caroline said feebly.

'Ian, Caroline asks if you can get the case and take it with you, please?' Sandra relayed to him. 'At least that way we know it is safe and she can then deal with Alex when she's up to it.'

'Sure can, good idea. Tell Caroline I'll take it with me. I'll bring it to her house later so that she knows it's safe. That way, she doesn't have to wait for me to get to the office. Send her home, Sandra. No excuses from her, and don't let her drive. You know how stubborn she can be.'

'Thanks for that Ian, very sensible. I'll take her home. Don't want her having a crash with Harley in the car,' she said, adding a hint of humour to the stress of the situation.

'Of course, it's all about Harley,' Ian laughed.

'And none of us would have it any other way, would we?'

'True that,' Ian said, ending the call.

Sandra would not take no for an answer and insisted on immediately driving Caroline and Harley home. Caroline joked with her it was for Harley's benefit and Sandra confirmed that, of course, that was the position. The King needed to be looked after and that's all there was to it. Not only did she drive them home, but she came into the house and fed Harley. She made sure Caroline was snuggled on the sofa under a thick patchwork blanket. Caroline had refused anything to eat or drink but Sandra had poured her a large glass of water and a glass of lemonade and opened a packet of ready-salted crisps. She put them on the table in front of the sofa.

'You need to stay hydrated,' she told Caroline firmly. 'And the lemonade and ready-salted crisps will replace the salts you have lost. We cannot have you being ill, especially because of that dopey bastard.'

Sandra had been quiet on the drive to Caroline's. Caroline had been grateful. She didn't need her ranting on about Alex, but she knew how mad Sandra was and rightly so. One slip-up and they were all in very serious trouble and they all knew that and took every precaution possible. Not Alex, the airhead. He was on a totally different planet in Alex's world where the sun was shining, and all was well. He clearly hadn't noticed his case had gone because he hadn't been in touch with Caroline at all. He normally rang when he had finished court, so that was a little odd, but she felt too ill to worry about it.

'Thank you so much, Sandra. I appreciate it and I will sort Alex out when I'm up to it, I promise.' Sandra tucked the blanket round her, flapping like a mother hen. She also tucked it round Harley who had wriggled his way next to Caroline. He gave her a grateful lick on her hand.

'I know you will, but I'm very angry with him. He's not a child, Caroline, but he continually acts like one. He has made you ill. That is unforgiveable. And he could have got us all sent to prison. Our lives would be finished. I trust you with my life. I wouldn't trust him with my dirty laundry. It's bad enough when he's a scatterbrain with normal files, making our working lives difficult. But this is a whole different level.'

'I know,' Caroline replied, thinking how cross Sandra would be if she knew this was not Alex's first time. She had put them all in jeopardy by not dealing with him properly, for that matter. Once was too much. She should not have let him continue to be an active part of it. Sure, they would still have to give him his cut to keep him quiet, so, he'd be getting money for nothing. But it was better than the alternative of getting them a lengthy prison sentence instead.

As Sandra went to leave the living room, Caroline's mobile, which was on the little table with the glasses of drinks and the crisps, started ringing. Sandra swept it up, frowning.

'It's security at the Crown Court. They're late, aren't they? Shall I answer it?'

'Yes,' said Caroline, frantically nodding and then wishing she hadn't, as another wave of nausea hit her.

It couldn't be good news that security was ringing at that time of night, but then they wouldn't be ringing if they had found anything they shouldn't have. They'd be ringing the police.

'Hi Caroline's phone,' Sandra said politely.

'Good evening. This is security from the Crown Court. Is it possible to speak to Caroline, please?'

Sandra looked over at Caroline, who nodded, so she passed over the phone.

'Hi, it's Caroline. How can I help?' she said, holding the phone in her right hand and massaging her temples with the thumb and ring finger of her left.

'Hi Caroline. It's Dominic here, security at the Crown Court. I tried to ring Alex on his mobile, but I couldn't get him, and he isn't in the building. I put a tannoy out for him and he hasn't answered. I've looked in all the usual places and he isn't here. He's left a file in courtroom three. The court clerk found it and handed it to me. I haven't opened it because I appreciate the information in there is confidential. I know it's your firm's because of the stamp on the outside. I didn't want Alex to worry he had lost it when he realises he doesn't have it. If you speak to him, tell him I have locked it in the cupboard at the security desk. It'll be perfectly safe overnight and I'll give it to him tomorrow.'

'Dominic, I cannot thank you enough for finding it and storing it safely. Also, for letting us know. I am sure Alex will be worried when he is trying to find it. If his head wasn't screwed onto his shoulders, I'm sure he'd have left that behind too,' she said, trying to make light of the situation, while she felt completely the opposite. She could feel her blood boiling and the veins in her forehead were pulsing. Her heart was racing.

Twice in one day. What the hell was up with him? she wondered. If she, or any of the others, caught up with Alex, she was certain his head and shoulders wouldn't be connected for very long.

'I know, but we all love him, don't we?' Dominic said affectionately.

'Don't we just,' said Caroline, thinking, *if I get my hands on him now, I'll throttle him.*

'What's the name of the file just so I can tell him?'

'Carrie Edwards 43112'

'That's great, thanks,' Caroline said at the same time as typing the information into a note on her phone.

'Have a lovely evening, Caroline.'

'You too, Dominic, and thanks again.'

'Anytime,' he said, ending the call.

'There won't be a next time,' Caroline said out loud.

Sandra had perched herself on the armchair nearest Caroline and had heard every word that Dominic had said.

'Has he totally lost his marbles?' she exclaimed.

'I don't know and I'm a bit worried, as well as being livid,' Caroline replied. 'He hasn't rung me, and he's clearly finished court. That isn't like him either.'

'Well, he's left without everything he needs, so perhaps he dare not ring you. He's lost his case, which presumably has drugs or money or both in it. He doesn't know that Ian has it, and he's lost that file. He won't remember he's left it in court. To be fair, if I was him, I wouldn't want to ring you either.'

'Do you think I ought to ring him to check he's OK or let him have a restless night worrying about it all?'

'I'd let him stew in his own juice; he's got to accept some responsibility for his actions, Caroline. He's not a child and pulling that silly grin he does might let him get away with murder with you, but it isn't going to save us if we are in the dock with him, is it?' she said gravely and honestly.

'I agree. I'll ring him first thing in the morning if I haven't heard from him. I'll be in a better state to handle him.'

'Absolutely, and I'll sleep a little easier knowing he's not getting a wink,' Sandra said mischievously. She kissed Caroline on the cheek and Harley on the top of his head before she left.

Fifteen minutes later, the doorbell rang. Caroline looked at the camera on her mobile and saw Ian standing there. Harley hadn't barked but was standing by the sofa wagging his tail.

'Clever boy. You know who it is, don't you? You don't need a ring doorbell,' she said, getting up.

As she opened the door, Harley pushed his way through so that he could greet Ian.

'Hello, lad,' Ian said, stroking the top of his head and ears. 'Hard day at the office for you today?'

'Woof, woof,' Harley replied, and both Ian and Caroline laughed.

'Come in,' Caroline said, opening the door wider so that Ian could get in with the case. 'I think he's saying it's been a very trying day and Alex needs shooting.'

'Well, he's not far wrong,' Ian agreed. 'Where do you want me to leave this?'

'Bring it through to the lounge. I want to open it and see exactly what he's left lying around.'

Ian followed her through to the lounge and laid the case on the floor. Caroline bent down to open it and had to steady herself on the armchair.

'You look terrible, Caroline,' Ian said, his voice full of concern. 'I didn't like to say anything when you first opened the door, but look at you, you can't even bend down without going giddy. Sit and I'll do it.'

'Thanks. I'm sure I'll be fine after a good night's sleep,' Caroline said, trying to sound more positive than she felt. At the same time, she thought, *fat chance.*

'I don't know how you'll get one of those with Alex and his antics,' Ian retorted. 'Do you want me to open these?'

'No, just show me them and I can tell if they are drugs or money. If they are to us, they are money, if they are from us, they are drugs.'

Ian whistled as he opened the case. There were five packages in there and he showed each of them to Caroline. 'Five packages, four with money, one with drugs,' Caroline exclaimed. 'If anyone had found this and opened these, we'd be dead. No way of talking ourselves out of this.'

'We'd be denying all knowledge. His case, his stupidity. He can take the rap.'

'He wouldn't though, I don't think. The police wouldn't think he was doing it on his own. They know him, and they know he couldn't organise anything like this, so they'd soon come sniffing around me,' Caroline said angrily. 'Do you want a drink of tea, coffee, something stronger?'

'I shouldn't. I need to get home to the kids, but I think a stiff whisky is needed,' Ian said, his voice cracking with anger and tears. 'I have so much to gain from this, but so much to lose if it goes wrong, Caroline. We all do. Why is he so fucking careless?'

'I don't know, Ian,' Caroline said, returning from the kitchen with a whisky glass and a nice bottle of single malt. 'Pour it yourself. Do you want a dash of water or some ice?'

'No, nothing should be added to spoil the taste of a good

single malt. Although, Alex has left a foul taste in my mouth that will affect it,' he said, pouring a finger of whisky and knocking it back in one. 'I needed that, thanks. Better take the glass and bottle back else I'll get arrested for drink driving to add to this fucking shit day,' he said, handing both to Caroline.

She took them to the kitchen and placed them on the island in the middle and returned to Ian. He was sitting on the floor in the lounge, stroking Harley's tummy.

'Ahhhhh, Harley,' Caroline said, walking in.

'He's dishing out the best therapy,' Ian said, continuing to stroke him. 'What are you going to do, Caroline?'

'I'm going to ring Alex in the morning, when I am feeling better, and tell him he's out. He can take his share of the money. We are going to have to pay him to keep him quiet. But he's not going to be involved in the actual operation at all anymore. If I tell Robert, he'll do him some serious damage. Alex is the weakest link and a real threat. Robert will neutralise him. As much as I am tempted, I don't want that. Alex can just sit back and take the money and keep out of it, so he can't fuck things up. We don't send drugs into prison from the cells anymore. The clients can come to you in the pub, rather than the Crown Court. We won't lose out and we'll all sleep better, knowing Alex can't screw things up any further.'

'I don't know how you put up with him, Caroline,' Ian said, looking directly at her. 'But I agree he cannot be involved any longer. We are all going to prison if this carries on.'

'He's been a good business partner. If things go according to plan and we don't go to prison, I won't have to be in business with him for much longer. Short-term pain for long-term gain. That's the way we are going to have to deal with it, and we are just going to have to put up with it. I can't have Robert finding out. I don't want fighting among us. I've enough to deal with.'

'Fair enough. I'm happy to do whatever you need, you know that. But, make no mistake, we do it for you, not for him. Mind you, we'd never have gone into this hairbrained scheme if it was him running it.'

Caroline laughed out loud. 'There wouldn't have been a scheme if it was left to him. If by chance there was and you followed him, I'd have been ordering psychiatric reports on you all.'

Ian laughed and then looked at her seriously. 'Don't keep anything from us, will you, Caroline? If you think he isn't listening, call a meeting of us all. He has to understand the seriousness of all of this. If push comes to shove, I won't think twice about letting Robert deliver that message if his thick skull has trouble taking it in. I've a family to protect. I'm doing it for them, and I won't let him put us in danger like this.'

'I promise you Ian, I won't let him off the hook and I will make sure he toes the line. If he doesn't, you and Sandra will be the first to know. Remember, Sandra knows, she won't let this go either.'

They walked towards the front door as Ian added, 'Rottweiler Sandra won't let it go. She'll just forget who it is she's supposed to be on your case about. It'll be Fred, John, whatever his name is.' They both howled with laughter. Just the tonic they both needed.

Caroline fell asleep not long after Ian left and awoke in the early hours. Harley was fast asleep on his bed next to the fireplace. The room was in darkness. Her throat was so sore when she swallowed it felt like sandpaper was raking it. The taste in her mouth was foul, and she remembered she hadn't brushed her teeth since she had been sick earlier. She felt her clothes sticking to her and touched her forehead. It was a bit clammy.

Perhaps you are coming down with something, she thought to herself.

She forced herself to sit up on the sofa and took sips of the water Sandra had poured for her earlier. It tasted revolting because of her mouth, but it at least soothed her throat a little. She started gulping it, realising how thirsty she was, and then slowed herself down, not wanting to be sick again. When she had finished the pint of water, she moved on to the lemonade. Having guzzled a few mouthfuls of that, she then belched.

Harley woofed, clearly disturbed by the noise in the dark.

'Sorry, lad,' she said apologetically. 'Just the lemonade. It's a bit too fizzy,' she told him, as if he would know exactly what she was talking about.

He came over in the dark. All she could see were the whites of his eyes, as she felt his wet nose nuzzling her hands.

'Good boy,' she said. Then she exclaimed, 'Blimey I bet you need the toilet, don't you?' She jumped up to let him out into the back garden.

The jumping was not a good idea, although she was pleased it was just her head that hurt. The sickness seemed to have passed.

Caroline let Harley out into the garden and went to the bathroom to brush her teeth. She splashed her face with cold water and looked at her reflection in the mirror. *God, I look terrible,* she thought. Her hair was damp and stuck to her head. Her skin was ghostlike, with a sweaty sheen to it. Dark circles and bags under her eyes completed the horror movie face looking back at her. She badly needed a shower but didn't feel up to it. That would have to wait until morning. Caroline slowly changed into her pyjamas and went to let Harley back in.

'I'm so sorry you didn't get a walk,' she said to him, wiping his feet and then leading him upstairs to bed. 'Mummy isn't well enough, but she'll make up for it tomorrow.'

Harley climbed onto the bed and got himself comfortable. Caroline snuggled in next to him and quickly fell into the deepest sleep she had had for ages. She had expected to toss and turn over the Alex situation, but fatigue won the battle.

CHAPTER TWENTY-ONE

DEVELOPMENTS

Caroline awoke from the deepest sleep she could remember, at just before six the following morning. She opened her eyes slowly, recalling the events of the previous day. She could feel Harley beside her. The warmth of his body on top of the duvet permeating through to her. She wished she could stay snuggled like that for the rest of the day, but sadly, it wasn't possible.

She did a mental check of how she felt physically. At least, lying down she felt considerably better than she had when she went to bed. No nausea and no headache. Her mouth still tasted revolting, and she felt weak, although that was probably in part due to having very little inside her. She slowly swung her legs over the side of the bed and gingerly stood up. All was well. Harley stirred and looked at her, not impressed that she had disturbed him.

'Morning H. Sorry to disturb you, but we've got another day in store for us at the fun factory.'

Harley looked at her as if to say his dictionary definition of "fun" was clearly very different from hers.

'Don't worry, it won't be for too much longer unless Alex gets us locked up or shot,' she said matter-of-factly.

Harley's expression of, *if we are relying on him, we're all dead,* just summed up the position perfectly.

Having had a shower and a coffee, Caroline felt much better. She decided to have a piece of toast. Breakfast for her was not a normal thing, but having missed dinner she made some toast.

Harley was delighted as he got a bit of crust. Feeling human again, she got in the car to head to the office and rang Alex. He didn't answer, which wasn't unusual. But it was strange that she hadn't heard from him after court yesterday, not even by text or WhatsApp. She didn't leave a message. He'd see the missed call and ring her back.

By the time Sandra arrived at the office, Caroline still hadn't heard from Alex.

'What bollocks did he come up with, by way of an excuse?' Sandra asked, after commenting that Caroline looked much better than the night before.

'I haven't been able to get hold of him,' Caroline answered. 'I rang him on the way into the office, but he didn't answer. I've rung him twice since. I've left a voicemail for him to ring me and texted and sent him a WhatsApp to call, but nothing.'

'That's strange, isn't it? Even for him?' Sandra questioned.

'Yes, it is. He's perhaps waiting for court to open to retrieve his file and case before he calls me. If I haven't heard from him by then I'm going to ring the court and get them to tannoy him.'

As if his ears were burning, her mobile rang. She could see it was Alex.

'I'll leave you to it,' Sandra said discretely, taking Harley with her and closing the door.

'What the hell happened to you?' Caroline said as soon as she answered. 'No call or message last night, and then your vanishing act continues this morning.'

'Good morning to you, too,' Alex said, trying to appear calm, but Caroline could hear a nervous edge in his voice.

'Don't try to make me feel bad, Alex. I'm not the one who disappeared and left a trail of havoc in his wake for me to sort out,' Caroline snapped.

She was trying to keep her voice even and calm, but she could feel her face turning beetroot red. The anger welling up inside her, waiting to explode out, like a volcano releasing its lava.

'OK, OK,' Alex interjected. His tone had changed. Caroline sensed he knew he was in a losing battle and that antagonising her would only make things worse.

'So why the radio silence?'

There was a long pause on the other end. 'Well …' said Alex weakly.

'Cat got your tongue? Not like you to be unable to come up with some patter,' said Caroline grimly. She had no intention of making this easy for him after what she'd gone through yesterday. 'It wouldn't have anything to do with your suitcase and a missing file, would it?'

'What do you know about it?' Alex asked breathlessly.

'Everything,' came the blunt reply. 'The more important questions are, what do you know and why haven't you been in contact? You clearly know there is some kind of problem.'

'I didn't know what to say to you,' Alex said honestly. 'I was in the cells and came up and my suitcase, which was on the table, had just vanished. No one knew where it was at the court. I've also misplaced a file. I assume that they haven't fallen into the wrong hands, otherwise we'd have had a visit from the police. But I haven't slept a wink all night. I felt sure the police were going to come bursting through my front door and arrest me.'

'Which is exactly what you deserve. I'm glad you didn't sleep. You made me physically ill yesterday. Sandra had to drive me and Harley home. And don't be under any illusion, if either the case or the file or both had fallen into the wrong hands, just because you haven't had a visit from the police doesn't mean you wouldn't be getting one. They'd take their time with surveillance and enquiries, waiting for you to expose us even further, which, with yesterday's antics, would be fucking inevitable.' Caroline's voice was shaking. She was so furious.

'I'm so sorry I made you sick, Caroline. I feel terrible about it.'

'No, you don't. You just feel terrible because you've cocked up and because I know about it. Ian has your case. He went in there to get the package out for Kris, who'd arrived at the pub and couldn't find you. You'd left the case wide open on the desk for anyone to nose in there. The packages might be well sealed, but together they still look suspicious. We don't want any prying eyes or nosy parkers. Worse than that, you left a court file in court three. Security couldn't find you, nor could they raise you on your mobile, so they rang me. Dominic commented he was glad our name was on the outside of the file, because he knew it was ours, and didn't have to look in it. I was glad he didn't have to look in it, for obviously different fucking reasons. Two serious cock-ups on the same day, Alex. Ian is aware. Sandra knows. I know. We are all fucking furious. You deserve the sleepless night. We don't. You are a liability, and it stops now. You get your money, but you play no further part in this. All you have to do is keep your fucking mouth shut. Think you can manage that?'

'But Caroline …'

'No fucking buts. I begrudge sharing the money with you when you'll be doing nothing, but that's a hell of a lot safer than you playing any part. None of us will get any sleep in our beds if we are constantly worrying about you and what you are leaving lying around, and where you are leaving it.'

'It won't happen again, Caroline,' Alex said, pleading.

'You are absolutely right. It won't because you won't have the opportunity again. It's not just me. It's the others, too. No one is going to put up with you having any involvement. And let's just hope Robert doesn't get wind of what's happened.'

'How would he unless you tell him?' Alex said sarcastically, but Caroline could tell he was nervous about it. Robert wouldn't think twice about organising a serious pasting for what he'd done.

'I won't tell him, you prat,' Caroline spat out. 'Not for your benefit, but he'll take it out on me. He didn't want you involved in the first place. But he has a way of finding things out through channels I don't even know about.'

'What are you going to say to him about why the drugs aren't coming to court anymore?'

'I'm going to say with cases overrunning, it's getting more difficult. With Ian across the road, it makes sense for them to go to the pub instead. He might be a bit worried about the increase in foot traffic at the pub, making it a bit more open to suspicion, but I'll persuade him otherwise. It is definitely better than the alternative of court.'

'What if he doesn't agree to it?'

'You'll have to hope that I haven't lost my powers of persuasion, won't you?' Caroline said nastily and hung up on him.

Caroline saw the relief on the faces of Sandra and Ian when she told them Alex was no longer an active part of the plan. In fact, it was clear they couldn't believe that he'd been so reluctant to give up.

'The arrogance of that man,' Sandra exclaimed.

'Pride comes before a fall,' said Ian, shaking his head in disbelief.

'And I'm determined to make sure we don't fall with him,' Caroline said.

Later on, she filled William and Michael in on what had happened and the decision she had made regarding Alex.

'For fuck's sake,' said William. His face was red with anger, having been turning so when he was listening to Caroline. His hands were shaking. 'What the fuck has he got between his ears? The clients have more sawdust than him. I don't know if I want to carry on with this. My nerves are shot to pieces.'

'We'll be fine now,' reasoned Michael. 'He's out of it. He can't say anything without getting himself in serious trouble and he's getting his money. No one else has given us any cause for concern. I think if we are all honest with ourselves and each other, we are happier that he isn't actively involved. So, perhaps this cloud has a silver lining. He's out of it and his mistakes haven't cost us.'

'Yet,' said William, still shaking.

'I understand William. really, I do. I was as sick as a dog yesterday. And while I don't see the silver lining that Michael always seems to find in things, I think we are all better off. I've got a video link with Robert later to tell him the line I'm feeding him, and we can carry on as normal,' Caroline explained.

'I think he'll be as relieved as us. If not more so,' Sandra said.

'Fingers crossed,' Caroline replied. 'That's the thing with Robert. He can be totally unpredictable at times.'

'Wasn't expecting a link today,' Robert said, smiling at Caroline, as he sat down in the video link booth at his end. 'Oh hi Harley,' he waved as he saw Harley crossing the room behind Caroline.

'I want to change things this end, so wanted to run it past you,' Caroline said, returning the smile.

She'd decided to make Robert feel like he was part of the decision, not that it was a fait accompli, which it clearly was. That way, she was more likely to get him on board.

'Oh yeah, in what way?' Robert enquired, leaning forward in his chair. His interest clearly piqued.

'The Crown Court is becoming more difficult for timing. Alex is never in the right place at the right time to hand over papers and collect money. Ian is in the pub. That side is working really well. So, I think, other than genuine emergencies, we divert people to the pub instead. What do you think?' she said, concentrating on his facial expression, trying to read him.

'I've heard rumblings he's keeping people waiting,' Robert said. 'I wasn't too worried. They are getting what they want, so they'll have to put up with it. But you know my views on Alex. He's a fucking idiot, so I'm happy with it. No, I'm fucking delighted to have him take a back seat. The further back, the better.'

Caroline was relieved that he wasn't asking more questions and agreed. However, to make it look like a genuine discussion, she padded it out a bit. She didn't want him ruminating about it later and getting paranoid.

'I've thought about the extra foot traffic at the pub, but there seems to be a reasonable amount there that's not to do with us.

Some regulars, some not. So, I really don't think it's going to make a difference to our potential vulnerability. I trust Ian and he agrees.'

'I trust Ian too,' Robert agreed, nodding his head. 'He's intelligent and speaks his mind. He's a risk taker, but not a bloody fool. A much safer pair of fucking hands.'

'Great. I'll get it started this end straight away then.'

'Cushty.' Robert grinned.

That word made Caroline smile inside. On one occasion, a regular and genuinely nice man with more than his fair of mental health issues rushed into the office.

'Caroline, your car is the Audi S4, isn't it? The white one on the side street round the corner?' he said breathlessly.

'Yes, it is,' she said. This is when she used to park there, rather than in the car park where she now parked because of this incident. 'Why?'

'I just saw a bunch of dancing monkeys trying to steal the wheels,' he said.

'What the fuck?' Caroline exclaimed.

'Oh, don't worry, Uncle Bruce has put them in their place. The word is out that's your car. It's cushty.'

'Caroline, did you hear me? How's everything else going?' Robert asked, jolting her back to the present.

'Fine,' said Caroline, amazed how calm she could be and how easily she could pretend everything was OK. Years of practising her court face now came in handy in a different way. 'Seb is making a success of it at the gym. You clearly knocked some sense into him,' she said, laughing. Robert cracked up.

'I'm surprised one punch was enough.'

'You clearly hit him hard enough. Ian is doing fine. William and Michael are totally under control. I am so glad we pay William the extra to keep tabs on Michael though, that would be a real headache otherwise.'

'Bet he's never turned that phone I gave him on,' Robert said, smiling.

'No more than he turns on his other one. They are no doubt both covered in cobwebs in the bottom of his bag.'

'Well, at least we won't have to worry about anything incriminating being on them, or him losing them,' Robert joked.

'True that,' Caroline said. 'What about your end?'

'All quiet on the western front. Dave and Louise seem to have got themselves a good little set-up. They aren't aiming big, so we haven't got to worry about them taking fucking risks they don't have to. Dave is getting the drugs to me pal Brian by dropping them in the laundry bag where he works. He's moving the product, no problem. Once a week, Louise and Dave sort their schedules so that they are both in the exercise yard. They exchange a few words, Dave says. No one will think anything of it, them being husband and wife after all. Dave slips out the package from under his jacket and passes it through the hole. Louise takes it and puts it under her jacket. Their backs are to the surveillance cameras, he says, and no other prison officers ever take any notice of them.'

'It sounds like they are being very sensible. Pretty much what we thought,' Caroline said, feeling relieved. 'Who does Louise deal with her end? I think you said it was Tasha?'

'Yes, you are right. Her contact is Tasha. Apparently, she was the brains of the operation behind her partner's drug dealing. All had been going well until their contact had a flat tyre on the M1, and she had to shift the drugs herself that night. The police stopped her as her brake light was out. They said they smelt drugs in the car. She says that's shit, but they searched it and found the drugs. She wonders whether the breakdown on the M1 was genuine, or whether she was set up. The police bailed her but went through her phone records and found evidence of drug dealing. She pleaded out before they could find more evidence that would have got her sent away for far longer. They think she is a reasonably small fish, so she got five years. It would have been more than double that if they'd known the truth, she says. Anyway, she feels she's been fucked over, so she won't do that to us.'

'And you are happy that makes her a safe pair of hands?' Caroline questioned.

'As far as anyone can be. She told Louise what had happened and that she desperately needed cash. Her two small children are being looked after by her sister while she and her partner are inside. But her sister has four children of her own and neither she nor her partner work, so money is fucking tight. Louise feels sorry for the kids and thinks it makes her an ideal candidate. It's better Louise isn't dealing with too many inmates, as the more who know, the more can tell. So, passing to Tasha and getting her to distribute lowers the risk significantly.'

Caroline knew they front-loaded the cost of the first batch, as Tasha didn't have the money to pay for it. However, her sister met Ian every week in the pub, and there had been no problems so far.

'They could have made more money by finding more people on the women's side to deal the drugs to, but that would increase the risk. Louise and Dave ain't fucking greedy,' Robert continued. 'They want to make enough, but not push it. They are in it for the longer game with a lower risk, and are making enough, and so are we.'

'Well, that's all very positive,' Caroline agreed, smiling.

'Me dad's getting proper fucking narky, though. Where are we up to?' Robert enquired.

'I've sent him four letters, including one with drugs in it. Let's see how we go. Hasn't he said he's had anything? That's a bit of a worry.'

Caroline felt her stomach heave again. Just getting over one problem and then another one loomed. It was like a storm where the waves kept coming, and she was a tiny boat trying to bob over them as best she could.

Caroline had been expecting Robert to mention his dad and the drugs every time they spoke, which was regularly regarding the people on bail. She was very concerned about the parcel with the drugs in it but hadn't wanted to raise it with Robert. Caroline knew he would then be putting pressure on her to send in more. She had opted to keep quiet and worry to herself, rather than encourage further conversation about it. Caroline had confided the same in Sandra when she'd asked her about it, Sandra understanding she was trapped between a rock and a hard place.

'He hasn't said he's had anything. Don't worry, I'll ask him about it later. He hasn't got a Dave, so it probably takes a bit longer. When did you send the first one?'

'About eight weeks ago, the first one. He should have had them all long before now. They all were guaranteed delivery the next day and had to be signed for. I told you this was so dangerous. Good job I didn't send him much, but anything at all is an incredibly serious situation. Also, he was on your case to get this up and running asap. So, why the radio silence from his end? This isn't good. I don't like this at all.'

Harley could sense the change in Caroline's demeanour and nuzzled her feet from under the desk. He always liked to be in physical contact with her if he was near her, and she found it comforting too, although it didn't reduce her stress levels on this occasion.

Robert could tell how stressed she was. He felt quite anxious about it himself but didn't want her to see he was worried. His dad had made it seem like he needed this up and running quickly and then had been impossible to get hold of since. Robert assumed the money he'd given him had sorted his issues out, but he didn't dare tell Caroline he hadn't heard from his dad. She seriously would be worried that the drugs had fallen into the wrong hands.

'Don't stress, Caroline. He's probably got the ones without the drugs and not even bothered to mention them. I'll sort it.'

'He should have got them all ages ago. Speak to him asap and get back to me. I don't need any more drama in my life.'

'Don't worry. As Seb would say, on it like a car bonnet.'

'And that fills me with total confidence – not,' Caroline said, cutting the link.

CHAPTER TWENTY-TWO

OPERATION DOG WALKER

Caroline had an extremely efficient system with all the dog walkers. None of them had let her down over the months they had been working together in this way. They were masters of discretion. When she met any of them – and she would see most of them at least once a week, if not more – no one mentioned the operation. There was not even a passing reference to it. All conversations related to the usual topics. Most commonly the dogs and what they'd been up to.

She'd only ever had a conversation with them, after the initial discussions to see who was interested, to discuss what day she'd be dropping their drugs in the poo bin. They could make sure they had the money ready in advance. She'd decided to give them all a different day and used different poo bins. That way, no one could easily establish a pattern unless she was being watched closely. She'd organised the poo bins for where they each most used them, so again, it would look less suspicious. Although, anywhere on the circuit would be OK, dogs were very much creatures of habit and tended to go in the same places, their favourite spots. She'd coordinated the drops with the stops, and it had worked like clockwork.

On a Saturday, she left her house for her evening walk with Harley at seven. She turned left from her house, taking him on a long loop around the street and through an alley, into the next close. They crossed over a busy estate road and headed towards the canal. However, instead of going that far, they turned left back into the other side of the estate and followed the road round to the little park. There was Harley's favourite tree, which he had to sniff round. Caroline assumed it was because it was a favourite of other dogs, too, so there were always plenty of good sniffs.

The tree was conveniently placed opposite poo bin number one. Subject to the amount of sniffing Harley did on the first part of the route, it would take, on average, about ten minutes to get from her home to the poo bin. While he was sniffing the tree, he would have done his business and so she would need to use that bin. Checking around to make sure that no one was about, she dropped Harley's deposit in the bin and collected the cash hanging on the hook. She then hung the drugs on the hook. The whole movement was very swift and unless you stood next to her, you wouldn't know what was happening.

Sometimes she saw Paula and Joe with Barney and Bailey making their second circuit, having already put the money in the first-time round. This was their boys' favourite stop as well. Although no one knew of the operation, and no one would want to go digging around in such an unpleasant environment, it was sensible not to leave the money or the drugs in there for too long. If they met, Paula or Joe used the poo bin and collected the drugs, but nothing was said. The normal dog walker chit-chat happened throughout. Sometimes they didn't meet, and often, they would meet on other days too, just as they always had. As far as Caroline was concerned, it was foolproof. There were no cameras, and every meeting seemed totally innocuous, because it was.

The only other time she'd had a conversation about the operation was with Joe. When she met up with him, he said he'd been ferreting about in the bin for the drugs as the handles on the bag had split. Even Barney and Bailey had been looking to see what on earth their dad was doing. Poo bags were strong, the handles not so. She'd commented that the way they hung on the outside of poo bins when they were left there, which disgusted her, you'd have thought they were, but clearly not so. Joe said they didn't normally have the weight. Caroline agreed a lesson had been learned, and she double-bagged them.

During their conversations, without referring to the drugs themselves, Paula and Joe commented things were going well. Their difficult financial position was improving, and they were getting back on track. Caroline was delighted for them. They were such a kind couple. Tom was very fortunate to have such supportive parents. She had many clients whose parents were not so supportive. In fact, many of them were not even on the scene. Without that help and love, their lives went in a very different direction.

Tuesday was the evening she left the drugs in the same place for Christine. She was a busy lady with commitments most evenings. Tuesdays worked well for her because she could be sure that she would be out just before Caroline. Although her dad walked Clive, Christine liked to have some alone time with him.

'Otherwise, I just feel like I'm paying his bills,' she said, laughing, on the day they finalised the arrangements.

'Rather his than one of those useless millennials. Look at his gorgeous face,' Caroline replied, kissing Clive on the nose. She received a big kiss back.

Christine was the only one Caroline had given Phillip's number to. Everyone else in the dog walker group needed the money now, whereas Christine wanted it to invest. She wanted her money to top up her pension and enable her to leave her job as soon as possible. Phillip was a financial advisor and an accountant. She'd made it very clear to him that Christine knew nothing about the other parts of the operation, nor the offshore accounts. All advice regarding her needed to be totally legitimate. The amounts were not huge, but regular and properly invested, would soon start to make her some real money.

Christine was the only one who'd had the quantity of drugs she was dealing increased. The others were all paying off debts or trying to keep their heads above water. That's all they had set out to achieve, and they were happy to be doing that. Christine wanted as much as possible, as fast as possible. Caroline had no idea who her buyers were, although she was pretty sure it was dealers connected to the school children. The amount she bought each week couldn't be for individual wraps, which is what she suspected Paula and Joe were doing, and Anthony's nephew and Marie's grandson. Christine was shrewd and intelligent. Caroline thought she was a bit higher up the food chain than that, on the level of those who were buying from them at court. She was pleased for her. It wouldn't last forever, so she was making out of it what she could.

Arrangements with Marie had been easy to make. All she did was collect the drugs to pass on to her grandson.

'I'm free all day every day, dear,' she'd said. 'You're the busy lady. You just tell me where to be and when and I'll work round you.'

'Yes Marie,' Caroline had replied. 'I have no doubt you're flexible, but have you discussed this with Oswald? Will Mr I Want be amenable to our plans?'

'He'll have to be,' Marie said, laughing. 'If he's not in the mood, I'll pop him into the basket with one of his bow ties on. He thinks he's the bees' knees wearing them, so I'm sure he'll be happy to be out showing off.'

'You spoil him, Marie,' Caroline said, grinning.

'Oh, and Harley's on direct dial to the RSPCA he's so neglected, is he?' Marie said, winking.

'Touché'

Caroline decided to spread the nights out a bit, so didn't drug drop on a Monday. She hated Mondays, always had since school, and Sunday nights weren't much better either. She had that pre-Monday school dread that built from lunchtime on a Sunday and had never left her. So, she decided that Sunday and Monday nights she would be drug free and could then decide if she wanted to go out in the evening with Harley, and vary the time if she wanted to.

Julie-Ann's day was Friday. It fitted in best with what the girls had on after school each day, and because it was the start of the weekend, the girls went to bed later. That way, Julie-Ann could take them out with Lola that bit later, and so fit in with Caroline's timetable. Caroline hadn't wanted to vary the time she went out each evening much. Dog walkers had habits that fitted in with their own lives, and there was very little that changed the routine. Plus, Harley seemed to have a stopwatch, because he knew exactly when it was time for walks. If she was a few moments late putting her shoes on and gathering his lead, he was by the front door reminding her, practically tapping his wrist.

Caroline left her drugs in the poo bin on the other end of the loop to the park, which was where Julie-Ann started the circuit. This was to make sure Julie-Ann had time to leave the money. It was in the last quarter on Caroline's route, unless she did it in reverse. Harley occasionally took her that way, for reasons she couldn't explain, but should she ever try to take him, it was a no-go.

He looked at her as if to say, 'it's my walk, I decide the route,' and with his strength he simply pulled her.

Julie-Ann often hadn't gone far past the bin when Caroline arrived, Lola having planted her feet and determined that five steps were enough for the evening. The girls were always stroking and fussing her and picking her up, so it didn't encourage her to walk very far.

Caroline had no idea who Julie-Ann supplied to. She was born and brought up in a neighbouring town, where a lot of her immediate family still lived. Like most towns, it had a drug problem, but the whole county was notorious for having city crime in a rural area. She assumed that Julie-Ann must have connections through family or friends but had never explored it further. Caroline had worried that out of all of them Julie-Ann might cause some issues. She wouldn't intend to, but she lived on her nerves.

However, she hadn't raised anything, and except for one week, collected the drugs and left the money every week without incident.

That one time, Caroline had gone to the bin, and there was no money.

Odd, she thought. *I wonder if one of the kids is ill, or if Julie-Ann is ill?*

She'd decided to have a further look on her second circuit, just in case Julie-Ann was running late. Even when the others were ill, they still managed to get to the bins. That was the benefit of them being so local, and of course, the dogs still needed taking out.

As she approached for the second time, she'd come across a breathless Julie-Ann. She was just depositing in the bin.

'I'm running a bit behind today,' she said, puffing.

'Oh, anything wrong?' Caroline had asked, a bit concerned.

'No, just Lady Muck decided she didn't want to walk at all today. So, she planted her feet on the wooden floor in the hallway and stuck there as if she'd been glued.'

'She's a proper madam,' said Caroline, tickling Lola under her chin.

Lola eyed her as if to say, 'and your point is what?'

'I've had to run here with her. She's over eleven kilos, you know. It doesn't sound much, but she soon gets heavy.'

'No need for gym membership then,' Caroline had said, and they both laughed.

That left Anthony on a Thursday. 'I'm free any day,' he said to Caroline, rather sadly. 'If you ever need anyone at your place, let me know.'

'I will do,' Caroline said. 'I'm so sorry about what they did to you.'

'Thanks. It's not that I particularly need the money, it's just I haven't made plans, so it's taking some adjustment. This thing with you is for my good-for-nothing nephew. I'm passing them on to him to make some cash to help my sister. I can't afford to support her, and she's supporting him, too. I collect them because I don't want to let you down. He's so unreliable he'll be late to his own funeral.'

'There seems to be a lot like him.'

'Too many. Anyway, it's fine by me, I'm out anyway with my baby, aren't I princess,' he said, bending down to stroke Millie, who looked up at him lovingly.

'She certainly thinks she's a princess, and she looks like one with all her bling and sparkle.' Caroline was referring to her pink collar studded with pink sparkly love hearts that matched her fluffy pink jumper.

'She acts like one, but I guess that's my fault. Good job she doesn't need to find a husband, I don't know who'd want to take her on,' Anthony said, laughing.

'I think Harley would give her a hard pass,' Caroline joked. 'She's far too high maintenance for him.'

As if he totally understood what was being said, Harley looked at Caroline in such a way and woofed that both Anthony and Caroline guffawed.

CHAPTER TWENTY-THREE

THE PRISONS

Robert got straight on his mobile to Richard.

'Alright son,' his dad said when he answered.

'Where the fuck have you been, Dad? I've been trying to get hold of you for weeks and you just vanished off the face of the fucking earth.'

'You watch the way you fucking speak to me, lad,' Richard responded angrily.

'It's been fucking eight weeks, Dad. You said you wanted in on this. It was urgent. You were fucking mad at the way Caroline was doing things and then I can't fucking get hold of you. I've been fucking worried.'

'No need to worry about me. I can take care of myself,' Richard said indignantly.

'That's not fucking fair, Dad. You were in a hole. You said so yerself. I bail you out and then you fucking disappear. I thought something terrible had happened.'

'I had a bit of trouble with the screws, but all sorted now. Nothing to do with you or this,' Richard replied, a little softer now.

'Have you had any letters from Caroline?'

'Yes, why?'

'For fuck's sake, Dad, you could have said. You know how fucking whittled she is about this. I had a link with her today and she says she's sent four fucking letters in. Have you had any? I say I don't know, and she starts fucking stressing as she's sent them guaranteed the next day. As far as we know, none of them have fucking got to you. I didn't dare tell her I hadn't been able to get hold of you. She'd have blown a fucking gasket.'

'You're as neurotic as she is. I've had two letters so far. The first had nothing in it I want, so I didn't think it was worth mentioning. The second I got this morning. It had her poxy £10 wrap in it, so we are good, just like I said we would be. It might take a bit longer in here, but solicitor's mail still gets through just the same. It's been delayed getting to me because of my situation, but it's all good now. Now can you ask the silly cow to send in more next time so that I can start shifting some proper gear and sorting my shit out?'

'I don't think I'll phrase it quite like that, otherwise, I think the chances of you getting anything are fucking zilch,' Robert said, laughing.

'Alright, posh it up a bit for her then,' Richard agreed, laughing too.

'Did the money I organised sort things out for you?' Robert asked.

'For now. But I've got to keep this moving, otherwise I'm in the shit again.'

'Well, now I know you got it OK, I'll sort it with Caroline, but if you need more cash in the meantime, let me know. We are on our way now, Dad. Things are on the up.'

'Thanks, son. Remember when you used to sit on my shoulders and touch the ceiling? You thought you were touching the sky.'

'Yes, I do. I was a bit scared of being up so fucking high, but I loved it. What made you suddenly think of that?'

'You talking of things being on the up. We had some good times, didn't we, Rob?'

'Yes, Dad. We had some real good times,' he replied, almost choking up. 'Shall I ring you tomorrow when I've spoken to Caroline?'

'Sure, speak to you later,' Richard said, hanging up. His voice was catching in his throat, too.

The next morning, Caroline was in reception telling Sandra how well it had gone with Robert.

'You know just how to charm him,' Sandra said, winking at her.

'For now,' Caroline replied. 'But when all said and done, he's a criminal, so I can't trust him completely.'

'Aren't we all?' said Sandra, and they both laughed.

At that moment, they heard the post being delivered through the door.

'Woof, woof,' said Harley, bolting that way. The nice postal worker always put a biscuit through the door for him with the post, and he wanted to make sure no one stole it from him.

'Harley, you've drooled on the letters,' Caroline jokingly chastised him, while he looked at her licking his chops.

She returned to the reception flicking through the letters, and when she saw one, her face fell.

Sandra saw it immediately. 'What's up?'

'We've had a letter back from Manchester prison,' Caroline said, ripping open the plastic.

It had clearly been marked to return to the sender, but someone had opened it. Her heart was pounding in her chest.

'Thank god it isn't the one with the drugs in it,' she said, dropping it on the desk and sinking into the chair.

'Why did they return it?'

Caroline picked it up again and looked at it carefully. 'I really don't know. There's nothing wrong with how we packaged it and it's clearly been opened, and the contents taken out. It's then been done back up and put back in the post, returning it to us.'

'Well, that was a lucky escape.'

'If the other one hasn't been stopped, too. Who knows? It could be with the police as we speak.' Caroline leant back in the chair, feeling faint.

Everything had been under control a week ago, and now, in the blink of an eye, it was one problem after another. At some point, their luck was going to run out, and she had a terrible feeling it was going to be sooner rather than later.

Caroline went back to her desk and took out her burner phone to ring Robert. It was dangerous to ring him, and she had never done it before, always waiting for him to ring her. She didn't know where he would be in the prison, and, of course, the phone ringing at the wrong time could cause him very serious problems. Her too, if anyone ever connected her to the phone, but it was a risk she felt she had to take. She had to know what Robert knew about what was going on with his father and the post up there.

He answered on the first ring. 'Caroline, what the fuck are you doing ringing this phone …'

'I know it's risky, but I have to speak to you.'

'Risky, you ain't fucking kidding. What's up? And it better be good?'

'Well, it's not good is it, if something's up? But I've had a letter come back from Manchester prison. It's one I sent to your dad. It's been opened and the contents have been disturbed, and it's been packaged back up to return to the sender. I don't know why they've done it, but I don't like it. They shouldn't be opening our post at all. I almost had a heart attack that it was the one with the drugs in, but it isn't.'

'Don't worry, he's got that one and another letter of yours.'

'Well, that means there is still another one floating about that he'll either get, will be returned, or might just float off into the ether. Thank god he got the one with the drugs, otherwise it'd be curtains. That's it, Robert. I'm not doing it anymore. No more communication with Manchester. I'm going to send your dad a letter saying having reviewed his case, I cannot assist him. He should seek alternative representation. We've escaped by the skin of our teeth, but this is far too close for comfort. I wasn't happy to start with. I should have followed my gut then.'

'What? So, you've had one letter returned and you want to pull the plug on the entire thing. Don't be so fucking melodramatic, Caroline,' Robert retorted angrily.

'Melodramatic! We've had more lives than the luckiest of cats. What do you not understand? They opened a letter that they shouldn't have done. I don't know why, and I don't care. They are not going to have more letters from me to open. I don't give a shit what your dad says. I'm not putting my neck further on the block than it already is, and that's all there is to it.'

'You can't just make fucking decisions like that. We run this fucking op together. Without me, there wouldn't have fucking been one.' Robert was shouting now.

'And without me, it would have finished the minute your arse got banged up in there. If you had your head on straight you would agree, but for reasons I don't understand, your dad is making you see things in a totally screwed up way. Wake up and smell the coffee, Robert, for fuck's sake. If we don't ditch him, we are going to end up banged up for as long as him. You tried. It didn't work, end of.'

'He's my dad,' Robert shouted.

'I know, but look at the fucking mess he's made of his life. He's not making a fucking mess of mine too,' Caroline shouted back, equally angry.

'Fuck you,' Robert yelled, and tossed the phone across the cell. It smashed against the wall, ending the call.

Robert was raging and started throwing things around.

'Bitch, bitch. Fucking bitch,' he shouted, punching his fists into the wall of his cell below the window, cutting his knuckles in the process. He was too angry to notice they were bleeding.

'What's going on, Rob?' Dave said, coming into his cell, a look of genuine concern on his face.

'Nothing,' Robert said, continuing to punch the wall.

'Funniest nothing I've ever seen,' Dave replied. 'Come on, mate, you're hurting yourself,' he said, moving towards Robert and gently taking hold of his right arm.

Robert flung him off a little more violently than he intended, yelling, 'Fuck off.'

After a few seconds pause he said, 'Sorry, Dave, didn't mean to fling you like that,' turning to face Dave who'd gone backwards several feet and had grabbed hold of the desk to stop himself falling over.

'It's alright,' said Dave, his voice a bit shaky. He was clearly taken aback by the force that Robert had used.

'It's nothing to do with you, mate, and it's nothing you can help with. We're all good, that's all that matters.'

'Of course, I am interested in that,' Dave said, regaining his composure. 'But I care about you, too. If there's something wrong I can help with, I wanna know, and I wanna help.'

'I know you do,' Robert said, his temper waning. 'I know you do. You've helped just by calming me down. I'll be alright, don't worry about me.'

'As long as you are sure?' Dave looked at him quizzically.

'Surey fucking sure,' Robert said, with a weak smile, as Dave backed out of the cell.

'And you just let a fucking woman tell you what to fucking do when it's your business in the fucking first place?' Richard yelled down the phone at Robert when Robert had relayed the conversation he'd had with Caroline.

'I've got no fucking choice, have I?' Robert screamed back. 'Or have you forgotten where the fuck I am? Can't just get out and sort it out myself, can I?'

Robert had replayed the discussion with Caroline in his head when he had calmed down. He could see how risky it was and how, because it was his dad, it had affected his perspective on things. However, he wasn't about to tell Caroline that, and it was his dad. For him, he was prepared to take some risks.

'Get on to the fucking supplier and get him to send them in to me direct then. I need them,' his dad yelled.

'How? The supplier isn't going to be able to get them in Rule 39. They aren't a fucking lawyer.'

'Fuck, fuck, fuck.'

'Hey Dad, don't worry. I've got money stashed. I can help you with whatever you owe. I can cover it, alright? We tried it. It didn't work out like we'd hoped, but I'm doing OK, so whatever you're into, we can sort.'

'Don't need fucking bailing out like a fucking child, Rob. I wanted to be in on this for the money and for something to be doing. You know how fucking brain-numbing this place is, but you're getting out, you've got a future. I've got nothing. My whole fucking existence is pointless.'

'Don't say that, Dad. It's not true. You're my dad, you matter to me.'

'Rob, I've hardly been in your fucking life. I've not done the things with you that dads do. We hardly fucking know each other when it comes down to it.'

'Dad, don't be like this …'

'Nothing more to say,' Richard said, hanging up on Robert.

Robert couldn't believe that his dad had just ended the conversation like that. He tried to ring him back, but the phone was switched off.

'Fuck, fuck, Caroline, what have you done?' he said to himself as he sat down on his bed. He knew he would never persuade Caroline to send anything into his dad after the conversation this morning. He'd never heard her like that, so agitated and angry. She'd made her mind up, and nothing was going to change it. He didn't have a good argument for changing it, anyway. He could see that now he'd thought about it. He understood his dad's disappointment, but it wasn't like it had properly got off the ground, so he couldn't be in that deep to anyone. If he was from his past, which he guessed it was from the debt he'd already paid for him, then he could help.

Why wouldn't his dad let him help? Too proud and stubborn, Robert thought, and then started smiling. *Guess I'm a bit of a chip off the old block.*

Later, having still not been able to get hold of his dad, Robert laid on his bunk with his eyes closed. He gave the appearance of being asleep, but he was far from it. His mind was racing. He was still furious about the way things had gone with the Manchester side of things, and his dad. He vacillated between being furious with Caroline for pulling the plug and understanding why she was so nervous. He had so wanted it to work out with his dad.

He was also very anxious about the way things had ended in the call with his dad. He had tried several times to get hold of him since, but he hadn't been able to. He was fairly certain his dad had destroyed the SIM. Other than writing to him, or trying to get hold of him inter prison, he had no other way of making contact. He didn't want to think about his life without any contact with his dad. Sure, it had been sporadic at best, and not the close relationship that he would have liked. But he thought this was the start of something great between them, a bond, a joint cause. In a nanosecond, his hopes had been dashed.

In the middle of the night, he was still mulling it all over. *He had to do something about it. He couldn't just let this opportunity slip away from him. How to resolve things, though? It was difficult without being able to get through to his dad. He'd just have to persuade Caroline to give it another go. After all, it wasn't the drugs package that had been opened. It might have been opened by mistake and returned to the sender to show the error, to be up front.* He couldn't think of any other reason the prison would have done it and not just given the documents to his dad. *Or was it the case they hadn't made it as far as the prison? Had the post office opened it for some reason and returned it to the sender? Was it not clear who to send it to?* He had all these questions swimming around in his head and no answers. *Caroline hadn't given any explanation as to what she had thought had happened. It was just a straight ending of the Manchester op, without thinking it through and working out all the angles.*

Should he get in touch with her? Get her to see the questions he had and see whether they could work through to some answers together? No, that would never work, he was sure of that. *She hadn't wanted this to go anywhere with his father in the first place. He hadn't understood then, and didn't understand now, why that was the case. Was it because she didn't feel she could control Richard? Well, she needed to understand that she couldn't control him, either. He might be in custody, but it was still his master plan. She was just in temporary charge of things out there. It wasn't for her to make unilateral decisions and dictate terms. She'd got above her station. She might be able to boss her staff around, and Alex. The fucking wet drip would never stand up to her, but he wasn't going to fucking stand for it. She needed to be shown that he was in charge. What he said went, and the Manchester side wasn't dead in the water. He'd make her contact the prison and find out what had happened. They'd work out a way to make sure it didn't happen again. Then he'd contact his dad, let him know it was a go and his dad would be back in touch again. He'd be happy things had returned to the way they should be.* Robert would win his admiration for standing up to Caroline, proving who's the fucking boss.

An idea started forming in his head. He could feel his heart rate quickening again, but this time not in rage, but in anticipation that he was taking charge of the situation. *It would take a bit of working out, and cost him a fair bit of cash. He'd need the right man for the job, but it would be worth it.* He knew exactly who to contact. *It would only take a couple of days to put into action.* He couldn't afford to let the grass grow. *Caroline needed to be taken down a fucking peg or two, and his dad needed to be reassured that all was well.*

In the morning, as Robert lay ruminating over Caroline and formulating a plan, Dave came into his cell.

'You awake, Rob?' he asked.

'Yep,' said Robert, making no effort to move.

'I think we might have a problem,' Dave said. His voice was low, and he sounded worried.

Robert swung his legs to the floor and sat up, looking at Dave. 'What do you mean we might have a fucking problem?'

'I can't be sure, but I have a feeling the last time Louise and I met at the wall we were being followed or watched. I thought it was just me imagination running wild, so I never said anything to anyone. Then I went to meet her at the wall yesterday and I had the same feeling. So, I didn't meet her. I carried on supervising the prisoners in the yard. She obviously wondered what the fuck was going on but didn't call or anything. She was sensible, didn't want to draw unnecessary attention to us. It's made me right paranoid, though. I didn't talk to her in the car about it. She tried, but I shook my head and changed the subject. When we got in the house, she started questioning me about what was going on, why I wouldn't talk to her. I told her about the feelings I've been having, and that I was worried the car was bugged.'

'What the fuck? Do you seriously think that's fucking happening?'

'I don't know, mate, I truly don't. But something's changed. I didn't feel like this before and now I do, and I can't shake it. I can't work out who is making me feel like this. I don't feel it's the same person monitoring me speaking to Louise, or the same person out in the yard. That's why I think it's bugs and AI rather than a person.'

'Are you sure you ain't been watching too many fucking late-night movies, Dave?' Robert asked. 'Not having a spliff of the wacky backy, are you?'

Dave laughed nervously. 'No, mate, I ain't. And when I explained it all to Louise, she said she felt things were a bit strange when I handed the drugs over. She wasn't sure that she was being watched, but she could feel the hairs stand up on the back of her neck and her palms went all sweaty, which she hadn't had before. I think I put the fear of God into her when I told her how I'd been feeling. I don't think it's in me imagination though, we both felt the same. Something's off.'

'Do you think that girl Louise is supplying to has fucking dropped us in it?' Robert hissed.

'No. Louise definitely doesn't think so and I have to trust her judgement. She says Tasha is solid and nothing about her has changed. No, I don't think that's where it's coming from. I'm not even sure it's got anything to do with us as such. Maybe everyone feels they are being watched more, but no one's mentioned it and I don't want to raise it.'

'No, don't. If you are being watched, that'll be a fucking red flag.'

'Exactly. I overheard my boss talking about a government inspection, so it might be to do with that. I'm hoping so.'

'Ahhhhh,' Robert said. 'Why didn't you fucking mention that before? It's got to be that. This shit hole got a fucking terrible review last time. It was all over the media. Not that anything fucking changed. It never does. I expect they are shitting it. They are going to get a worse review this time, cos things have definitely got fucking worse since I was last in here. When is it, do you know?'

'I think it's in about a month. We haven't been told yet. Nothing unusual in that either. We usually find out that things are changing from the bloody telly.'

'What do you want to do? How do you want to play it?' Robert enquired.

'I think we've got to stop it now. I don't want to, but as Louise said, it's too dangerous. We can't risk getting caught and going to prison. That would finish Dad off. We've earned a nice bit for him, thanks to you. I don't want it to end, because I don't know what we are going to do for him long term, but I just can't run the risk. I think it's time to quit while we are ahead.'

Robert's heart sank. *Another part of the op going fucking*

sideways, he thought to himself, boiling with fury.

He clenched his fists. 'We'll put it on hold for now,' he said grimly. 'You find out when this fucking inspection is. After that, we start up again. This isn't a job where you can just give fucking notice, Dave. We are in business with people who call the fucking shots, they don't take them. We owe them money. There will be drugs in the pipeline to us that need paying for. You can't just say that's it, mate, you've fucking had enough.'

Dave could see that Robert was about to lose it. However, he continued telling Robert that he was very scared and so was Louise. They'd taken the risks they were prepared to take, but this feeling had frightened both of them to death. They hadn't slept a wink last night and didn't want to be like that for the rest of their careers. Dave felt sure one of them would have a heart attack or nervous breakdown, he explained.

'We are grateful to you, Robert, for making us a part of it,' he continued, trying to justify their position and get Robert's approval. 'But surely everyone has to accept the goalposts move. We found ways to do this because we know the system and found the loopholes. Those are closing. It's too dangerous. No one wants those sorts of risks being taken, surely?'

'These people don't give a fucking shit about the likes of you and me. They care about their product being moved and the dough. They expect us to work round the fucking problems, come up with fucking solutions. We wait till this inspection. Then things'll go back to normal as they always do and then we start up again. This is not a fucking negotiation, Dave. It's not a fucking choice. You have no fucking power. If you don't do as you are fucking told when you are fucking told, I'll just put those that need to know in touch with you. Then you'll see what fucking choices you have.'

'Rob, mate, come on,' Dave pleaded.

'I warned you, Dave. I'm no fucking mate of yours. There are no mates in this game. You wanted in, you're fucking in. You don't get to pick when you fucking get out. I'm giving you the best you are going to get, a pause, so you don't get caught. That's it. We got people to answer to. We answer and provide what we are supposed to. Or your fucking throat gets cut. Welcome to the fucking real world. Now fuck off before I do something you'll fucking regret.' With that, Robert got off his bunk and came towards Dave. He could tell that his tone and attitude frightened Dave, and he meant to. His demeanour was cold and threatening. Dave went to say something but thought better of it and left.

Robert was fuming when Dave left. *Who the fuck does he think he is?* he yelled inwardly. *Thinks he can call the shots as and when it suits him. Get his cash, then fuck off as if nothing ever happened. I should never have brought Caroline or Dave, or any of them, into this. They don't understand the fucking rules. They just think they can pick and choose when to get involved as and when it fucking suits them. Well, they fucking can't.*

His burner ringing interrupted his internal rant. He didn't recognise the number, but that wasn't out of the ordinary. The people who had access to his number were always changing theirs. The risky business they were involved in meant keeping the same number for too long on the outside could be dangerous.

'Hello,' he said gruffly.

'What the fuck do you think you're playing at?' was the response down the phone. It wasn't a voice he recognised. It was deep and angry.

'Who the fuck is this?' Robert asked, angry at the way the voice was speaking to him.

'Someone who shouldn't be having to make this fucking phone call. You need to get your side of things under fucking control.'

'What the fuck are you talking about?'

'Some packages coming from the court have been light, and it seems to have been going on for some time.'

'What do you mean, they've been light? My guys are reliable. They weigh it, they cut it, they weigh it again. No way they are fucking skimming,' Robert said defensively.

'Might not be them guys,' the voice growled back. 'Seems to be only the drugs coming from the Crown Court. It's taken a while to look into this, which I fucking shouldn't have to. Your man there seems to have a fucking side op.'

'What the fuck? Alex, you fucking prick,' Robert said.

'Alex, that his fucking name?'

'Yes. He's a cocky twat, but I never thought he'd be fucking stupid enough to try something like this. It won't happen again. I'll fucking sort this out once and for all.'

'You fucking better had, and now, else fucking Alex is going to get a visit and he ain't going to fucking like it.'

'Consider it sorted.'

'It fucking better be.'

Robert was puce with rage. *What the fuck is going on?* he asked himself. *Caroline is controlling things and not doing what she's told. Alex seems to have gone off script and he ain't fucking clever enough to be doing that.*

He wondered if Caroline was involved. *It wouldn't surprise me,* he thought. *She certainly ain't the person she used to be. The power has gone to her fucking head.*

He decided that even though Caroline had chosen Alex as a business partner, she would not have set up a sideline with him, given he was Mr Unreliable. They were both going off script independently. Caroline trying to control things and drop the Manchester part. Alex setting up his own business. *How fucking dare he?* He could feel his pulse throbbing in his temples. He was so mad. *Then Dave trying to stop his part.* He could see the whole thing starting to collapse around him. He had to get control of the situation, and fast. *Caroline was the key to the money on the outside.* He had to get her in line and get her to get everyone else in line. *No more Mr Nice Guy. It was time to remind her who she was dealing with.*

CHAPTER TWENTY-FOUR

THE ATTACK

Caroline parked in the car park and walked towards the office. She had overslept and so was later than she wanted to be. It was such a rarity for her. She always woke before the alarm clock, feeling as if she'd only been asleep for twenty minutes. On her way to work, she'd dropped Harley at doggy daycare. He went every Friday. It was his treat. He loved the staff and enjoyed the ball games. There were couches to lounge on, treats to be had, and paddling pools to play in when the weather was warm. He preferred people to dogs, but Caroline knew he had quite a doggy following, including a female Alsatian he'd taken a particular shine too. Today was bath day too, which he enjoyed.

'Have a fabulous day at the spa, Harley,' she said when she dropped him off. 'Mummy will go to work and earn the pennies to pay for it.'

He looked at her as if to say, 'Alright. You do what you need to do. I'll be fine here,' and went in without so much as a backwards glance.

It wasn't a particularly bright day, but it wasn't cold, Caroline thought, as she climbed the two steps to the office door and searched in her handbag for the key. She chastised herself regularly for not putting it in a particular pocket in her bag. Then she wouldn't have this constant searching, which she did every day. As she was rummaging about, she heard a voice behind her, and felt something in the small of her back.

'Don't say a fucking word. Don't make a sound, otherwise you're fucking dead.'

Caroline froze. She didn't know what to do. Her legs started to shake, and her heart was pounding as if it was going to burst right through her chest.

'Open the door, like normal,' the cold voice instructed.

Caroline fumbled through her bag, trying to find the key.

'Hurry the fuck up,' the icy voice growled. Although there was an accent, her brain was too scrambled to place it.

Caroline found the key and tried to put it in the lock, but her hands were shaking so much she had to use both of them to steady the key enough to connect it with the lock. She turned it and opened the door. The alarm sounded, and she went into the corridor, the man right behind her. She could feel his hot breath on the back of her neck, making the hairs on it stand up on end. He jabbed her in the back with whatever he held there, Caroline couldn't tell through her jacket. She took a deep breath as she tried to steady her hands to tap the small buttons on the alarm keypad. She got it wrong the first time, and it carried on beeping.

'Turn the fucking thing off. You ain't going to get any help by letting the alarm ring out, you stupid bitch. You'll be on the floor before your brain realises it.' The threat made her blood run cold.

Somehow, and Caroline didn't know how, she managed to turn the alarm off. 'What now?' she stuttered.

'Your office. Now,' he instructed, pushing her as she turned to the right, went through reception, and into her office. He pushed her roughly towards the desk, releasing her from his immediate grasp. Caroline turned round and gasped. Facing her was a man in his forties. He was clean shaven and had dark close-cropped hair. He was very muscly and well over six feet tall. Caroline was no match physically for him. Not that it mattered what he looked like. The gun in his hand gave him the advantage of this situation.

'What do you want?' Caroline asked, sounding far braver than she felt. She was leaning on the edge of her desk to steady herself, fearing she would fall to the floor without it. Her legs were so weak she could barely feel them.

'It's not what I want, it's what you need to do. Listen carefully, because you are only going to get this message once. The next time, you won't even know about the bullet that kills you. Or maybe we shoot you after we've shot your beloved dog,' he said, smiling menacingly at her. 'I was hoping he'd be here today. Send the drugs to Richard. Stop trying to control things you are not in control of. Do your bit. Play your fucking part, and nothing will happen. Pull another fucking stunt like you have, or refuse in any way, and it's over …' he paused. 'For you. Got it?'

Caroline opened her mouth and closed it again. Her mouth felt so dry, her tongue was sticking to the roof of it. His eyes were fixed on hers. She could feel herself sweating as if she had a fever. A river running down her back.

'It's too dangerous. We almost got caught. I can't run that risk. We'll all end up in prison,' she whispered, but stammering.

'If you don't fucking do it, you are going to end up in your casket. So, I think the odds have suddenly improved, don't you?' As he said this, he pistol-whipped her to the left side of her head, causing her to fall in a state of unconsciousness to the floor.

Caroline didn't know how long she passed out for, but when she came round, she was lying on her right-hand side, parallel to her desk. The man was leaning over her. He was staring directly into her eyes, his face practically touching hers.

'And get your fucking business partner under control. Skimming on the side ain't a fucking option. He was warned from the start. He won't be warned again.'

'What are you talking about?' Caroline asked, her voice barely audible and raspy.

'You fucking know and remember snitches get stitches, made into bitches and put into ditches,' he snarled, before cracking her on the side of the head again, sending her back into unconsciousness.

'Caroline, Caroline!' Alex shouted, when he came into the office and saw her lying on the floor. 'What the fuck has happened?'

He could see that she was bleeding heavily from the left side of her head. He felt for a pulse, not sure where in her neck he was supposed to find it, but eventually felt it. When he looked closely, he could see her chest rising and falling as she was breathing, but it was very shallow and silent. He shook her but didn't get a reaction out of her.

'Fuck, fuck,' he repeated, while hurrying to the kitchen to find some kitchen towel to hold against her cut to stem the blood.

By the time he returned, Sandra came in through the front door. She followed Alex into the office and gasped. 'What the bloody hell has happened here?'

'I don't know, I only just got here myself and she was like this,' Alex said, clearly panicking. Sandra took the kitchen towel off him and held it to Caroline's head.

'Is she breathing?' she asked Alex anxiously.

'Yes,' he said confidently. 'But I couldn't get a response from her.'

'Caroline, Caroline,' Sandra called, gently shaking her. 'Can you hear me?'

Caroline stirred slowly. She tried to open her eyes and immediately shut them again. 'Head hurts,' she said, her voice very weak.

'Thank God you are still with us,' Sandra exclaimed. 'We need to ring an ambulance. That wound needs stitching, and you'll have a nasty concussion, at the very least.'

'No ambulance,' Caroline whispered.

'Caroline, you need one. You are badly hurt,' Sandra said, as she pulled out her mobile from her handbag.

'Sandra, no ambulance,' Caroline said quietly, but firmly. 'That will alert the police, and we can't have that. Alex can get me up and run me to the hospital. I don't have to tell them what happened, but they have to treat me. I'll get the stitches and rest my head.'

Caroline looked at Sandra, making it clear that this was not negotiable, and then shut her eyes again. The light was increasing the intensity of the headache she already had. It felt like a pneumatic drill was banging away inside her brain.

'Can you stand?' Alex asked Caroline uncertainly.

'Only one way to find out,' she said, trying to lift herself up with her right arm. She immediately fell to the floor, groaning.

'What's the matter?' he asked, looking very worried.

'I feel really sick and dizzy. My head is pounding, and it's worse when I try to open my eyes.'

'This is extremely dangerous,' Sandra said. 'You need to be carefully moved by someone who knows what they are doing, and that definitely isn't Alex. He breaks or drops everything he touches, and you are damaged enough.'

'Thanks for the vote of confidence, Sandra,' Alex huffed, knowing she was right.

'You can't keep the wheels on your trolley,' Sandra retorted. 'Caroline's special goods, and she needs handling delicately. That word is not in your vocabulary, so don't pretend to me for one moment it is.'

At that moment, the front door opened again, and in walked Ian and Seb. They'd reached the car park at the same time and walked to the office together. Their arrival saved any more squabbling.

'What in god's name has happened to you, Caroline?' Ian shouted, rushing past Sandra and Alex to kneel in front of her.

'I've been pistol-whipped,' Caroline said feebly. She felt weak, and she was shaking from head to foot.

'You've been fucking what?' Ian said with a look of incredulity on his face.

Sandra's mouth dropped open too, and Alex's eyes were as wide and round as saucers, as they each took in what Caroline said. They'd been so busy trying to treat her, they hadn't got round to what had happened to her.

'Who and why?' Alex asked.

'I don't know who,' Caroline explained. 'I didn't recognise him. The why appears to be because I won't send drugs into Manchester prison to Richard.'

'But you can't,' Sandra said immediately. 'The post got opened. It's too risky. Even an idiot can see that.'

'Clearly not,' Caroline whispered. 'I said it was too dangerous. We might get caught. I was told the alternative would be a bullet in my back and a resting place in my casket.'

'He said that to you?' Seb questioned. Caroline could see he felt so sorry for her. They all understood how frightening it had been for her. She felt quite calm. She wondered if she might be in shock.

'Yes, he did. After he threatened to hurt Harley.'

'What a nasty piece of work,' Sandra said angrily. Caroline knew she'd be as cross about the threat to Harley as she would be to Caroline herself, probably more so.

'How would Richard know about Harley?' Ian questioned.

'I don't know,' Caroline replied. 'Unless Robert has mentioned him in one of their conversations, which is very possible. He's always taking the mick out of how much I love Harley, and how I treat him like a person. So, when he's been bitching about me, he might have mentioned it.'

'So, do you think Richard has put a hit out on you then?' Alex said, wringing his hands.

'It looks very much like it,' Caroline groaned, still lying on the floor with her eyes closed. The pain was excruciating.

Ian looked from Alex to Sandra to Seb. They were all looking at each other in disbelief. All struggling to believe what they had just heard. It was like something out of a movie, and they didn't like the script.

'You need looking at, Caroline,' Ian said, taking control of the situation.

Sandra was still holding the large wad of kitchen towel to

Caroline's head. She removed it and the bleeding had slowed down. But the cut was large and would need stitching, Ian told Caroline. He added he worried about the concussion. That wasn't something to be messed about with, either.

'I know,' said Caroline. 'We were just talking about taking me to the hospital when you arrived. We can't call an ambulance. I'm too worried they will alert the police, or an officer will notice from across the road. They don't usually see anything we think they ought to, but it'll be sod's law on this occasion they come over here. I know there's nothing lying around to incriminate us, but if they think I've been attacked and don't want to do anything about it, they'll get suspicious. We really don't want that aggravation in our lives. We've got more than enough.' Caroline spoke as firmly as she could, the workforce of drills and heavy machinery still banging away relentlessly in her skull.

'I'll take you,' Ian said immediately. 'I'll get my car and pull it down the alley at the back. Then we'll take you out through the back garden, away from any potentially prying eyes. There's enough of us to help you. Seb can come with me to help get you out the other end.'

'I love a man with a plan,' Caroline smiled weakly.

Ian rushed off and got his car. Somehow, the four of them managed to pick her up off the floor, and then Ian carried her to the passenger seat of his car. On more than one occasion, Caroline felt as if she was going to pass out again, but she willed herself to stay with it. Ian and Seb kept her talking the whole way to the hospital, which took about twenty-five minutes with the traffic. Ian was effing and jeffing every time they arrived at a red light. Caroline knew her voice was getting weaker; she was struggling to stay awake. Seb craned his neck from the passenger seat to keep an eye on her and kept telling her to open her eyes. She knew he had her best interests at heart, but it hurt so much to open them. It was impossible to keep them open. They felt so heavy, and she felt so tired.

Finally, they arrived, and Ian pulled up right to the front door, in a disabled space. He shot out of the driver's side and flung open the back door. Seb was by his side instantly.

'Never seen you move so fast,' Caroline said, trying to smile.

It was a standing joke in the office that, although Seb was tall and lanky, he moved at the speed of a very slow snail.

'Look what it takes to make me move,' he replied. 'Bit dramatic, even you must agree,' he said, grinning at her.

'And it might have made him move quick, but I feel like I'm having a heart attack. So, let's not bother with an action replay,' Ian retorted.

He sent Seb off to find a wheelchair. Caroline protested, but he was hearing none of it. He told her she was so weak he feared she'd be out cold in the car park the minute they tried to move her. Caroline had to concede he was right. It took the pair of them to manhandle her out of the back of the car and into the wheelchair. Fortunately, it wasn't as rammed in A & E as it had been when she'd been on previous occasions with her mum, who'd been very poorly. She was sent off for a head X-ray and MRI scan. When it was determined she was just going to have a very nasty headache for a few days, she was stitched up and sent home. Caroline lied, telling them she had someone at home, as with a concussion the doctor told her it was dangerous for her to be left alone, in case the sleep became deeper than that.

'Right, straight home it is then,' Ian said, helping her back into the car.

'No, back to the office,' she said immediately.

The painkillers she'd been given were taking the edge off. The jackhammers and pneumatic drills had now become chainsaws. Still very painful, but far more tolerable.

'You have got to be joking?' Ian was incredulous.

'No, I'm not. I can't be left on my own for twenty-four hours. I'm going to ring my friend and see if she can come and stay over this evening. But today you lot can keep an eye on me. We've also got to work out what we are going to do about what's happened. I don't think I'm going to get another gun in my back today, but it won't be long if I don't send the stuff into Manchester. I've got no intention of doing that. We'll all be in prison, so it's a nonstarter.'

'What are we going to do, then?' asked Seb.

'I don't know. I need to think this through. We all do. Who do we think sent this thug? Richard or Robert, or both?'

'I think Robert genuinely likes you, Caroline. You've supported him most of his life. Far more than anyone else. Do you seriously think he would do this to you?' Ian questioned.

'After what I experienced this morning, I'd believe it if you told me it was a Martian sent from outer space. It seems that unbelievable.'

'What in god's name are you doing here?' Sandra exclaimed, as Caroline walked, assisted by Seb, through the door to reception. Ian was parking the car.

'Don't even start,' said Seb emphatically. 'Ian and I have already had that battle with her and lost.'

'I'm fine. The X-ray and MRI say so. I've got a concussion and I've been nicely patchworked,' Caroline said, trying to play it down.

'And she told them she had someone at home to look after her because she cannot be left on her own for twenty-four hours,' interjected Seb.

'Alright, grass,' Caroline said, smiling.

'Well, that was just downright naughty, Caroline,' Sandra said, motherly but sternly. 'And dangerous. You are not looking after yourself properly. Not only is there a madman threatening to kill you, but you might inadvertently kill yourself by not waking up. What were you thinking of?'

'Don't panic. I've come back here so I can think things through and discuss with every one of you what you think, and what we should do. We need to have a plan to deal with this. I'll get a friend to stay overnight. I'll be fine.'

'You will be,' Sandra said firmly, 'because I'm staying with you. No ifs or buts or I'm phoning that hospital and telling them you are going to be on your own. Otherwise, you'll say you've got a friend and you won't have. I know you.'

'Yes mum,' Caroline said, knowing when to quit. This was a battle she wasn't going to win. 'You only want to make sure that Harley is properly looked after.'

'Well, of course,' Sandra said, as if that was obvious. 'What sort of aunty would I be if he wasn't in the forefront of my mind all the time? I have to say I am relieved he was at daycare. I don't know how he would have reacted, but I certainly think he would have tried to protect you. In fact, I know he would, and he'd have got hurt, or worse.'

'I know. I thought the same. That's why I think it's Robert who's responsible. He knows Harley goes to daycare on a Friday. I can't think he's passed that information on to Richard. Robert knows the fear of hurting Harley would get me to do more than if he was here and actually got hurt. It'd be too late then to bully me.'

'It might have just been luck,' Ian said, joining the conversation. 'Given the threat he made about Harley, he might have just taken him out if he'd caused a problem.'

'Well, that doesn't bear thinking about,' said Caroline, shuddering. 'Now, can someone make me a cup of tea? Let's see if we can round up Alex, Michael and William on a conference call of some sort to discuss what we are going to do. It's lunchtime, so we stand a chance of getting hold of them, well William at least.'

Caroline, Sandra, Ian and Seb sat in Caroline's room. Caroline leant back in her chair with her eyes closed. She was feeling much better than she had, but the light still bothered her. Her mobile was on loudspeaker on the desk. Patched into the call were William and Michael, tucked away safely in William's car for privacy, and using his mobile, of course, and Alex, who was alone in the robing room in the Crown Court.

'How are you, Caroline?' Michael asked straight away, clearly very worried. 'We've been so concerned about you.'

'I'm better than I was. Thanks, Michael,' Caroline informed him.

'From what I've heard, that's not saying a great deal,' said William. 'You must have felt absolutely terrified. I think Alex thought you were dead when he first found you.'

'I did,' said Alex gravely. 'I'm still shaking from it. I have never been so scared in my life as I was finding you like that.'

'I know. I was petrified at the time,' said Caroline quietly. 'But I think the shock is setting in now. I feel cold and I'm shivering. What we must decide is how we are going to deal with this.'

'It sounds to me like we are damned if we do and damned if we don't,' said William seriously. 'It's a no-win situation, Hobson's choice. If we send the drugs into Manchester, there's a high chance we'll get caught. It's worse now, because we don't appear able to trust Richard, so the risk is higher. Or you get seriously hurt, or worse.'

'Or Harley,' interrupted Sandra.

'Which, of course, would be worse,' said Caroline, smiling, and knowing that in some ways Sandra meant it like that. But then it would be worse for Caroline if something happened to her beloved boy.

'Who do you think set it up, Caroline?' asked Michael. Michael was always a rational thinker. He was clearly as concerned as the others, but able to keep a more level-headed approach. Everyone else was obviously anxious and agitated. He was more composed.

'My initial thought was Richard. From what Robert let slip, he is clearly indebted to some dangerous people, as well as wanting to get involved in a bit of drama and excitement in his life. He's serving life, so he has nothing to lose, and that always makes someone a very loose cannon. But part of me, my gut feeling if you like, thinks it's Robert. I know he and I go back a long way, but when all is said and done, he's a career criminal. He'll throw anyone under the bus he needs to in order to save his own skin. Also, his dad has a hold over him. It's almost like Robert is trying to make up for lost time, to create a relationship between them that has never been there. I can't imagine Richard was at all happy with my decision, and I did think it was odd he didn't contact me directly. After all, in the database, he's a legitimate client. Then I thought maybe he was leaving it to Robert to handle. Robert hasn't spoken to me since the conversation when I told him I wasn't sending the drugs to his dad. He was livid. That was a few days ago now, and I haven't been able to get hold of him on his burner since. It's constantly off.'

'Hang on a minute,' she continued. 'I'm such an idiot. I've got the ring doorbell footage on my phone. You should be able to see me and him at the door. Let me have a look. Yes, here it is. I'll take a screenshot of him. You can see his face quite clearly. He had an accent that I still can't quite place. Since the attack I've been racking my brains, but I don't think I recognise him. It all happened so quickly and was so terrifying.'

Caroline forwarded the screenshot to Alex and William, and brought it up clearly on her phone so that those in the office could see it.

Everyone leaned over, looking intently at the picture.

'I know him,' Ian said. 'What the fuck is his name?'

Caroline could see him frantically scrambling through his brain, trying to make the connection.

'How do you know him?' Alex enquired. 'He doesn't look familiar to me.'

'He does to me,' added Michael. 'I think I dealt with him at the police station a few months ago. He was arrested for a nasty set of offences if I am remembering it rightly. It was alleged he had shot through the front door of a rival drug dealer with a sawn-off shotgun. Worse still, he'd got the wrong house, because it was a young woman and her baby who lived there alone. I imagine they were petrified. Now what's his name?'

'What a nasty piece of work he is,' William said, echoing everyone's thoughts.

'That's right,' Ian said, rubbing his chin. 'I had him after that. He'd found the right house and was being investigated for GBH, waterboarding. Of course, they were never going to make that stick. They won't get any statements to support the allegation.'

'So, we are dealing with someone truly dangerous who could carry out their threat to Caroline, then?' Sandra said gravely.

'Sadly, yes, we definitely are, and I've just remembered his name, Paul Chamberlain.'

'Ah yes,' Caroline said. 'I remember you both telling me about him. Are you both certain it's him?'

'Absolutely,' both Ian and Michael said in unison.

'What do we know about him, then?' Alex asked, and she could hear him tapping away on his laptop. 'He's local, originally from Wolverhampton, so that might be the accent you heard, Caroline?'

'Yes, I think so. Now thinking about it, it was Brummie but not, if you know what I mean.'

'Well, if he's local surely that means that Robert instigated it. At least the instruction of him. Richard might have put him up to it, but what are the chances of him knowing someone in the area? He didn't come back here, did he, after he got out for the murder? He didn't connect much with Robert at that time. It would be one hell of a coincidence if he just happened to know someone here with the right credentials to do something like this from this area. My money's on Robert, I'm afraid,' William reasoned logically, ever the seasoned lawyer.

'Why threaten to kill me, though? If he kills me, the operation ends. He stands to lose a lot. His old man doesn't.'

'Who's saying he's thought it through like that, with logic? You've said yourself how much of a hothead he can be at times. Also, he probably thinks you'll go through with it because you'll be too frightened. He doesn't think you will risk your life by refusing to do it,' William continued pragmatically.

'Well, he doesn't know me very well, does he?' Caroline said matter-of-factly.

'He thought he'd frighten you, and you'd just do it. He hasn't got the intellect to follow things through like we just have,' Michael agreed.

'The question is now, what do we do about all of this? Do we confront Robert?' Ian asked.

'I don't think we have a choice,' Caroline said. 'It's going to come to a head one way or another. I'm not sending the drugs to Manchester. He's going to find out about it. So, either I front it out with him, or I wait for the bullet to come. I have to try to reason with him, make him see sense.'

'Good luck with that,' Ian said, shaking his head. 'I think reasoning, logic and common sense went out the window when he thought it was a good idea to hire a hitman on the person running the op for him.'

'And even if you can,' Sandra interjected, 'you can never trust him again. This whole thing is over.'

'Oh yes, it's over alright. I just have to make sure I escape with my life intact.'

'What's stopping him coming after you when you pull the plug on the op, though?' Seb asked. 'Surely he's going to be pissed about that?'

'Nothing,' Caroline said, shrugging her shoulders. Then she stopped. 'Oh, hang on a minute, I might have the answer there.' She flipped her phone to another app.

'What are you doing?' Alex asked.

'My brain feels like scrambled egg, so I forgot I installed a camera to watch the safe.'

'What? How come I didn't know about it?' Alex was indignant.

'I didn't deliberately keep it from you, or from anyone,' Caroline said sincerely. 'When Robert was out and helping us with the drugs and money in the office, he helped me put them in the safe. He was always watching me, and I thought he was trying to see the combination. I changed it regularly, but I suppose I was worried he was a proper criminal at heart, different to us, and would screw us over if he felt like it. It wouldn't take much to break in here. So, I installed the camera. I've never needed to look at the recordings since I did it. To be honest, I'd forgotten all about it.'

While she was explaining this, she had found the app and loaded the feed from the time the gunman forced her into the office. It was difficult to watch, but all of them in the room could see what took place. The others gasped when Caroline was hit, and Alex, William and Michael listened.

'I feel sick,' said Sandra as the colour drained from her face.

'Jesus, he absolutely belted you,' Ian said, horrified.

'That is the worst thing I have ever seen,' Seb said quietly, his eyes wide with disbelief.

There was silence from the others at the end of the phone as they digested what their colleagues were watching in the office.

'OK, there's no point dwelling on it. We've got to keep moving forward,' Caroline said rationally.

It was the only way she could cope. Watching it again had been more horrifying than experiencing it the first time. It only reinforced to her that if she did not get out ahead of this, her life was in serious danger.

'I agree it's Robert who has set this up,' she continued, setting out her point of view. 'Too much of a coincidence for Richard to have independently found someone local. He'd use his own contacts. So, either they are in it together or Robert has done it to prove himself to his dad. Either way, his dad has nothing to lose, so we have no way in there. Robert has a lot to lose. He's made a lot of money. Enough for this all to stop and to live happily ever after. He's not serving a long sentence, and we all agree he hasn't thought this through. He has no idea about this camera. He knows about the ring doorbell, but that shows a face, not an offence. He knows we'd never go to the police anyway if it required us to give any form of account or explanation.'

'How does it help, though?' Ian asked. 'Like you say, we can hardly go to the police.'

'We don't need to. This footage seals his fate. He hasn't banked on us investigating. I don't go to court and the police station much these days. I don't see the clients. He has counted on me not recognising him, which I didn't. Without this footage, what am I going to do even if I do? Nothing. I'd have to give evidence, and he knows I can't do that. With this, though, showing what happened, and you guys being able to identify him, we track down this client. We show him this footage and tell him if he confirms who sent him, that'll be the end of it for him. He'll tell us for sure. Otherwise, that footage finds its way to the police. I don't have to make a statement. It's as clear as day and he'll be serving a double-figure sentence. I'm sure he'll confirm it's Robert. Then I will deal with Robert. I'll go in and see him in prison.'

'What if he won't see you? He'll probably refuse to come to the visit,' Michael questioned.

'Yes,' Caroline mused. 'I hadn't thought of that. I know, I'll ask Phillip to come with me. I'll get him to let Robert know he needs to come and see him, and he can book me on to the visit, too. That way, we know Robert will keep the visit. When there's his money involved, he'll be there.'

'OK,' said Alex. 'I think this is as good a plan as we have. Do we all agree?'

'Yes,' everyone said in unison.

'It had better work,' Sandra said grimly. 'I don't like scary movies, and this is worse than most I've seen.'

'It'll work,' Ian said firmly. 'It has to.'

They agreed Ian, Seb and Michael would pay Mr Paul Chamberlain a visit. Alex said he didn't trust himself not to lose it completely, and William needed to sort the afternoon court. Caroline said it didn't need to be done immediately, but everyone disagreed. They all had adrenaline coursing through their veins because of what had happened and needed to do something proactive about the situation. Ian and Michael could identify him. Seb was a bit of extra muscle, and Michael was the voice of calm and reason to prevent the situation from getting out of hand. He had promised Caroline he would do his best to keep the other two under control, although Caroline conceded it was one hell of a task.

Ian knocked loudly on the front door.

'That's a police officer's knock if ever I heard one,' Michael said, grinning.

The front door opened, and a young woman in her twenties answered it. She was dressed in a onesie. They all looked at each other and it was obvious they shared the same thought, *a terrible outfit for this time of day*. She was probably one of the people who wore it in the supermarket. She had sliders on her feet.

'Is Paul in please? Michael asked pleasantly.

'Who wants to know?' she replied curtly.

'He'll want to know otherwise the next knock will be from the cops,' Ian said harshly.

'Paul, there are some men here for you. Come and sort your shit out!' she yelled, and went back into the house, leaving them on the doorstep.

Ian took that as an invitation to come in, and he did just that. He stood in the hallway, followed by Seb. Michael waited on the doorstep.

'Ever the gentleman, such manners,' Ian commented. Michael smiled at him.

It was a small hallway with the stairs to the right and a door into the rest of the house directly in front. It needed a good clean and a lick of paint, and the stair carpet had seen better days. It was very worn in places. They could hear the sounds of young children squabbling from within the house, and the female's voice shouting expletives at them to be quiet.

They then heard footsteps from upstairs, and Paul came bounding down the stairs. He looked shocked to see Ian in his hallway.

'Alright, Ian,' he said nervously. 'What you doing here? Didn't think legal aid stretched to home visits,' he said, laughing nervously.

'It doesn't,' Ian responded sharply. 'But you know me. I'll always go the extra mile for the client, and I've some footage I couldn't wait to show you.'

With that, he thrust his mobile towards Paul's face, the footage playing on it. He wished it was his fist cracking into Paul's skull instead.

Paul watched without saying a word. His eyes got wider and wider as he watched the footage and the full implication of what it meant to him became clear.

'What the fuck?' he exclaimed.

'Exactly,' shouted Ian. 'What the fuck do you think you are doing, beating up my boss and threatening her with a gun?'

He couldn't help himself. He grabbed hold of Paul's shirt at the front, pulling him closer, until their noses were almost touching.

'If I'd had my fucking way, you'd be drinking your food for the rest of your days through a fucking straw. But Caroline, she's a lady, and she won't hear of such things unless we absolutely need to.'

Spittle was landing on Paul's face. He was clearly frightened as Ian continued to eyeball him.

'Not so brave now, are you?' Ian spat at him.

'What do you want?' Paul asked. 'I've a missus and two kids. I can't go to prison,' he whined.

'I think you should have fucking thought of that before you did this,' Seb answered him venomously.

'Now, now,' said Michael calmly, moving from the step into the already crowded hallway. 'There's always a deal to be cut.'

'Oh, hi, Michael, didn't see you there,' Paul said thankfully. He was obviously pleased to see someone who he didn't think was going to try to snap his neck. 'What can I do?'

'Well,' Michael continued in his calm, level voice. 'If you tell us who ordered this, that'll be the end of it.'

'I-I-I can't do that,' he stammered.

'Well, either you do, or this goes straight to the cops,' Seb threatened. 'I don't give a shit either way. In fact, I'd quite like you to go to prison. Caroline's well liked and well known. You'll have to watch your back the whole time, and it'll be a long fucking time.'

Ian increased the grip on the front of Paul's top. Paul was in no doubt Ian was struggling to control his temper.

'I won't have to give a statement, will I?'

'No. I just need to record you confirming who it is. The footage and the recording will never find their way to the police if you do that. It's a very good deal for you.'

'Too fucking good. It's a no brainer,' Seb added.

'OK, OK, but let go of me. You're hurting.'

'Not as much as I'd like you to, or as much as you fucking deserve,' Ian said, releasing him so violently he stumbled back onto the stairs.

Ian switched his phone to the recording app and said, 'Speak.'

'It was Robert Jones. He called me and told me exactly what to do and what to say. I don't know why I had to do what I did, but I owe him, so I couldn't get out of it. Please tell Caroline I didn't want to. I've nothing against her. You guys have been good to me, but I didn't have a choice.'

'There's always a choice,' Ian said firmly, after the recording had finished. 'You made yours and it was a bad one. We don't want to hear your fucking name again. We don't want to see you, and if you ever go near Caroline or any one of us …'

'I won't, I swear,' Paul whimpered.

Ian then punched him hard in the face. 'That's from Sandra for threatening Harley,' he said, as they all left.

Caroline had to laugh when they returned to the office and told the story. In spite of the seriousness of it all, it was funny, especially the punch on behalf of Harley.

'Did you really say that about Sandra and Harley?' Caroline said.

'Too bloody right he did,' she replied. 'No one threatens our boy.'

Three days later, Phillip and Caroline drove to the prison to see Robert. Phillip had insisted that he pick Caroline up and drive her when she contacted him to tell him what had happened. He was horrified. Of course, Robert was a career criminal. They all knew that. But he believed that there was honour among thieves, and Robert would not turn on one of his own team, and especially Caroline.

'I am still struggling to believe it,' he told Caroline, as he drove his Porsche two-seater sports car along the single lane carriageway from her office to the prison.

Caroline didn't know much about cars, but she knew that this one was lovely. It was navy blue and looked sophisticated. Exactly the sort of vehicle she imagined Phillip to own.

'And the huge egg and stitched wound on the side of my face are costume make-up then?' she said, laughing.

'You know what I mean,' he said, laughing too. 'And I don't know why we are laughing. It isn't a laughing matter. But he's spoken so fondly about you over the years. You've been more of a parent to him, more of a mother figure to him, than anyone else. I honestly thought you were one of the most important people in the world to him, so God help the rest.'

'And you may be right,' Caroline said sadly. 'And we have to laugh, otherwise we'd cry and probably not stop. But the simple truth is, Robert had a terrible upbringing. His father was involved in crime from the day dot. When he got sent to prison, Robert was a small child. His mother wasn't great before that, but afterwards she was totally hopeless. Robert's childhood was appalling, and his fate was sealed. He went into a life of crime. The worst thing that could have happened to him was his dad showing up again in his life. Robert still hankers after the dad he had when he was a child. He wants to go back to those happy times. His dad made him feel like he'd let him down when I pulled the plug, and he couldn't cope with that. He had to prove himself to his dad.'

'You almost sound sorry for him.'

'In some ways I am. He is trying to create a relationship with his father that can never be real, no matter how hard he tries. But you are right, I never thought he would threaten me like this.'

'I don't feel as sorry for him as you do. It's not all about upbringing, the nature/nurture debate. He's had people looking out for him, which is more than some, and then he stabs one of the most important in the back, or round the head, literally. There's no excuse for that.'

The way Phillip was speaking made it sound like he was talking from experience and Caroline didn't want to push it.

'As long as he backs off, that's all that matters. I don't want to be looking over my shoulder, thinking that he's going to send someone else after me. We might have put the frighteners on Paul, but he could soon find someone else.'

'I had no one when I was growing up to look out for me. Pure grit and determination got me where I am. There's no point crying over what should have been or what you think you should have had. Life is what you make of it. There is no excuse for his behaviour, and I will make it clear to him. If he is coming after you, he's coming after me too.'

'You don't need to do that, Phillip. You are on the fringe of this. Don't drag yourself in any deeper.'

'If he can do this to you, he can do it to any of us. We have to stand together.'

'Thank you so much. I really do appreciate it,' Caroline said gratefully.

'Assuming he does come to his senses, what are you going to do?' Phillip enquired.

'I honestly don't know. I've made a lot of money, but I don't think it's enough to retire in the way I'd hoped. I haven't thought further than trying to get Robert off my case. I've been so busy running everything, and then with this happening, I haven't even checked.'

'You could carry on running things without Robert. You could at least keep the gym part running, and that made Robert a lot of cash. You could scale it back and cut Robert out of the loop. His punishment for his actions,' Phillip said.

'No,' Caroline said firmly. 'I'm not meant to be in this world in any other way than representing people. I've had a glimpse into the dark side, a look at the excitement, but it's a bit too dangerous for me. No, I'm going to cut my losses and escape while I literally have all of my limbs intact. I've come a little too close to death for comfort.'

They parked in the visitors' car park and showed their identification to secure their entry to the visitors' room. Then they went through metal detectors and physical searches. The sniffer dog took a lot of interest in Caroline, probably able to smell Harley. They then had an unpleasant wait in a smelly waiting room before they finally sat at the table on the visitors' side. The legs of their chairs were bolted to the floor. Robert came through the inmates' side and did a double take when he saw Caroline sitting at the table, laptop with her. She'd had to apply for special permission for that, which had been granted reluctantly, when she'd explained she was his solicitor. When asked why she hadn't booked a legal visit, Caroline explained the accountant needed to be present too, and he couldn't go in as a legal visit. It had taken several emails, telephone calls and forms to secure the access, but they had achieved it, and it would be worth it.

Robert turned to try to leave the visitors' room, but Phillip beckoned him over earnestly.

'Well, I think that's a pretty good indicator of guilt,' he

muttered to Caroline under his breath.

'I agree,' she said. 'He looks like he wants a big hole to open up and eat him.'

'And he hasn't seen the footage yet.'

'Hi, Phillip, alright, Caroline,' Robert said, joining them at the table and sitting down on his side. 'Wasn't expecting to see you,' he said, looking directly at her.

'I wanted to show you the new work I've had done to my face,' she said, staring at him. 'I wasn't expecting it, and I don't think it'll catch on fashion wise, but I thought as you paid for it, you might want to see it for yourself.'

'What are you fucking talking about?' he yelled defensively.

'I wouldn't yell if I were you,' Phillip said firmly. 'If you get thrown out of here, our next stop is the police, and you won't want that.'

'What are you fucking talking about?' Robert hissed. 'You wanted to see me Phillip, what about?'

'Everything OK over here?' an officer enquired.

'Fine,' they all said in unison, and the officer went off, but kept a close eye on them.

'I wanted to see you because of what you did to Caroline. She's a client of mine too, and look at the state of her,' Phillip whispered angrily.

'What makes you think I was involved?' Robert questioned. The coldness in his tone surprised them both.

'Because someone you know, who you used to care about, has been seriously assaulted, and you haven't even asked how she is. It is obvious you didn't want to see her, and that tells me you're involved. You don't need to be Einstein to work this one out,' Phillip growled at him.

'And what has it got to do with you?' Robert's voice was icy now.

'Everything. We are a team. Turn on one, you turn on us all. What's saying you won't come after me next? No, Robert. There's a line and you've crossed it. I hope it was worth it because this is the end of the road for us. We are done.' Phillip sat back in his chair and glared at Robert.

'You fucking bitch,' Robert spat at Caroline. 'It was all running smoothly until I got you on board. I should never have trusted a fucking woman.'

'No, Robert,' Caroline said equally coldly. 'It was all running alright until you got angry and stopped thinking. That's what happened with the attack that landed you in here, and that's what has caused this. And believe it or not, cameras are your downfall again.' She stopped speaking and showed him the video. 'Don't think I won't go to the police. I don't need to make a statement. The footage speaks for itself. And Paul, well, he doesn't want to go down, of course, but he's quite happy to put your name in the frame if it'll get him a shorter sentence. And it will, much shorter. He's got the contact between you on his phone.' She played him the voice recording. 'See, you don't engage your brain when you get angry, do you? You never learn.'

'You wouldn't,' Robert said, looking at her, fear in his eyes.

'Wouldn't I? Before this happened, I could never have imagined it. But then, before this, I'd never been threatened by a man with a gun in my back and pistol-whipped to within an inch of my life. So yes, I think I would, because sometimes, Robert, things happen in life that change a person. This is one of those times. I am not the person I was. I am the person I need to be to get me through this. This ends now. Me and you. We are done. I never want you to contact me again. The operation finishes now. It's your fault, you sort it. I'm having nothing to do with it. No more drugs to the gym or my house. Any outstanding money is to be delivered, then we are done. It's all over.'

Robert looked at Caroline, the realisation of what he had done finally hitting him.

'Caroline, please,' he begged.

'I mean it, Robert. Finish your sentence. Get on with your life.

It's up to you what direction it takes. Follow your father, and you can see where that ends. Or take a different path. I don't want to know, and I don't care. And if you ever threaten me in any way, or anyone I care about, especially Harley, this footage and the recording of Paul go directly to the police. Your fate will be sealed. Understood.'

Robert nodded. Caroline almost felt sorry for him, but knew she could never trust him again. All good things come to an end. It had been good for a while to take herself out of herself and do something totally reckless and exciting. But play with fire and you get burnt and she had been. It was time to put it all behind her.

'I think you'll be fine,' Phillip said, as they walked back to the car. 'You controlled him brilliantly, and he knows exactly what will happen if he screws up. I think he's terribly sad to lose you. Even I felt a bit sorry for him.'

'I did too, but I can never trust him. I'd be forever looking over my shoulder, and I don't want to live like that. It was good while it lasted, but *c'est la vie*. And he threatened Harley. That was deliberate and cruel. He knows what he means to me. I want to thank you too. I couldn't have done it without you getting me in, and without you giving me the confidence to front it out like that.'

'You've got more balls than most men, Caroline. You'd have managed without me fine, but I was more than happy to help,' he said, grinning. 'Let me also help you by crunching the numbers for you and see how we can best use the money you've amassed to make your life easier and less stressful.'

'You'd be a genius if you can,' she replied. 'But stress and me seem to go hand in hand, unfortunately.'

CHAPTER TWENTY-FIVE

CAROLINE'S ESCAPE

Caroline and Phillip returned to the office after their visit to Robert to update everyone. Caroline hadn't telephoned on the way back, preferring to tell them face to face that it was over. The situation had been resolved.

Harley greeted her as soon as she walked through the door with a tail wag so vigorous it was spinning windmill like.

Phillip let Caroline take the lead. He could see how much her colleagues cared about her, and how impressed they were by the way she dealt with Robert, and the whole situation.

'Are we sure he's definitely got the message?' Michael asked.

'Absolutely,' Phillip assured them all. 'We have also ensured that he contacts everyone necessary. No need for us to do anything at all. Our involvement ends now except for collection by Ian of the remaining money. Any blowback is Robert's and his alone. He's in no doubt about that, and in no doubt what will happen if he tries to come after any of us. For my part, I'm sorry it's over. It's been lucrative for all of us, and I've enjoyed it. I shall, of course, still look after the company, and each of you individually, for as long as you need me.'

Caroline knew everyone was reassured to hear that. Phillip was an extremely good accountant and had assisted all of them.

'Well, I guess it's back to the day job then,' William said wryly.

'Yes, afraid so,' Caroline said. 'We've made a fair bit, but I don't think it's enough for any of us to run off into the sunset.'

'Some of us don't want to,' Michael said, smiling. 'I'm quite happy exactly where I am.'

'Well, I think you're the only one,' said Seb, groaning and laughing at the same time.

'For once, Seb, I think you might be right,' Sandra said, giggling.

Unbeknown to everyone involved, the minute she'd agreed to the venture, Caroline sold her house. Her next-door neighbour, Hannah, who always seemed to know everything that was going on in the street, had told her a property developer owned two of the houses in the street and rented them out. Caroline couldn't remember the details. She was sure Hannah had told her about them right down to the tiniest minutiae, in the way that only Hannah could. She'd say, 'well long story short,' and you knew it would be anything but. It would be feature length with all the add-ons. When she said that, it was Caroline's cue to zone out. Hannah meant well enough, but blimey Caroline thought lawyers could talk. They really didn't hold a candle to Hannah.

However, that had been a useful piece of information. She'd spoken to one of those neighbours when she next saw them and got the contact details for the developer. Caroline asked him if he'd be interested in buying her house but renting it to her for the foreseeable. She'd explained the house was quite large for her and Harley. She would, in time, be looking for something else and perhaps a holiday home by the sea. With it being so difficult to buy a house, not being able to put an offer in until you had an offer on yours, she didn't want to miss out by being tied down if she found something.

The developer bit her hand off. Her house was a pretty, detached house, in excellent condition, and to have a solicitor as a tenant made life simple for him. He was interested, but insisted Caroline was tied into a six-month contract that automatically renewed, unless either side gave notice. That period was three months. He didn't want to be left in the lurch, and if she was buying somewhere else, it would take about that length of time, anyway. The transaction had taken less than eight weeks. A record in the current climate it had appeared.

Of course, he didn't know the real reason Caroline might leave in a hurry. Although the new venture offered very lucrative rewards, she'd worked hard for what she had in the house. Caroline wanted to get out of it what she could and that is what she'd done. She'd been drawing some of it out of the bank, and now had a stash of cash in her go bag if she needed it. Caroline pulled the bag out now, counting how much was in there, playing back the last few days in her mind. She thought about how much her life had changed in the last year and how much she had changed. It was right what she had said to Robert. She couldn't go back to being the Caroline she had been before their venture. That person simply didn't exist anymore. The day of the assault she'd given notice, she couldn't stay.

Counting her money, she thought back to a time when she attended the police station in the middle of the night. When she first started attending the police station, even if it was late, she used to make sure she was wearing smart clothes and her hair and make-up were perfectly done. However, she soon became a seasoned attender where that was simply not sustainable. Dragging herself out of bed night after night meant that she soon ditched the glamour for reality. She would yank on a tracksuit, comb her fingers through her hair and would only have make-up on if she had been too tired to take it off the night before.

Caroline started laughing to herself as she remembered this one occasion when she was in custody, representing a client. She returned to the custody desk to be greeted by the custody officer, laughing. He told her another client of hers had just been booked in and had asked whether she could represent them. The custody officer told the client of course she could and asked the client why she had questioned it. The client said she thought Caroline had been arrested. They had both laughed out loud at this. Caroline said to the custody officer that she must look worse than normal, or at least she hoped that was the case. She was laughing now, thinking what the custody sergeant and client would think of her now, and how, if things had gone differently, she might have been arrested, or worse.

Caroline met some friends later that evening at the local pub. She didn't want to. She didn't particularly feel like socialising, but she felt she ought to make an effort. It was a very pleasant walk along the canal for Caroline, which afforded Harley the opportunity to do his usual trick when he wanted to go swimming and Caroline didn't want him to.

'No,' she said firmly, when he looked from her to the canal and back again. She knew exactly what he was asking, and he knew exactly what she was telling him. He, on the other hand, had no intention of doing what she said, and she knew that. As a result, he just fell on his right-hand side straight into the water.

Then he looked at her as he came to the surface as if to say, 'well I'm wet now, so I might as well stay in and have a swim.'

When she arrived at the pub, Tina and Ali were sitting in the garden.

'I can see Harley did his usual,' Ali said, laughing. Harley was grinning, looking thoroughly pleased with himself, still soaking wet.

'Oh yes. He takes as much notice of me as everyone else,' Caroline replied, laughing too. 'Worse still, he's had a good shake all over me. It's a good job it's warm so we can both dry off.'

She sat down at the table and Tina promptly poured her a large glass of red, saying, 'I'm amazed you have turned up.'

'I know. I'm a crap friend, but I promise I'll do better,' Caroline said, smiling.

The other two looked at her, and she knew they were both thinking, *things will never change.*

'Your cut looks incredibly sore,' Ali commented.

'It's fine,' said Caroline, downplaying it.

All she'd told them was she'd been assaulted by a client. Caroline hadn't gone into any details on their group chat, and she only told them because it was impossible to hide it. She'd considered not going out, but she'd put them off so many times that she was running out of goodwill.

Peter and the Wolf, she'd thought to herself. *If I hadn't made so many excuses in the past to get out of things, I could have used this genuine reason not to go, but I've stuffed myself, so that'll teach me.*

Caroline caught a whiff of Harley. *I'd better bath him when I get home,* she thought to herself.

Harley then positioned himself at the side of Tina. He wanted to make sure he was in the prime spot to get treats from her. She never met up with Caroline without being the best aunty and providing plenty of "snacky snacks", as she called them.

Caroline stood up to go to the toilet. As she did so, a piece of clingfilm came out of her shorts pocket with some pills wrapped up in it.

'What are those?' Tina asked.

'The painkillers I've been prescribed,' Caroline answered, bending to pick them up.

'I thought you said it wasn't that bad?' Ali chipped in.

'And why are they done up like that?' Tina said, laughing. 'Looks a bit dodgy, doesn't it?

'Just a bit now you mention it,' Caroline agreed, laughing too. 'I didn't want to bring a handbag, so I just took a few out of the pot they came in and wrapped them to keep them safe.'

'Good job you are so squeaky clean. No one would ever suspect they were anything other than totally legit.'

Caroline just grinned and winked, thinking, *if only you knew ladies, if only you knew.*

After their visit to the prison to see Robert, Phillip, true to his word, reported back that Caroline had banked over three million pounds. It hadn't taken too long for Caroline and Robert to start earning the £45k each a week while he was out, and then for the shorter time he'd been inside before it had all fallen apart. She'd had her dog walker sideline too, of course. Her money had been earning a good bit of interest in the respective banks, and by his calculations, she could retire and buy herself the home in Spain she dreamed of. Caroline hadn't realised she'd amassed so much, although she did look at it periodically in each bank. She'd been too busy running things to take too much notice.

Following that revelation, Caroline did her dog walk each night that week with Harley. She collected the money and deposited the drugs. However, as well as the drugs in the bags, she added a note, explaining that next week would be the last drug drop. She apologised for the short notice, outlining she had been attacked. Caroline made it sound as if the attack was from the drug supplier and so she couldn't get them anymore. In a way, that was true. Robert was the drug supplier. He was what had got her into it, and he had organised it all. Her explanation was a bit simplistic because, of course, they didn't know of all the moving parts and the bigger picture, but it was basically right.

The following week, with the final payment from each of them, she had received little notes. Everyone was concerned as to how she was. When they'd seen her, they'd commented on her head, as you would expect them to do in the normal course of events, but she'd just said she was fine. All of them had thanked her for her help, and all of them had said it had helped enormously.

Paula and Joe had made enough to get back on track. The relatives of Anthony and Marie had benefited while it lasted, and Julie-Ann and Christine had saved a nice little nest egg. When Caroline saw Julie-Ann, she told her she had a good financial advisor who could help her invest the money if she wanted to. Caroline hadn't realised Julie-Ann had been holding on to it. Julie-Ann explained she wanted to use it for some nice holidays for the girls, so she wanted to hang on to it and keep it off the radar with the benefits she got. Caroline didn't want to expose Phillip by suggesting that he had ways to keep things off the books or expose her own knowledge further. She decided it was in everyone's interests, especially hers, to keep it simple.

Over the next few weeks Caroline thought back over what had been an unbelievable few months in her life. As quickly as it had started it had finished, and it all seemed a dream that had happened to someone else. Her scar was tender from her pistol-whipping, a more unpleasant reminder that it had been her reality, if only for a short period. She didn't feel good about herself. She'd allowed herself to cross the line, to go from helping people to possibly hurting people for her own self-gain. She knew what the terrible consequences of taking drugs were. Not just the physical, but the mental and psychological anguish too. And not just for the drug takers, but for their friends and families and the wider community too. She'd gone from a vocation driven by helping people to personal greed whatever the cost. She tried to justify it to herself that she had helped others and that if it wasn't her someone else would be doing it anyway, but deep down she knew she'd allowed her own personal pity and wallowing to enable her to be easily influenced when she should have used her strength and morals to say '*No*'.

'Still, it's over Harley, we can escape and spend time together. That's all I want, to be with you.'

Harley looked at her lovingly as if to say, 'I'll always be yours,' and she snuggled her face into his.

A few weeks later, Caroline asked Alex if she could have a word.

'How are you feeling now?' he asked her, slumping in his seat opposite her.

'On top of the world, Alex,' she said sharply. She saw his quizzical look at her demeanour. 'I'm back in control of things, and that suits me. And don't think I don't know about your little sideline,' she said, glaring at him. Harley was at her side, staring at Alex too. He hadn't gone to greet him as he usually would.

'What?' he said defensively.

'Don't get all defensive and don't try to deny it. That's one of the reasons I got beaten up. You just had to, didn't you? Couldn't make do with the money you were making, couldn't just play your part. The reason you only had such a small part was because you fucked it up and I knew you couldn't be trusted. And this proves it. Did you honestly fucking think that no one would know you were skimming? These weren't £10 bag users. These were the big guns, you twat. You nearly got me killed, and you nearly got yourself killed. If I hadn't found a way out of this for us, they'd have come for you by now.'

'You always have to be in control, always think you are better than everyone else,' Alex retorted.

'No, I don't. I never wanted to be in charge of this place, you know that. I just ended up doing it. And all round you've benefited from me running it. What you can't accept is that you can't, and this sideline of yours, I suppose, was your way of trying to prove to yourself you can. Well, that worked out really fucking well, didn't it?'

'I am sorry, Caroline. I didn't mean for you to get hurt.'

'I know, but you didn't think, that's the trouble. You didn't think of anyone but yourself. You can't run any type of business like that, Alex, and I won't be here to pick up the pieces. It's time you dropped the little boy act and grew up. You've a little boy of your own. He nearly didn't have a father. This is the real world Alex, and we deal with dangerous people. You've got to stand on your own two feet and take responsibility and face the consequences that come with it.'

Caroline had arranged a meeting, and they were in the Crown Court room. It did not escape anyone's attention that this was where they had been when the operation had first been outlined. Harley was lying on his bed, licking his paws. This was the first time they had all been together since the meeting when she had returned from the prison with Phillip. Since then, everyone had had a chance to come to terms with the inevitable changes that had taken place and consider their own finances and the way forward.

'How are we all doing?' Caroline asked.

'It seems weird,' William said. 'It's like it never happened, like a dream. No one has mentioned anything at court. None of the clients we dealt with. It's like their memories have been erased.'

'Or time has changed, and we are in a parallel universe,' Michael added.

'Or it was all just a figment of our imaginations,' Ian agreed.

'The scar on the side of my head would say otherwise, and on a positive note, our bank balances too,' Caroline responded.

'You are right about that,' Ian agreed. 'I haven't made as much as I had hoped, but I've a very nice nest egg for the kids' university fees and my pension. All I need to do is keep ticking over and that's fine by me.'

'My position hasn't changed,' Michael said. 'And yes, I know I'm in the minority, but that's the way I like it,' he added, and they all laughed.

'I've made enough to pay off all my student debt, and a substantial house deposit,' Seb said proudly.

'Ah, the baby's grown up,' Sandra joked.

'I wouldn't go that far,' Ian interrupted. 'He blew the microwave up at lunchtime, putting tinfoil in it.'

'For the love of God,' Caroline laughed.

'Well, he makes you look good, Alex, so I suppose that's something,' William jested wryly, and they all laughed. 'I've topped my pension up nicely,' he added. 'I want to reduce my hours to part time, please. I can find myself a nice work-life balance, have some quality time, but get out from under the wife's feet to sustain marital bliss.'

'I have a newborn, so although I've made a few bob, we want a bigger family, so retirement is still a long way off for me,' Alex said.

'I only stay for Harley, so I'm in Caroline's hands,' Sandra added, and all eyes turned to Caroline.

'Well, I obviously don't have a family like some of you do, although of course I do have my precious boy.' She bent down to stroke him, and he nuzzled into her affectionately. 'My near-death experience has taught me I work too hard, and play too little, and that needs to change. None of us are getting any younger, especially Harley, and I need to make the most of it. I'm quitting. I'm off to Spain.'

'You dark horse,' said Ian. 'You've got it all sorted in a heartbeat.' His voice was full of admiration. 'I'm thrilled for you. I know we all are. You so deserve it.'

'Here, here,' William said, and they all clapped and cheered.

All except Alex, who looked incredulous.

'What about me? You can't just leave the business like that?'

'What about you? You've made some money, you've a good practice and good staff. You'll have to put on your big boy pants and get on with it. Like I told Robert, we're done. You know why and I'm out. Now. The buck stops with you.'

Everyone felt the atmosphere in the room change, the temperature plummet, and no one quite understood what was going on between Caroline and Alex, or why.

'So, what's the place in Spain like?' Sandra asked, dying to know, and trying to change the subject and lighten the mood.

'It's got a pool for Harley, and a permanent spare room for Aunty Sandra, and another one for anyone else who wants to stay. It's perfect.'

'It sounds it,' Sandra agreed. 'I'll get my bags packed.'

'Awesome. We'll see you on the flip side,' Seb quipped.

'Not if I see you first,' Caroline responded, blowing them all a kiss as Harley added a parting woof.

ACKNOWLEDGEMENTS

I would like to thank my family and friends for their support in writing this, my first book. In particular, Sally, Tina and Jo who read the first draft and made helpful comments to move it from that to this.

Being a part of the criminal justice system for over twenty-five years has given me a unique window into the lives of people that otherwise I would never have met.

Criminal defence solicitors are a rare and unique breed. The poor pay and anti-social hours demand it. The characters are fictitious, but all of their qualities and quirks I have seen first hand. Indeed, some are my own!

It is a demanding vocation, but while my working life has been hectic, it has also been interesting and varied.

The main thanks must go to my clients. Without them, I wouldn't have had the successful career I have had or gained the knowledge and life experience I have accumulated this past quarter of a century. They have been as different as the offences they have committed, but have reminded me on a daily basis how fortunate I am.

Printed in Great Britain
by Amazon

47276853R00158